PENGUIN  CLASSIC

RAMEAU'S NEPHE
D'ALEMBERT'S DRE.

DENIS DIDEROT was born at Langres in eastern France in 1713, the son of a master cutler. He was originally destined for the Church but rebelled and persuaded his father to allow him to complete his education in Paris, where he graduated in 1732. For ten years Diderot was nominally a law student, but actually led a precarious bohemian but studious existence, eked out with tutoring, hack writing and translating. His original works, *Pensées philosophiques* (1746), *Lettre sur les aveugles* (1749), and *De l'interpretation de la nature* (1753), display a preoccupation with the mind-body dichotomy. In the early 1740s, however, he had met three contemporaries of great future significance for himself and for the age: d'Alembert, Condillac and J. J. Rousseau, who were to assist him in the compilation of the *Encyclopédie*, which Diderot edited right up to its completion in 1773. His boldest philosophical and scientific speculations are brilliantly summarized in a trilogy of dialogues: *Entretien entre Diderot et d'Alembert, Le rêve de d'Alembert (d'Alembert's Dream)*, and *Suite de l'entretien* (1769). In *Le neveu de Rameau (Rameau's Nephew)*, written in 1761 or later, he gave to prose fiction a new creative scope. Towards the end of his life he visited St Petersburg at the invitation of Catherine II, to whom he bequeathed his library. He died in 1784.

LEONARD TANCOCK spent most of his life in or near London, apart from a year as a student in Paris, most of the Second World War in Wales and three periods in American universities as visiting professor. Until his death in 1986, he was a Fellow of University College, London, and was formerly Reader in French at the University. He prepared his first Penguin Classic in 1949 and, from that time, was extremely interested in the problems of translation, about which he wrote, lectured and gave broadcasts. His numerous translations for the Penguin Classics include Zola's *Germinal, Thérèse Raquin, The Débâcle, L'Assommoir* and *La Bête Humaine*; Diderot's *The Nun, Rameau's Nephew* and *D'Alembert's Dream*; Maupassant's *Pierre and Jean*; Marivaux's *Up from the Country*; Constant's *Adolphe*; La Rochefoucauld's *Maxims*; Voltaire's *Letters on England*; Prévost's *Manon Lescaut*; and Madame de Sévigné's *Selected Letters*.

DENIS DIDEROT

RAMEAU'S NEPHEW

AND

D'ALEMBERT'S DREAM

Translated with Introductions by
Leonard Tancock

PENGUIN BOOKS

PENGUIN BOOKS

Published by the Penguin Group
Penguin Books Ltd, 80 Strand, London WC2R 0RL, England
Penguin Putnam Inc., 375 Hudson Street, New York, New York 10014, USA
Penguin Books Australia Ltd, 250 Camberwell Road, Camberwell, Victoria 3124, Australia
Penguin Books Canada Ltd, 10 Alcorn Avenue, Toronto, Ontario, Canada M4V 3B2
Penguin Books India (P) Ltd, 11 Community Centre, Panchsheel Park, New Delhi – 110 017, India
Penguin Books (NZ) Ltd, Cnr Rosedale and Airborne Roads, Albany, Auckland, New Zealand
Penguin Books (South Africa) (Pty) Ltd, 24 Sturdee Avenue, Rosebank 2196, South Africa

Penguin Books Ltd, Registered Offices: 80 Strand, London WC2R 0RL, England

www.penguin.com

This translation first published 1966

049

Printed and bound in Great Britain by Clays Ltd, Elcograf S.p.A.
Set in Monotype Baskerville

ISBN-13: 978–0–140–44173–4

www.greenpenguin.co.uk

MIX
Paper from
responsible sources
FSC
www.fsc.org   FSC® C018179

Penguin Books is committed to a sustainable
future for our business, our readers and our planet.
This book is made from Forest Stewardship
Council™ certified paper.

CONTENTS

Foreword   7

Denis Diderot   9

Introduction to *Rameau's Nephew*   15

RAMEAU'S NEPHEW   33

Notes on *Rameau's Nephew*   127

Introduction to *D'Alembert's Dream*   133

Biographical Note on the Characters   141

Conversation between D'Alembert and Diderot   149

D'ALEMBERT'S DREAM   165

Sequel to the Conversation   225

Notes on *D'Alembert's Dream*   235

FOREWORD

THE two works of Diderot contained in this volume, although both in dialogue form, confront the translator with different problems. *Le Neveu de Rameau*, in form as in other respects unique, veers bewilderingly in style from the inflated, rhetorical and bombastic to the simple, slangy and coarse, and often the face value of what is said is not the author's intention, for he is being ironical as well as humorous. It is true as a general rule that a translator must use the language of his own time, but some compromises have to be found when dealing with a very topical and allusive conversation taking place in an age of wigs, snuff-boxes and sedan-chairs. I have been greatly helped by conversations with a friend and colleague at University College London, Dr André Lequet.

Le Rêve de D'Alembert, on the other hand, while fairly straightforward stylistically, is a challenge to the non-scientist. He has to use terms scientifically acceptable today, but not so technical or modern as to be absurd in the mouths of these eighteenth-century speakers. Moreover scientific terminology was still very vague in Diderot's day, and in any case the dialogues aim largely at making abstruse scientific facts or hypotheses comprehensible to the laity by means of analogies and parables in simple language. The work is, after all, as much a plea for religious and sexual emancipation as a scientific treatise. In trying to execute this feat of tightrope-walking I have been supported by a colleague with expert knowledge of eighteenth-century French scientific writing, Dr W. A. Smeaton, Reader in History and Philosophy of Science at University College London, who has looked through my attempts and to whom I am extremely grateful.

It should of course be made clear that these friends are not responsible for errors of meaning, judgement or taste, which are mine alone.

The drudgery, but also the fun, has been shared by my wife.

At the end of the texts will be found some notes which it is hoped will help the reader to appreciate some of the allusions to persons and events. The notes have no claim to completeness – biographies of some of the minor and despicable hack-writers mentioned, for instance, in *Le Neveu de Rameau*, would do nothing but tell the reader that this was a despicable and minor writer, which he knew already. Complete notes would be as long as or longer than the text.

October 1964   L.W.T.

DENIS DIDEROT

DENIS DIDEROT (1713–84), son of a master cutler, was
born in Langres, in eastern France, where he was educated
by the Jesuits until he was fifteen. He came to Paris in 1728
and finished his education there, graduating at the University in 1732. Thenceforth he was to remain in Paris,
with only one significant break in 1773–4 when he went to
Russia, for the remaining fifty-two years of his life, and he
became just as much the Great Parisian as his English
contemporary Samuel Johnson became the Great Londoner.
Little is known about his life until about 1742, but legend
(and Rameau's nephew) speak of his teaching subjects,
such as mathematics, which he learned as he went along,
writing sermons for lazy preachers, and other such ex-
pedients which may have contributed to his astonishing
versatility. From 1742 onwards he became something of a
literary hack and in addition to original work did various
translations from English, including that of a medical
dictionary, which probably accounts for his lifelong interest
in medical and biological research, one of the fruits of which
was to be *D'Alembert's Dream* over twenty years later. It was
his work as a translator which prompted a syndicate of
publishers to entrust to him, after one or two false starts
with others, the task of translating *Chambers's Cyclopaedia*, a
fairly modest compilation, into French. But like so many
things Diderot touched, the simple publishers' project
rapidly enlarged itself until the work became the first great
Encyclopaedia of the modern world, running to seventeen
folio volumes of text and eleven supplementary volumes of
plates, and taking in all about twenty-five years to reach
completion. In 1747 Diderot became joint editor with
D'Alembert, the distinguished mathematician, and the

9

enthusiasm throughout the progressive half of France and in most of Europe was immense. The greatest literary figures in the land were proud to be collaborators – Voltaire, Montesquieu, Jean-Jacques Rousseau, who undertook the music articles, Daubenton, assistant of the great Buffon, the articles on natural history, and countless small manufacturers, artisans, craftsmen, in fact anybody who could supply information of a technical kind, offered help in what became virtually a national effort. It soon became clear, from the *Prospectus*, written by Diderot, and the *Discours préliminaire*, by D'Alembert, that the tendency of the work was to be materialistic, progressive and hostile to all religious and social vested interests. The opposition of the other half of France soon made itself felt, and the forces of reaction used every conceivable means, often foul and sometimes dastardly, to try to suppress the *Encyclopédie*. The struggle proved too much for D'Alembert, who deserted Diderot in 1758, after the completion late in the previous year of Volume 7, and Diderot alone carried the immense weight of editorial responsibility, dealing with business problems and the unremitting attacks of enemies, and writing many major articles and countless small ones, until the completion of the last volume of plates in 1773. These twenty-five years of ceaseless, grinding work would have been more than enough for the average man, but Diderot in addition carried on at least two other careers – those of creative writer and art critic – and was into the bargain one of the greatest talkers of his age. An eternal adolescent, he was bursting with enthusiasm and curiosity about the worlds of science, art, music, the theatre and technology, full of the excitement of discovery, always elaborating some new theory, arguing with the wrong-headed, an idealist and a realist, sublime but not averse to the smutty joke, a down-to-earth materialist yet haunted by moral scruples and a highly developed social sense, a scientist always in a state

of febrile emotion and seldom far from tears, a deadly
enemy but the kindest and most companionable of men.

These varying interests and emotions kept him busy
throughout the years on a multitude of non-Encyclopaedic
writings, most of which cannot be labelled clearly as
belonging to any single genre: novels quite different from
the conventional forms, philosophical dialogues and essays
on scientific and biological subjects, a long series of critical
accounts of the Paris art salons which virtually mark the
birth of that peculiarly French genre of art criticism done
by distinguished men of letters – later to be used with so
much effect by such divergent types as Baudelaire and
Zola – some tedious and pedestrian plays, but some dramatic criticism of the first importance, and the *Paradoxe sur
le comédien*, a discussion of the art and craft of acting still
relevant today and recently heatedly argued over by some
of the leading French actors. And finally *Rameau's Nephew*,
a work belonging to no recognizable genre, neither novel
nor play nor essay nor, in spite of its sub-title, satire, and
unique in French literature.

Few of these works were published in Diderot's lifetime,
partly, no doubt, because he never had time to put them
into a final form and see them through the press, and
partly, we cannot help suspecting, because in an age of
brilliant talkers he seems to have been one of the most
brilliant and, his enemies would have said, time-wasting;
but mostly because the matter of many of these writings
was so subversive, anti-religious or scandalous that they
would never have survived the censorship. They were,
however, circulated among a not very small group of
friends, and they worked like leaven in the formation of new
opinions, in the campaign for knowledge and truth used as a
means of social progress known to us as the Enlightenment.

Of the three giants of eighteenth-century French literature Diderot is the most attractive as a man. A Jack-of-all-

trades of genius, he lacks the dazzling polish of Voltaire and the poetic sweep and overwhelming eloquence of Jean-Jacques Rousseau, but neither has he the spiteful pettiness of the one nor the morbid self-centredness of the other, and he was far broader in his interests and scarcely less deep. For Voltaire was really a practical man, most at home when dealing with some real issue, righting some real wrong, while metaphysical speculation bored him and he ended up by saying that there are mysteries we lack the equipment to solve. Rousseau was a complex character who rationalized his own condition, experiences and above all grudges and resentments into 'systems', which he imposed with his spell-binding style and with the intolerance of the bigoted puritanical type. Each was one-sided and a little inhuman. Diderot was as near to being universal as modern man can be, and never lost his human touch. Even at his most discursive he is never boring, for he has the gift of communicating his own enthusiasm and of opening up new prospects. He is a friend one loves listening to because his talk never grows stale.

RAMEAU'S NEPHEW

(LE NEVEU DE RAMEAU)

INTRODUCTION TO *RAMEAU'S NEPHEW*

I

RAMEAU'S NEPHEW is a masterpiece alone of its kind and not a little mysterious. Almost every aspect of it, dating, intention, meaning, is open to debate, and tentative conclusions about one aspect are often flatly contradicted by another.

The framework is easy enough to see. Jean-François Rameau, nephew of the great composer Jean-Philippe Rameau, had come to Paris, like his uncle, from Dijon. He was an eccentric character – though not, it seems, as wildly so as he is portrayed in Diderot's dialogue – who made a precarious living in Paris as a teacher of singing and keyboard playing, and was apparently well known as a hanger-on in grand houses and the more fashionable cafés. In the story he meets Diderot one day in the garden of the Palais-Royal, then the fashionable promenade of both the *monde* and the *demi-monde*, and they fall into conversation. Rameau is depressed because in a moment of irritation he has spoken his mind in the house of Bertin, the wealthy *Trésorier des parties casuelles* (from which title some obvious coarse jokes can be expected) and offended the latter's current mistress, Mademoiselle Hus, an actress of the *Comédie française*, and this momentary dropping of the mask has lost him the comfortable position of sycophant and tame jester to the household, sometimes referred to as Bertinhus. The conversation wanders along various main roads and byways, social, musical, literary, educational, political, moral and philosophical, with breaks for hilarious mimicry and pantomime by Rameau, until the latter remembers that he has to put in an appearance at the opera, when the two men part on a non-committal note.

Behind this very readable conversation, with the frolics and outrageous opinions of an exuberant personality, who is a great comic creation of Rabelaisian proportions, there is an extremely complicated and difficult work which raises questions not yet all clearly answered by the researches and criticisms of generations of scholars. One man's guess is almost as good as another's. Therefore what follows in this introduction is not a statement of established facts, but one man's guesses or opinions, and the reader may well have some quite different ones, for like most literary masterpieces, especially those that deal with human character in depth, this text can be mused over and 'interpreted' for a very long time.

2

Here are some of the questions it raises: When was it written? Is the text we now possess the good one? What did Diderot mean by calling it a satire? Satire of what? Is the reader expected to take the side of 'He' or 'I'? If 'I' represents Diderot, then why is the more important and interesting role given to 'He', Rameau's nephew? Are we to conclude that the part of 'I' is simply a foil or 'feed' to provoke interesting reactions from 'He'? But if the real interest is in the portrait and opinions of 'He' are we to assume that Diderot endorsed the nihilism and cynicism of this man's views? If so, this runs counter to most of the official opinions expressed by Diderot throughout his public life as a writer and editor of the *Encyclopédie*. Such being the case, is this a revelation of the real Diderot, written for himself alone or a few friends? Is it a sort of confession of hypocrisy and cynicism – the kind of mood we all fall into sometimes, when we deliberately pour scorn on all the things we normally profess to stand for and respect, when in a moment of truth we admit to ourselves that all we have done and appeared to believe in has been nothing but a smokescreen, an official attitude worn like a mask in order to earn a living? Or, yet again, is this dialogue an elaborate piece of polemic, an attack on Diderot's enemies in the great war of the *Encyclopédie*? Or a ruthless exposure of the filth and corruption of the society of his time? Or even a battle in the little war, *La Guerre des Bouffons*, which was raging in the opera houses between champions of Italianate and French music – the French equivalent of the Tweedle-dum–Tweedledee fusses in London a little earlier between Handel and Bononcini? If it is a musical tract it has got seriously out of hand, for the musical part proper is relatively small, whereas some of the moral, social and philosophical implications are of the first importance.

Arising from this last group of speculations there is this most baffling question: If the thing is an attack on Diderot's literary and ideological enemies, if it is a satire aimed against certain types of corrupt people, if it is a move in the war over Italian and French music, why did Diderot not publish it? It is all very well to say that he was reticent about publishing his works, especially those with dangerous implications such as the horrifying sexual ones of the *Supplément au Voyage de Bougainville* or *Le Rêve de D'Alembert*, but you cannot have it both ways and say in the same breath that this text is an attack on some very real enemies who are mentioned by name and that he never intended to publish it because of its dangerous moral implications. If he never intended to publish, why the scathing personal abuse of definite enemies? It seems rather stretching a point to suggest that Diderot wrote this brilliant piece of invective for the private satisfaction of knowing that it might possibly be published after his death and after that of most of the people attacked. But of course limited private circulation of the work might be the answer to that question. Or again, can we take a simpler view and say that the sub-title *Satire* just means a realistic picture of contemporary life? If that is so, however, we are left with other difficulties, for this monstrous creation is anything but a 'realistic' picture of the ordinary and uninteresting man Rameau's nephew was in humdrum life, and we are still required to explain why Diderot never published it and why all the complicated moral, artistic and philosophical questions should occur in a mere Hogarthian picture of eighteenth-century coarseness. Not, surely, as mere by-products of the richness of Diderot's genius, with no other *raison d'être*?

Nor is the list of conjectures exhausted. Is it a dialogue between the respectable, law-abiding side of each one of us and the anarchist, irresponsible, wholly self-centred side? A splitting of Diderot's own character into these two parts, opposed in a piece of dialectics? Or, yet again, a stock-taking on Diderot's part in the matter, always uppermost in his mind, of the conflict between two irreconcilable eighteenth-century ideas, both of which he believed in with equal enthusiasm: on the one hand an intense, emotional belief in moral purpose, the goodness of man, progress, enlightenment and, on the other, absolute materialism, involving as it must hopeless, pessimistic, amoral determinism, in fact a restatement of the ancient dilemma between free will and fatalism? If so, determinism has a good run.

Finally, have we been looking for complications which are not there? Is this text merely a wonderful portrait, like an immensely inflated *Character* of La Bruyère? A portrait of a half-crazy crank on to which Diderot has embroidered all sorts of ornamentations and arabesques in the way that he apparently did in conversation? But this seems too simple an explanation to be plausible.

3

From speculations let us turn to the adventure story of the text itself. The fate of Diderot's papers and manuscripts is too complicated to be discussed here in any detail, nor would such detail be relevant. But some of it must be known for a proper understanding of the work itself, and in the case of *Rameau's Nephew* it is a fine tale of mystery, chance and roguery almost worthy of a detective story.

After Diderot's death his manuscript material survived in three main lots, with a fairly substantial 'leakage' into a fourth:

1. *Naigeon.* Before his departure in 1773 for the long and hazardous journey to Russia at the invitation of Catherine the Great, Diderot deposited with his friend and literary executor Naigeon a large quantity of manuscripts. These were utilized by Naigeon for the first collected edition of *Œuvres de Diderot* in 1798. *Le Neveu de Rameau* does not appear in this edition, neither is there any mention of it in the list of Diderot MSS. offered for sale by Naigeon's heirs to Madame de Vandeul in 1816. The Naigeon papers were dispersed after 1820, and here begins one of the mysteries which bedevil the Diderot story, for vast numbers of wandering manuscripts may still turn up anywhere in the world.

2. *Russia.* The Empress Catherine helped Diderot financially, and delicately suggested that the money might be regarded as payment in advance for his library and papers, which were to be sent to St Petersburg after his death. Accordingly, after 1784, Diderot's daughter Madame de Vandeul fulfilled her side of the bargain and had a complete set of copies made of all the MSS. in her possession, and these went to the Hermitage Library and are still in the State Library in Leningrad. It was only natural that Diderot's daughter should prefer to send copies to the

Empress and keep the originals herself, and some of the Russian material is faulty and obviously copied in haste.

3. *Vandeul*. The collection of MSS. in the possession of Madame de Vandeul was held tenaciously by the family until the death, in 1911, of Albert de Vandeul, the last direct descendant of Diderot. All through the nineteenth century the Vandeul family was not only uncooperative but obstructionist, and although the existence of these papers was known to all scholars, access to them or reproduction was forbidden. Finally, after 1911, they passed to the Le Vavasseur family (collateral descendants from a female Vandeul) who at last permitted Professor Herbert Dieckmann to make a critical inventory of them, published in 1951. There are two manuscripts of *Le Neveu de Rameau* in this collection.

4. The substantial 'leakage' referred to above was to Diderot's friend Grimm, to whom he gave or lent various MSS., some of which Grimm published in his *Correspondance littéraire*. This was a monthly literary review of which only about fifteen copies were made and circulated privately to a few privileged subscribers, such as certain European royalties, and which contained copies of texts unpublishable because of their scandalous or subversive nature. Diderot's two longest works of fiction, *La Religieuse* and *Jacques le Fataliste*, were first circulated semi-clandestinely in this way. When he finally left Paris Grimm took with him some of these papers, which were dispersed in Germany after his death.

The first time our text was ever heard of except by those who may have been in Diderot's confidence was in 1805, when in Leipzig there appeared *Rameaus Neffe*, described as a translation by Goethe from a French manuscript lent him by Schiller. Goethe, it seems, returned the manuscript to Schiller and then all trace of it was lost. The mystery of this manuscript was long thought to be as supernatural as that of the Stranger who commissioned Mozart's *Requiem*, and the explanation is probably equally prosaic, for almost certainly it was a copy made clandestinely in St Petersburg by a German officer who had passed it on to Schiller.

The second edition of the work is one of the prize pieces of impudence in literary history. In 1821 two gentlemen named De Saur and Saint-Geniès published in Paris *Le Neveu de Rameau. Dialogue.* This was none other than Goethe's German text re-translated into French and palmed off as a newly discovered Diderot work. Madame de Vandeul was naturally furious and lent a manuscript of hers to Brière, who published it in Volume 21 of his edition of Diderot's complete works in 1823. We now know that the Vandeul manuscript used for this, the first proper French edition, was very faulty, but it was the source of subsequent editions for some sixty years, modified more or less wisely according to the tact and scholarship of editors. Nor need we stop over an edition by Tourneux in 1884 based on the Hermitage manuscript.

And then, in 1891, over a century after Diderot's death, there was a sensational discovery. Georges Monval found in the boxes of a bookseller on the Quai Voltaire in Paris a perfect manuscript in the beautiful, clear writing used by Diderot when he was making fair copies. This manuscript was in Volume 186 of a 300-volume collection, bound in vellum, which had been formed by a Marquis de la Roche-foucauld-Liancourt. This gentleman had spent a great deal of time between 1815 and 1848 in Germany, and collected rare eighteenth-century items which he had had bound together in these volumes and edifyingly described as *Tragédies et Œuvres diverses.* In reality they seem to have been a *cache* for erotica and works of a more or less scandalous nature. The Monval manuscript is by far the best text and is the source of all good later editions down to that by Jean Fabre in the series *Textes Littéraires Français* (Geneva, Droz,

1950) from which this translation is made. The Monval manuscript eventually found its way into the Pierpont Morgan Library, New York. It is a safe guess, but not more than that, for nothing to do with this work is indubitable, that this was a final copy given or lent to Grimm by Diderot.

4

Not only the subject-matter of the work, but the extreme care so obviously taken by Diderot in writing out this Monval manuscript gives the lie to the legend that Diderot's writings, apart from Encyclopaedic work, were thrown off as diversions, that this work, for instance, was just a huge joke, a bit of Rabelaisian horseplay. A manuscript in the hand of his last years, with scarcely any alterations or crossings-out except one or two stylistic second thoughts, throws new light upon what one might have been tempted to call slips, inadvertencies and contradictions in the text. Are we justified in dismissing the form of *Rameau's Nephew* as a muddle that runs on and on? The mystery deepens when it is realized that there is no reference to this work in the correspondence either of Diderot himself or of his friends. We are therefore driven back to the text as the only evidence of when the work was written or with what aim in view. And the dating, if it could be done accurately, would be a guide to aim and meaning.

But it cannot be done accurately. Internal evidence – references to people and events – might very conveniently narrow the date of composition down to the spring of 1761, were there not also many other references and allusions to events much later. The musical references, in particular, and the onslaught on Palissot tie it down to early 1761, but what of Voltaire and the part he played in the Calas affair in 1765? Some critics have tried to explain these awkward discrepancies by the theory that Diderot dashed off the original dialogue in 1761 but continued to touch it up over many years, and that the many allusions to later events are there either because Diderot was careless and did not remember what he had put (strange assumption, even about an author as busy as Diderot), or because new events occurred which were so apposite as examples that he deliberately put them in without bothering about the general shape. But it is difficult to believe that any author would knowingly leave glaring inconsistencies in a work simply because he felt himself above such *minutiæ*. It may be of interest to have just a few of these contradictory arguments juxtaposed:

Arguments tending to date the composition: The event which is ostensibly behind the whole episode, the fact that Rameau had just lost his position as sponger and clown in the establishment of Bertin and his mistress Hus, cannot have happened later than the very beginning of September 1761, for on 2 September this irregular *ménage* broke up. The liaison was notorious throughout Paris and its end was the sensation of the moment. But reference is made to Rameau's child and its upbringing. We know that the child died in June 1761. Moreover, the Nephew refers to the latest thing being done at the Opera, *Hercule mourant* by Dauvergne. This was first performed at the beginning of April and ran all through that month. These and many other details suggest that the first form of the dialogue must date from about April 1761, and the extremely circumstantial nature of the whole conversation indicates that Diderot wrote it up immediately after the encounter in the Palais-Royal.

Arguments tending to make nonsense of this exact dating: The negative argument that the conversation never took place at all, and that this is simply a novel, hardly seems to be valid in the face of the remarkable accuracy of the details and personal allusions. But apart from the Voltaire–Calas reference there is the muddle over Rameau the Uncle. In this dialogue Philippe Rameau is clearly meant to be alive, dead and then alive again. In reality he died in September 1764. And what of the existence of the *two* Frérons, father and son? The younger Fréron was only a child in 1761.

So one could go on. Can any conclusions be drawn from this apparent confusion? Clearly there was a primitive text to which Diderot added as the years went on. Fabre puts the final touching-up as late as 1777 or even 1779. But why the disparities? It simply will not do to say that they are there because Diderot did not notice or that he put them there just to annoy us. The only reasonable explanation which does not make him out as having been a fool or a very laboured joker is that his aim in constantly repolishing *Le Neveu de Rameau* was quite divorced from chronology or even from realism. It was artistic, critical, philosophical, moral. Which brings us back at last to the original questions: what is this text, and what was Diderot's object in writing it?

5

There are many possible objects, some of which are grouped here under four main headings, but the arbitrariness of the list is betrayed by the uncertainty of the frontiers and the proliferation of subdivisions:

1. An attack upon the enemies of the *Encyclopédie* and of progress?

If so, 'He', Rameau, embodies impure literary and artistic criticism, that is to say opposition to what is manifestly good and true for reasons of self-interest. Rameau is in the employ of the anti-Encyclopaedic faction, he is the vile creature used by the Court, the corrupt financial circles and the corrupt Church to do the dirty work so that they may keep their own hands clean. The *Encyclopédie* threatens their vested interests in ignorance, superstition

and obscurantism, and they pay unprincipled parasites
such as Rameau or venal hack-writers, many of whom are
mentioned by name, to destroy by any means, however
foul, the reputation and influence of decent and progressive
people.

2. A battle in the musical war?

A feud divided the partisans of the 'French' style of opera
in the Lully tradition, of which Jean-Philippe Rameau was
the greatest living exponent, and the 'Italian', represented
here by various fashionable Italian composers such as
Pergolesi and, for this purpose, Hasse, referred to as the
Saxon. It was obviously a clever move to put the attack into
the mouth of the great Rameau's unsuccessful and dis-
gruntled nephew, especially as Philippe Rameau was
notoriously mean, hard and disagreeable as a man. In this
Diderot's own motives were not quite pure, for the elder
Rameau, nothing if not a conscientious and scholarly
musician, had protested against some of the *Encyclopédie*
articles on music, which was not surprising since they came
from the pen of a man of genius in other fields who unfortunately was also a cranky amateur musician, Jean-
Jacques Rousseau. This of course marked down Rameau as
an enemy in Diderot's mind, even though Jean-Jacques,
most vain and touchy of men, had long since flounced out
of the Encyclopaedic team and left Diderot in the lurch.

But what does the musical criticism of *Rameau's Nephew*
amount to? A declaration in favour of certain recent
developments in the conventions of opera, and the fact that
many of the composers Diderot champions against Rameau
and the French tradition happen to be Italian is really
beside the point. The real division is between formalism
and naturalistic effects, and the 'Italian' style (in Pergolesi,
Handel and, for that matter, Gluck) seemed to Diderot a
more faithful portrayal of real emotions. Philippe Rameau

was fundamentally a great instrumental composer, interested in forms, harmonic effects and orchestral colour, as was recently shown by a beautiful production of his opera-ballet *Zoroastre*, which was staged at the Opéra-Comique in Paris in September 1964 to mark the bicentenary of his death. The plain fact is that Diderot knew next to nothing about music. Neither, for that matter, did he know much about the technical side of painting, which did not prevent his making some successful incursions into the field of art criticism, but in musical matters this technical deficiency is more serious, because Diderot simply considers opera as dramatic work, and the music as the equivalent of language and gesture in a stage play. As he demanded verisimilitude in drama so he wanted naturalistic effects in music which, logically, would make Tchaikovsky's *Grand Overture 1812* ('with full pyrotechnic effects') or somebody's impression of a storm at sea 'realized' on a theatre organ far greater pieces of music than the later Beethoven quartets. Moreover, by ignoring the very great qualities of Philippe Rameau's music and condemning it on purely dramatic and linguistic grounds, Diderot is as guilty of impure criticism as a dramatic critic who judges a play in terms of political ideology and not as drama.

This leads to regions not strictly in the territory of musical criticism at all, but the move is characteristic of Diderot's inquiring mind. It is interesting to find a Frenchman willing to admit that few European languages strain and distort the human singing voice as badly as French. It is a matter of vowel sounds, and one has only to think of the difficulty of singing, for example, the words *en murmurant* softly on a high note, or compare the Italian and French forms of Gluck's *Orfeo*, in order to assess the relative values of the two languages from the singer's or audience's point of view.

From this it is but another step to an attack upon the

libretti provided by French poets, with some penetrating observations, less valid today, but not wholly invalid, on the unsuitability of French, with its self-conscious intellectualism, its preoccupation with logic and clarity, its syntax, grammar and prosody, as a basis for lyrically expressive, free-flowing music.

In a word, the musical arguments in this dialogue are light in weight, they apply only to opera and then are mainly concerned with verisimilitude, which is the least important thing about opera.

3. A discussion of moral values?

The most profound issues raised by the two men in their discussion are certainly the moral ones. The crucial problem which each of the great eighteenth-century French writers tried to solve in his own way, and which none of them solved quite satisfactorily, is this: in varying degrees each was committed to a materialistic philosophy, and this means determinism. But they were equally committed to an emotional faith in progress, civilization, the social virtues of public spirit, kindness, unselfishness. But the logical end of determinism is cynical opportunism, for how can there be moral responsibility if our lives are predetermined by the laws of chemistry and physics? Diderot in his official writings is illogically both a materialistic fatalist and a sentimental moralist. Can this dialogue be interpreted as an attempt to face up to his dilemma behind closed doors? Does 'He' carry materialistic jungle law as far as it will go, and are the objections raised by 'I' real ones or merely conventional protestations? From this point of view the dialogue might be likened to an intimate talk in a pub between two politicians who agree to drop masks and their public *personae* and speak the truth for a few minutes. In their quiet corner they admit that their official party beliefs are merely a screen behind which the real business

of life is carried on, namely to enjoy the benefits of an easy
and lucrative career. But one is more timid than the other,
and goes through the motions of virtue and high ideals.
The other, spurred on no doubt by his friend's pusillanimity,
soars aloft on higher and yet higher flights of cynicism and
nihilism. What is the use of noble ideals and the good life
after you are dead? Why be a great artist and starve in a
garret? The enjoyment of this life, the only one we have,
is all that matters to the individual, and moral values are
illusory. The comical reaction of 'I' to all this – half
conventional horror, half grudging admiration – pushes
'He' to the extreme limits of materialism in a declaration
that the final meaning, the only real joys in life, are physical
intake of food and drink, the pleasures of the bed and a good
daily evacuation of the bowels. From this it is but a step to
the vanity of all so-called culture and education, since
education teaches useless subjects and teachers are by
definition ignorant and second-rate, for were it otherwise
they would be doing something more profitable to themselves. Rameau candidly illustrates this by an hilarious
demonstration of his own charlatanism as a teacher of
music. After some conventional tut-tutting by 'I', we learn
that in every profession it is not knowledge or skill, but the
tricks of the trade, the externals of proficiency, the professional manner, which bring success. Finally there is a
long discussion of the familiar theme: is happiness possible
without virtue? Rameau ingeniously begs the whole
question by saying that happiness comes from living according to nature, *one's own nature*. This turns one of the most
cherished ideas of some eighteenth-century thinkers upside-
down – the notion that nature is right because she is pure,
simple, undefiled. Human nature, such people say, is
essentially good, and has only been corrupted by evil
political forces and social exploitation. Yes, says Rameau,
nature is indeed always the best guide, and she counsels free

rein for such perfectly natural human traits as sloth, lies, hypocrisy, greed, sensuality. Look at a natural animal or child and deny that if you can.

4. Literary and artistic questions?

So homogeneous is the dialogue, like a piece of cloth woven in many colours, that one should really go back to the beginning each time and follow each thread through. But the task would be not only difficult but useless, because the threads change colour as they go along, and sometimes get inextricably mixed with other threads. There is no point in following through the threads of purely personal literary controversy against such people as Palissot, the Frérons and the rest. But one fundamental 'official' theory of Diderot, and indeed most of his contemporaries, was the moral purpose of art. Over and over again, in his aesthetic works, dramatic and art criticism, Diderot had repeated his conviction that the object of any artist should be to make vice hateful and virtue attractive. But if 'He' in the dialogue in any way expresses the inner thoughts of Diderot himself, here is a flat denial of official doctrine amounting to intellectual suicide. For what do we find? 'He', Rameau the nephew, reads carefully the 'moral' plays of Molière, the portraits of La Bruyère, in order to pick up tips on how to be a successful swindler, hypocrite or whatever it may be. Here we are in very deep water indeed, for if a work of literature, in order to achieve its moral purpose, must faithfully portray immoral types, who is to say that exactly the opposite effect to the one supposedly intended is not going to be produced upon the reader? And, next and inevitable step, what is to prevent the unscrupulous from utilizing this obvious fact in order to sell pornographic literature disguised as a purity campaign? The speech beginning: 'Well, what I find in them . . .' (p. 82) is like a glimpse down into the depths of one's own soul that makes one

either sick or relieved to be honest at last. It is the overthrow of all moral values. How many 'uplifting' works of
art are by this searchlight revealed as bottles of strong
aphrodisiac labelled as tonic-water? How many authors, or
even preachers, find a vicarious satisfaction for their lusts
in describing in delicious detail the false allurements of sin?

From here there is but another step to the corruption of
all critics, who have to toe the party line of the periodical
for which they are writing, and from there, by way of
naming some of these critics and their literary reviews, to a
passage which is a stroke of genius: 'HE: That's true. But
all the down-and-outs are united in front of food...'
(p. 84). This ridiculous episode between Fréron and the
Abbé Laporte blends almost all the elements of a complex
work into one wonderful fugal passage. The abbé is the
prime cause of the quarrel with Bertin and Mademoiselle
Hus which had landed Rameau on the streets just before
the encounter with Diderot, and the intertwined themes
which come together here include the literary satire, the
social satire, the philosophical argument, the moral question, the cynical nihilism of Rameau, the fictional framework, the real life-story of Rameau, the realistic novel, the
comic masterpiece, the picture of manners and last, but
doubtless not least in Diderot's own mind, Diderot's personal grudge against the literary clique which had booed his
own dramatic efforts. And even the coarseness and
obscenities in the dialogue are now revealed as part of the
plan, for it transpires that much of the opposition to the
Encyclopédie and the cause of progress is motivated by the
crude sexual intrigues of some influential people.

The danger of developing, even in such a rapid survey as
this, some of the subjects touched on in this conversation,
is that one might think it is a treatise on various abstruse
artistic, social and moral questions and therefore dull. The
very opposite is the case. Rameau the nephew, whatever

he may have been in real life, is here one of the great comic creations of literature, worthy to be mentioned with Falstaff and Don Quixote and, like them, comic because tragedy is never far away. Towards the end of their conversation, when Rameau has returned to his theme that there is nothing in life but sensual enjoyment and that the true way of life is that of total selfishness, 'I' (Diderot) suddenly asks the simple and searching question: 'Do you love your child?' Like a pinprick this deflates the vast balloon of Rameau's philosophy. He tries to make his answer square with the philosophy, but whether or not it is true that we live only for eating, drinking, fornicating and evacuation of the bowels, it suddenly appears that Rameau is a human being, ready to sacrifice and if need be to die for his child. Even, he says, if my child should rob and kill me, which he might easily do if he lives out his father's theories, yet I must die for his happiness. For that also is nature.

In real life no argument has a really neat and conclusive ending, least of all a discussion ranging over vast and varied fields. The end of this one must be inconclusive for the deepest philosophical reasons, but it must also be so because human behaviour and artistic truth demand it. The two men in a pub, or on a seat in a garden – it is no longer quite clear where they are – become aware of the time, and they have to end abruptly on the sort of note real people always come back to: 'Oh well, I dunno.'

RAMEAU'S NEPHEW

SECOND SATIRE

Vertumnis, quotquot sunt, natus iniquis
(Horace: *Satires*, II, 7)

COME rain or shine, my custom is to go for a stroll in the
Palais-Royal every afternoon at about five. I am always to
be seen there alone, sitting on a seat in the Allée d'Argenson,
meditating.[1] I hold discussions with myself on politics, love,
taste or philosophy, and let my thoughts wander in complete abandon, leaving them free to follow the first wise or
foolish idea that comes along, like those young rakes we see
in the Allée de Foy who run after a giddy-looking little
piece with a laughing face, sparkling eye and tip-tilted
nose, only to leave her for another, accosting them all, but
sticking to none. In my case my thoughts are my wenches.
If it is too cold or wet I take shelter in the Café de la
Régence[2] and amuse myself watching people playing chess.
Paris is the place in the world, and the Café de la Régence
the place in Paris where this game is played best, and at
Rey's the shrewd Legal, the crafty Philidor and the
dependable Mayot sally forth to battle. There the most
amazing moves can be seen and the poorest conversation
heard, for if you can be a man of wit and a great chess-
player like Legal you can also be a great chess-player and
an ass like Foubert and Mayot. One day after dinner there
I was, watching a great deal but saying little and listening
to as little as I could, when I was accosted by one of the
weirdest characters in this land of ours where God has not
been sparing of them. He is a compound of the highest and
the lowest, good sense and folly. The notions of good and
evil must be strangely muddled in his head, for the good

qualities nature has given him he displays without ostenta-
tion, and the bad ones without shame. Moreover he is
blessed with a strong constitution, a singularly fervid
imagination and lung-power quite out of the ordinary. If
you ever run into him and his originality does not hold your
interest, you will either stuff your fingers into your ears or
run away. God, what awful lungs! Nothing is less like him
than himself. At times he is thin and gaunt like somebody
in the last stages of consumption; you could count his teeth
through his cheeks and it is as though he had had nothing to
eat for days on end or had just come out of a Trappist
monastery. A month later he is sleek and plump as though
he had never left some millionaire's table or had been shut
up in a Cistercian house. Today, in dirty linen and ragged
breeches, tattered and almost barefoot, he slinks along with
head down and you might be tempted to call him over and
give him money. Tomorrow, powdered, well shod, hair
curled, beautifully turned out, he walks with head high,
showing himself off, and you would almost take him for a
gentleman. He lives for the day, gloomy or gay according to
circumstances. His first care when he gets up in the morning
is to make sure where he will be dining; after dinner he
thinks where to go for supper. Night has its own peculiar
worry – whether to tramp home to his little garret, assuming
that the landlady, sick and tired of waiting for the rent, has
not demanded the key back, or whether to go to earth in an
inn just out of town and there await the dawn with a crust
of bread and a pot of ale. When he has less than six sous in
his pocket, which sometimes happens, he falls back on a
cabby he knows, or the coachman of some noble lord, who
gives him a shake-down on some straw beside his horses.
In the morning he still has some of his mattress in his hair.
If the weather is mild he walks up and down the Cours or
the Champs-Elysées all night. He reappears with the day-
light, already dressed yesterday for today and sometimes

34

from today for the rest of the week. I don't think much of these queer birds myself, though some people make boon companions of them, and even friends. They interest me once a year when I run into them because their characters contrast sharply with other people's and break the tedious uniformity that our social conventions and set politenesses have brought about. If one of them appears in a company of people he is the speck of yeast that leavens the whole and restores to each of us a portion of his natural individuality. He stirs people up and gives them a shaking, makes them take sides, brings out the truth, shows who are really good and unmasks the villains. It is then that the wise man listens and sorts people out.

My acquaintance with this particular one went a long way back. His talent had opened the door of a certain home where there lived an only daughter. He swore to her father and mother that he would marry her. They shrugged their shoulders and laughed in his face, saying he was mad, but I saw it become an accomplished fact. He used to touch me for a few crowns, which I gave him. Somehow or other he had wormed his way into several good homes, where there was always a place laid for him, but on condition that he did not speak unless permission had been given. He held his peace and ate in a rage. Kept under restraint in this way he was wonderful to behold. If he felt like breaking the agreement and opened his mouth, at the first word all the company cried: 'Oh, Rameau!' Then his eyes glittered with rage and he fell to eating again with renewed fury. You were anxious to know this man's name, and now you do. He is a nephew of the famous musician who has delivered us from the plainsong of Lully that we have been chanting for over a hundred years, who has written so many unintelligible visions and apocalyptic truths on the theory of music, not a word of which he or anyone else has ever understood, and from whom we have a certain number of operas in which there is harmony, snatches of song, disconnected ideas, clash of arms, dashings to and fro, triumphs, lances, glories, murmurs and victories to take your breath away, and some dance tunes which will last for ever. Having buried the Florentine master[3] he will himself be buried by the Italian virtuosi, which he foresaw. Hence his gloom, misery and surliness, for nobody, even a pretty woman who gets up to find a pimple on her nose, is so cross as an author threatened with outliving his own fame. Witness Marivaux and the younger Crébillon.

He accosts me . . . 'Aha, there you are, Mr Philosopher, and what are you doing here among all this lot of idlers? Are you wasting your time, too, pushing the wood about?' (This is a disparaging way of referring to the games of chess and draughts.)

I: No, but when I've nothing better to do I enjoy for a moment watching those who push well.

HE: In that case you don't enjoy yourself very often, for apart from Legal and Philidor the others know nothing about it.

I: What about Monsieur de Bissy?

HE: He is to chess what Mademoiselle Clairon[4] is to acting. They each know everything there is to know about their game.

I: You are hard to please, and I see you tolerate only men of genius.

HE: Yes, in chess, draughts, poetry, eloquence, music and other nonsense of that kind. What's the use of mediocrity in that sort of thing?

I: Not much, I admit. But a large number of men must go in for them before a man of genius emerges. He is one in a million. But that's enough of that. It is ages since I have seen you. When I don't see you I scarcely give you a thought, but it is always a pleasure to see you again. What have you been up to?

HE: The same as you, I and everybody else does: good, bad and nothing. And then I've been hungry and eaten when the chance came along, and after eating I have been thirsty and had a drink, sometimes. In the meantime my beard grew, and when it grew I had a shave.

I: That was a mistake. A beard is all you need to be a sage.

HE: I grant you that. I have a lofty, furrowed brow, blazing eyes, prominent nose, a wide face, black, bushy eyebrows, a good mouth with full lips and a square jaw. If this great chin were covered by a long beard it would look most impressive in bronze or marble, don't you think?

I: Side by side with Caesar, Marcus Aurelius or Socrates.

HE: No, I should look better between Diogenes and Phryne. I am as impudent as the one and I am fond of consorting with the others.

I: Are you still in good health?

HE: Yes, usually, but not all that good today.

I: What? And you with a paunch like Silenus and a face –

HE: A face you would take for his behind. The spleen which has dried up my dear uncle is apparently fattening his dear nephew.

I: Speaking of your uncle, do you see him sometimes?

HE: Yes, going past in the street.

I: Doesn't he ever do anything for you?

HE: If he ever did anything for anybody it was without realizing it. He is a philosopher in his way. He thinks of nothing but himself, and the rest of the universe is not worth a pin to him. His wife and daughter can just die when they like, and so long as the parish bells tolling their knell go on sounding intervals of a twelfth and a seventeenth everything will be all right. He's quite happy. That is what I particularly value in men of genius. They are only good for one thing, and apart from that, nothing. They don't know what it means to be citizens, fathers, mothers, brothers, relations, friends. Between ourselves, we should resemble them in every respect, but not wish the species to be too numerous. We need men, but not men of genius. My goodness no, them we certainly don't want. They change the face of the globe, yet even in the smallest things stupidity is so rife and so powerful that you can't change it without the hell of a fuss. Part of their conception does come about, part remains as it was. Hence two gospels – a Harlequin coat. The wisdom of Rabelais's monk is true wisdom for his own and everybody else's peace of mind: do your duty after a fashion, always speak well of his reverence the Prior and let the world go its own sweet way. And it does go quite well, since the majority is satisfied with it. If I knew anything about history I would show you that evil has always come here below through some man of genius. But I don't know any history because I don't know anything. Devil take me if I have ever learned anything or if I am any the worse for it. One day I was at the table of a Minister of the Crown who has brains enough for four. Well, he demonstrated as clearly as one and one make two that nothing was more useful to nations than lies and nothing more harmful than truth. I don't recollect his proofs very well, but obviously it followed that men of genius are pernicious and that if a child bore on his brow the mark of this dangerous gift of nature he should be thrown to the wolves.

I: And yet people like that who are so against genius all claim to possess it.

HE: I am sure they think they do in their heart of hearts, but I don't think they would dare own up to it.

I: That's because of modesty. So from then on you developed a terrible loathing for genius?

HE: One I shall never get over.

I: But I have seen the time when you were in despair at

only being an ordinary man. You will never be happy if you are equally worried by the pros and the cons. You should make up your mind and stick to it. Still, I agree with you that men of genius are frequently peculiar or, as the saying goes, great wits are oft to madness near allied, and you can't gainsay the fact. Periods which have not produced any will be despised. Geniuses will bring honour to the nations in which they have lived; sooner or later statues are erected to their memory and they are regarded as benefactors of mankind. With all due respect to the noble minister you were quoting, I think that although a lie may be useful for a moment it is necessarily harmful in the long run, and that, on the contrary, in the long run truth necessarily does good even though it may be harmful at the moment. From which I should be tempted to conclude that the man of genius who shows up a common error or who establishes a great truth is always worthy of our veneration. It may happen that such a man falls a victim to prejudice and the law, but there are two kinds of laws: some absolutely equitable and universal, others capricious and only owing their authority to blindness or force of circumstances. These last bestow only a momentary disgrace upon the man who infringes them, a disgrace which time turns against judges and nations for ever. Who is disgraced today, Socrates or the judge who made him drink the hemlock?

HE: And a fat lot of good it has done him! Was he condemned and put to death any the less for that? Was he any the less a seditious citizen? Because he despised a bad law did that do anything to prevent his encouraging fools to despise a good one? Was he any the less impudent and eccentric as a person? Just now you yourself were within an ace of admitting to a very unflattering view of men of genius.

I: Listen, my dear man. A society ought not to have bad

39

laws, and if it had only good ones it would never be in the position of persecuting a man of genius. I did not say that genius was inseparable from wickedness or wickedness from genius. A fool is more likely to be a wicked man than a man of intelligence. Even if a genius were usually difficult to live with, touchy, prickly, insufferable, even if he were an evil man, what would you conclude from that?

HE: That he ought to be drowned.

I: Steady, my dear fellow. Now look, tell me – I won't take your uncle as an example, for he is a hard man, brutal, inhuman, avaricious, he is a bad father, bad husband, bad uncle; but it is not quite certain that he really is a man of genius, that he has taken his art very far or that his work will count ten years from now. But Racine? There was a genius for you, but he was said to be none too good as a man. And what about Voltaire?

HE: Don't press me too hard. I am logical.

I: Which would you prefer: that he had been a worthy person, tied to his counter like Briasson, or to his tape-measure like Barbier,[5] giving his wife a legitimate baby once a year, a good husband, good father, good uncle, good neighbour, an honest tradesman but nothing more; or that he had been a rogue, a traitor, ambitious, envious, spiteful, but the creator of *Andromaque, Britannicus, Iphigénie, Phèdre, Athalie*?

HE: Well, for him it might have been better if he had been the first of these two.

I: That is infinitely truer than you think.

HE: Oh, that's just like all you people! If we say something good it is just by accident, like lunatics or visionaries. Only people of your sort realize what you are saying. Yes, Mr Philosopher, I do know what I am saying, and I know it as well as you know what you say.

I: Well, then, why for Racine?

HE: Because all those fine things he created didn't bring

him in as much as twenty thousand francs, whereas if he had been a worthy silk merchant in the Rue Saint-Denis or the Rue Saint-Honoré, a wholesale grocer or an apothecary with a good connexion, he would have amassed a huge fortune and while doing so would have enjoyed every possible kind of pleasure. From time to time he would have given a coin to some poor devil of a clown like me for making him laugh or for procuring, upon occasion, a girl to make a nice change from the eternal cohabitation with his wife. We should have had some excellent meals at his home, played for high stakes, drunk excellent liqueurs and coffee, gone for excursions into the country. You see I was perfectly aware of what I was saying. Yes, you can laugh. But let me tell you that it would have been better for everybody round him.

I: No question about that, provided he hadn't made dishonest use of the wealth he had acquired in legitimate trade, and that he had kept out of his house all these gamblers, these parasites, these dull toadies, idlers and useless rakes, and provided that he had got his shop boys to wallop the officious person who comforts husbands with a nice change from the usual cohabitation with their wives.

HE: Wallop, sir, wallop! You don't wallop people in a well regulated city. It is a respectable way of life, and lots of people go in for it, even titled folk. And what the devil do you expect people to spend their money on if not to have a good table, good company, good wines, pretty women, pleasures of all descriptions, amusements of every kind? I'd just as soon be a pauper as possess a large fortune and have none of these enjoyments. But to come back to Racine. The man has only been any good to people he didn't know and after his death.

I: Agreed. But just weigh the bad against the good. A thousand years from now he will still draw tears, still be the admiration of men in all countries of the world. He will inspire kindness, compassion, tenderness. People will ask who he was and of what country, and they will envy France. He hurt a few individuals who are dead and gone and in whom we take little or no interest, but we have nothing to fear from his misdeeds or failings. No doubt it might have been better if he had received from nature the virtues of an upright man as well as the talents of a great one. He is a tree which has stunted some others growing near by and smothered plants growing at its feet, but it has raised its head to the heavens and its branches have spread far and wide. It has given shade to all who came, come or are to come seeking rest round its majestic trunk. It has produced exquisite fruit in never-failing abundance. Or again we could wish that Voltaire had the gentleness of Duclos, the ingenuousness of Abbé Trublet or the uprightness of Abbé d'Olivet,[6] but since that cannot be, let us look at the really interesting side of it and forget for the moment the point we occupy in time and space; let us cast our eyes over the centuries to come, the most distant lands and nations yet to be born. Let us think of the good of our race, and even if we are not generous enough ourselves let us at least forgive nature for having been wiser than we are. If you throw cold water on Greuze's head you will probably put an end to his talent at the same time as his vanity. If you make Voltaire less sensitive to criticism he will no longer be able to probe down into the soul of Mérope, and will cease to touch your heart.

HE: But if nature were as powerful as she is wise why, when she made them great, didn't she make them equally good?

I: But don't you see that with such a line of argument you overthrow the universal order of things, and that if everything were excellent here below nothing would stand out as excellent?

HE: You are right. The main thing is that you and I should exist, and that we should be you and I. Apart from that let everything go as it likes. The best order of things, to my way of thinking, is the one I was meant to be part of, and to hell with the most perfect of worlds if I am not of it. I would rather exist, even as an impudent argufier, than not exist at all.

I: There is nobody who doesn't share your opinion and criticize the existing order of things without realizing that he is thereby denying his own existence.

HE: That is true.

I: Let us therefore accept things as they are. Let us establish what they cost us and how much they bring in, and leave alone all the things we don't know enough about either to praise or to blame, and which are probably neither good nor evil but only necessary, as many good people think.

HE: I don't follow much of what you are holding forth about. It is apparently philosophy, and I warn you that I give that a wide berth. All I know is that I would like to be somebody else, at the risk of being a man of genius, a great man. Yes, I must confess something tells me I would. I have never heard any of them praised without feeling secretly furious. I am envious. So when I hear something disreputable about their private lives I listen with pleasure. It brings us nearer together and makes my own mediocrity more bearable. I tell myself: 'You would never have written *Mahomet*, that's a fact, but neither would you have perpetrated the eulogy of Maupeou.'[7] So I have been and still am angry at being mediocre. Yes, yes, I am mediocre and angry. I have never heard the overture to *Les Indes galantes* played, never heard *Profonds abîmes du Ténare, Nuit, éternelle nuit*[8] sung, without ruefully telling myself: 'That's what you will never do.' In fact I was jealous of my uncle, and if at his death there had been some fine compositions for keyboard still unpublished, I wouldn't have hesitated to remain myself and be him too.

deep abyss
of Tenare

I: If that's all that's worrying you, I shouldn't bother.

H.E: Oh, it's nothing. These things are just passing phases.

(He fell once again to singing the overture to *Les Indes galantes* and the air *Profonds abîmes*, and then went on):

Something inside there is talking to me and saying: Rameau, old chap, you would like to have composed those two pieces, and if you had composed those two you could do two more, and when you had done a certain number you would be played and sung everywhere, and you could hold your head high as you walked along. Your own mind would tell you your own worth, and people would point you out and say: 'That's the man who wrote the pretty gavottes,' (thereupon he sang the gavottes, then, looking like a man whose overwhelming joy has moved him to tears, he added, rubbing his hands): 'You would have a fine house (measuring the house with his arms), a good bed (nonchalantly stretching himself thereon), good wines (tasting them and clicking his tongue against his palate), a fine coach (raising one leg to step into it), pretty women (fondling their bosoms and gazing at them voluptuously), a hundred lick-spittles would come and pay court to me every day (he seemed to see them all round him – Palissot, Poincinet, the Frérons, father and son, La Porte – and he gave ear to them, swelled with pride, bestowed his approval on them, smiled, treated them with disdain or scorn, sent them packing, called them back and then went on): And so it is that you would be told in the morning that you were a great man, you would read in the *Trois Siècles* that you were a great man, and by the evening you would be convinced that you were one; and the great man, Rameau the Nephew, would fall asleep to the soft murmur of eulogies in his ears, and even in sleep he would look well satisfied, his chest would fill out, rise and fall with pleasure and he would snore like a great man.

(And while saying all this he sank softly upon a seat, closed his eyes and mimed the happy slumbers he was imagining. Having sampled the sweetness of this repose for a few moments he awoke, yawned, rubbed his eyes and went on looking about him for his fawning flatterers.)[9]

I: So you think the happy man sleeps well?

HE: Of course I do! As for me – poor devil – when I get back to my garret and tuck myself into my pallet I am all shrivelled up under my coverlet, my chest tight and my breathing difficult. A sort of feeble whine can just be heard, whereas a financier makes his dwelling re-echo and the whole street is filled with thunder. But at present it is not my wretched snoring and sleeping that are worrying me.

I: And yet that is wretched enough.

HE: What has happened to me is far worse.

I: Well, what?

HE: You have always taken a certain amount of interest in me because, although I am a chap you really despise, I amuse you at the same time.

I: Yes, that's true.

HE: Very well, I'll tell you about it.

(Before beginning he fetches a deep sigh and puts both hands to his forehead. Then he recovers an appearance of calm and says:)

You know of course that I am an ignoramus, a fool, a lunatic, rude, lazy and what we in Burgundy call an out and out shirker, a rogue, a gormandizer . . .

I: What a panegyric!

HE: It's true in every detail. Not one word can be knocked off. No argument about that, *if* you please. Nobody knows me better than I do myself, and I haven't said it all.

I: I don't want to offend you, so I will agree with everything.

HE: Very well then, I have been staying with some people

who took to me precisely because I was gifted with these qualities to an unusual degree.

I: How very odd. Up to now I had thought that one either concealed them from oneself or condoned them in oneself, but despised them in others.

HE: Conceal them from oneself, is that possible? You can be sure that when Palissot is quite alone and communing with himself he tells himself quite a different tale. Rest assured that when he and his colleague are together they admit quite frankly that they are nothing but a pair of arch scoundrels. Despise them in others, indeed! My folk were more just and their characteristics were such that I was a tremendous success with them. I lived like a fighting cock, fêted and sorely missed if I was a moment away. I was their dear Rameau, their pretty Rameau, their Rameau the lunatic, impertinent, ignorant, lazy, greedy old fool. Not one of these pet names but earned me a smile, a caress, a tap on the shoulder, a box on the ears, a kick, a toothsome morsel chucked on to my plate during meals, at other times a certain liberty I could take without its being of any consequence, for I am a person who isn't of any consequence. People do what they like with me, in my company, in front of me, without my standing on ceremony. And think of the little presents that rained down upon me! Clumsy dog that I am, I have lost the lot! Lost the lot through having a bit of common sense for once, just once in my life. Ah, never again!

I: Well, what happened?

HE: An incomparable piece of folly, incomprehensible, unpardonable.

I: Well, what folly?

HE: Rameau, Rameau, did they take you on for that? The stupidity of having shown a bit of taste, intelligence and reason! Rameau, old man, this will teach you to remain what God made you and what your patrons expected you to be. And so they seized you by the scruff of the neck, showed you the door, and said: 'Be off with you, and don't show your face here again – the fellow has pretensions to sense and reason, it seems! Clear off! We've got those qualities ourselves, anyhow.' And so off you went, biting your nails; it is your accursed tongue that you should have bitten off first. For want of realizing that, here you are out in the street, penniless and with nowhere to lay your head. You were stuffed with food and now you are going back to garbage; well housed and now you will be only too glad to be given back your garret; you had a good bed and now the straw awaits you between Monsieur de Soubise's coachman and friend Robbé. Instead of the cozy and quiet slumbers you used to enjoy you will hear the whinneying and stamping of horses with one ear and with the other the thousand times worse noise of dull, harsh and barbarous doggerel. Hapless, ill-advised fool, possessed by a million devils!

I: But couldn't you manage to make it up again with them? Was it such an unpardonable blunder on your part? If I were in your place I should go and see these people. They need you more than you think.

HE: Oh, I am sure that now they haven't got me there to make them laugh they are dull dogs with a vengeance.

I: That's why I should go and see them. I wouldn't leave them time to manage without me and turn to some respectable amusement, for who knows what may happen?

HE: That's not what I am afraid of. That won't happen.

I: However marvellous you may be, somebody else can replace you.

HE: Not at all easy.

I: I realize that. All the same, I should go along with that ravaged face, those wild eyes, shirt torn open, tousled hair, in fact in the really tragic state you are in at the moment. I should throw myself at the goddess's feet, glue my face to the ground, and without raising myself address her in a low, sobbing voice: 'Forgive me, Madame, forgive me, I am an unspeakable wretch. It was just an unfortunate moment, for you know I am not given to common sense, and I swear I will never go in for it again for the rest of my life.'

(The funny thing was that while I was holding forth to him in this way he was doing the actions. He flung himself down with his face pressed to the ground, he seemed to be holding the point of a slipper between his hands, and he wept and sobbed, saying: 'Yes, my little queen, yes, I promise, never in my life, in my life.' Then suddenly rising to his feet he went on in a serious and thoughtful tone:)

HE: Yes, you are right. I think that is best. She is kind hearted. Monsieur Vieillard says she is so kind! I know myself that she is. And yet to have to go and eat humble pie in front of the bitch! Beg for mercy at the feet of a miserable little performer who is constantly booed by the pit! I, Rameau, son of Monsieur Rameau, apothecary of Dijon and a man of substance who has never bowed the knee to anyone! I, Rameau, nephew of the man they call the great Rameau who, ever since Monsieur Carmontelle drew him stooping and with his hands under his coat-tails, can be seen in the Palais-Royal walking bolt upright and with his arms up in the air. I who have composed keyboard pieces which nobody plays, but which may well be the only ones to go down to future generations who will. I! I, indeed! That I should go and ... Look, Sir, it can't be done. (Placing his right hand on his heart): I can feel something there rising in revolt and saying: 'Rameau, you will do nothing of the kind.' There must be a certain dignity connected with man's nature and which nothing can stifle. A mere nothing will arouse it. Yes, a mere nothing, yet there are other days when it wouldn't upset me in the least to be as abject as you like, and on those days I would kiss this Hus girl's arse for twopence.[10]

48

I: Ah, but you see, my friend, she is fair, pretty, young, soft and plump, and so it is an act of humility to which one more delicate than you might stoop upon occasion.

HE: Let's get this clear: there is arse-kissing literally and arse-kissing metaphorically. Ask fat old Bergier, who kisses Madame de la Marque's arse both literally and metaphorically – and my goodness, in that case I should find both equally unpleasant.

I: If the way I'm suggesting doesn't appeal to you then have the courage to be a pauper.

HE: But it is hard to be a pauper while there are so many wealthy idiots you can live on. And then the self-contempt; that is unbearable.

I: Do you know that sentiment?

HE: Of course I do. How many times have I said: 'Well, Rameau, there are ten thousand good tables in Paris, each laid for fifteen or twenty, and of all those places, not one for you! Pursefuls of gold being poured out right and left, and not one single coin drops out for you! A thousand silly little wits with no talent or merit, a thousand little creatures devoid of charm, a thousand dull wire-pullers are well dressed and you go naked! How can you be such a fool? Couldn't you flatter as well as the next man? Couldn't you manage to lie, swear, perjure, promise, fulfil or back out like anybody else? Couldn't you go on all fours like anybody else? Couldn't you aid and abet Madame's intrigue and deliver Monsieur's love-letters like anybody else? Encourage that young man to speak to Mademoiselle and persuade Mademoiselle to listen to him, like anybody else? Couldn't you drop a hint to the daughter of one of our *bourgeois* friends that she looks dowdy and that some nice ear-rings, a little make-up, some lace and a dress in the Polish style would suit her down to the ground? That her dainty feet were not meant for walking in the street, that there is a rich gentleman, young and handsome, with a gold-braided coat,

a magnificent carriage, and six tall lackeys, who happened
to see her as she was passing by and thinks she is charming,
and that from that day on he has lost all appetite for food
and drink, cannot sleep any more and is dying? – But what
about Daddy? – Yes, of course, your Daddy will be a bit
upset just at first. – And then Mummy, who is always telling
me to be a good girl? – Old wives' tales that don't mean a
thing.– And my confessor? – You'll see no more of him, or
if you persist in the quaint idea of going and telling him the
story of your amusements, it will cost you a few pounds of
sugar and coffee. – He is a stern man, and has already
refused me absolution for the song *Viens dans ma cellule*. –
That was because you had nothing to give him, but when
he sees you all in lace . . . – Shall I have lace, then? – Of
course, all kinds . . . and wearing lovely diamond ear-rings.
– What, shall I have diamond ear-rings? – Yes. – Like those
of that *marquise* who sometimes comes and buys gloves in
our shop? – Yes, just like those; a fine coach with dappled
grey horses, two tall flunkeys and a little nigger-boy, and
the outrider in front; make-up, patches and a train-bearer. –
At the ball? – Yes, at the ball, the opera, the theatre. . . .
(Already her heart is bounding with joy. . . . You fiddle with
a bit of paper between your fingers . . .) – What's that? –
Nothing. – Oh yes, I think it is. – It's a note. – Who for? –
For you, if you are at all interested. – Interested? I should
think I am. Let's have a look . . . (she reads it). A meeting,
that's out of the question.– On the way to Mass? – Mummy
always goes with me. But supposing he came here one
morning rather early . . . I always get up first and am down
at the counter before anyone else is out of bed. He comes,
she likes him, and one fine day, at twilight, the damsel disappears and I get my two thousand crowns. . . . And to
think, old man, you possess talents like that and yet go
without bread! Aren't you ashamed of yourself, you old
misery? I recalled a lot of rascals who didn't come up to

my ankles and yet were rolling in money; I had a fustian coat and they were covered in velvet; they supported themselves on sticks with gold handles shaped like ravens' beaks and wore rings on their fingers with Aristotle or Plato stones. How did they begin, though? Most of them as third-rate musicians, and today they are petty nobles. Thereupon I felt brave, with soul uplifted, wits sharpened and equal to anything. But those happy moods were only of short duration, apparently, for so far I haven't been able to make much headway. Anyhow, that is the theme of my frequent soliloquies, and you can paraphrase them how you like so long as you conclude therefrom that I do know what self-contempt is, or the torment of the soul that comes from neglect of the talents heaven has vouchsafed us, which is the cruellest of all. It were almost better that a man had never been born.

(As I was listening to him acting the scene of the pimp and the maiden he was procuring, I was torn between opposite impulses and did not know whether to give in to laughter or furious indignation. I felt embarrassed. A score of times a burst of laughter prevented a burst of rage, and a score of times the anger rising from the depths of my heart ended in a burst of laughter. I was dumbfounded at such sagacity and such baseness, such alternately true and false notions, such absolute perversion of feeling and utter turpitude, and yet such uncommon candour. He noticed the conflict going on inside me and said: What's the matter?)

I: Nothing.

HE: You look upset.

I: Well, so I am.

HE: What do you advise, then?

I: Change the subject. Unhappy man, to have been born or to have fallen into a state so vile!

HE: I quite agree. But don't take my state too much to

heart. When I took you into my confidence it was not in order to upset you. I managed to put a little by while I was with these people, for, remember, everything was found, absolutely everything, and I was allowed so much for my little extras.

(Then he began banging his forehead again with his fist, chewing his lip and rolling wild eyes ceilingwards, adding: But it's all over now. I put a little aside, time has gone by and anyhow that much is saved.)

I: You mean that much is lost.

HE: No, no, saved. You get richer every minute. One day less to live or one crown more, it all comes to the same. The important thing is to evacuate the bowels easily, freely, pleasantly and copiously every evening. *O stercus pretiosum!* That is the final outcome of life in every sphere. At the last day all are equally rich, whether it is Samuel Bernard[11] who, thanks to thefts, pillagings and bankruptcies, leaves seven millions in gold, or Rameau who will leave nothing, Rameau whose hessian shroud will be provided by charity. A dead man can't hear the bells tolling, and it's no use a hundred priests chanting themselves hoarse for him and a long line of blazing torches stretching in front and behind, for his soul is not walking in the procession with the master of ceremonies. To rot under marble or to rot under earth is still to rot. To have your coffin surrounded by choirboys in red or choirboys in blue or nobody at all, what difference does it make? And then look at this wrist of mine; it used to be as stiff as the devil. These ten fingers were like so many rods set in a wooden metacarpus, and these tendons were like old catgut, drier and stiffer than that which has been on a turner's wheel. But I have so pulled them about, strained and broken them in. So you won't work, won't you? Well, I say you damn well will, and that's that.

(While saying this he seized with his right hand the fingers and wrist of his left and turned them backwards and forwards until his fingertips touched his arm; his joints cracked and I was afraid they would be dislocated for good.)

I: Mind what you are doing, you will maim yourself.

HE: No fear, they're used to it. For ten years I've been giving them a dreadful time of it. Whatever they felt about it the buggers just had to get used to it and learn to hit the right keys and flit over the strings. And so they work all right now. Yes, quite all right.

(At the same time he takes up the position of a violinist, hums an *allegro* of Locatelli, his right arm moves as though bowing and his left hand and fingers seem to fly up and down the neck. If he plays a wrong note he stops, tightens or loosens the string, plucking it with his nail to make sure it is in tune, then takes up the piece again where he broke off, tapping the time with his foot; head, feet, hands, arms, body all play their part. In this very way you have sometimes seen Ferrari or Chiabran or some other virtuoso in similar convulsions at the Concert of Sacred Music, presenting a picture of the same torture and giving me almost as much pain, for is it not a painful thing to see torment in somebody who is supposed to be giving a representation of pleasure? If he must act the part of a victim being tortured, for goodness sake draw a curtain between this man and me and hide him from me. If in the middle of all this agitation and shouting there occurred a piece of double-stopping, one of those passages in harmony when the bow is drawn slowly across more than one string at the same time, his face took on an expression of ecstasy, his voice grew gentle and he listened to himself with rapture. And the chords really were heard by his ears and mine. Finally, putting his fiddle back under his left arm with the hand that had been holding it, and lowering his right hand with the bow, he said: Well, what do you think of that?)

53

I: Marvellous.

HE: Not too bad, I think. Sounds just about as good as the others.

(Thereupon he crouched like a player sitting down at the keyboard. Take pity on yourself and me, I said.)

No, no, as I've got you here you shall listen. I don't want a testimonial given without knowing what for. You will now praise me in more convincing tones, and that will bring me in another pupil.

I: I go about so little, and you will tire yourself to no purpose.

HE: I never get tired.

(Seeing that it would be quite pointless to pity the fellow, whom the violin sonata had left bathed in sweat, I decided to let him get on with it. So there he was, seated at the keyboard, with his legs bent and his head turned ceiling-wards, where you would have said he could see a score written out, singing, improvising, playing something by Alberti or Galuppi, I don't know which. His voice went like the wind and his fingers flew over the keys, sometimes abandoning the top part so as to do the bass, sometimes leaving the accompaniment to take up the top part again. One passion after another flitted across his face – you could see tenderness, anger, pleasure, grief and feel the *pianos* and *fortes*. And I am sure that somebody better versed than I would have recognized the piece from the tempo and character, his facial expressions and the snatches of song that escaped him from time to time. But what was so odd was that every now and then he fumbled and made a fresh start as though he had done it wrong and was annoyed at no longer having it at his fingers' ends.

So you see, he said, rising to his feet and wiping the drops of sweat that were running down his cheeks, that we also can strike a tritone or an augmented fifth, and that we are familiar with consecutive fifths. Those enharmonic passages

54

that dear uncle has made such a fuss about aren't really all that difficult, and we shall manage all right.)

I: You have put yourself to a lot of trouble to show me how very proficient you are. A man like me would have taken your word for it.

HE: Very proficient? Oh no. As far as the tricks of my trade are concerned, I know them fairly well, and that is more than is necessary. For in this country need anyone know the subject he teaches?

I: No, any more than people need know what they learn.

HE: That's very true, good Lord, very true. Now, Mr Philosopher, put your hand on your heart and tell the truth. Time was when you weren't as well off as you are today.

I: I'm not all that well off even now.

HE: But you wouldn't still be going to the Luxembourg in summer, you remember –

I: That'll do, yes, I remember.

HE: In a grey plush coat.

I: Yes, yes.

HE: Threadbare on one side, with a frayed cuff, and black woollen stockings darned up the back with white thread.

I: All right, all right, have it your own way.

HE: What did you do in those days in the Allée des Soupirs?[12]

I: Look pretty silly.

HE: After that you used to trot along the road.

I: Quite right.

HE: You used to give maths lessons.

I: Without knowing a word about it myself – isn't that what you're driving at?

HE: Exactly.

I: I learned through teaching others, and I turned out some good pupils.

HE: That's as may be, but music isn't the same thing as algebra or geometry. Now that you are a well-to-do gent –

I: Not so well-to-do.

HE: – And have feathered your own nest –

I: Very little.

HE: You take on tutors for your daughter.

I: Not yet. Her mother sees to her education. Anything for peace and quiet at home.

HE: Peace and quiet at home? Damn it, you only get that when you are servant or master, and the thing to be is master. I once had a wife, God rest her soul, but when, on occasion, she answered back, I rose up on my spurs, loosed my thunders and said, like God: 'Let there be light,' and there was light. And so in the space of four years we didn't have words ten times. How old is your child?

I: That is nothing to do with it.

HE: How old is your child?

I: For God's sake leave my child and her age out of it and get back to the teachers she is to have.

HE: Really, I've never known anything so pig-headed as a philosopher. Would it be possible, by dint of the most humble supplications, to learn from the esteemed philosopher roughly how old his respected daughter might be?

I: Well, let's say eight.[13]

HE: Eight! She should have had her fingers on the keys these four years.

I: But perhaps I was not all that anxious to bring into her educational programme a subject that takes up so much time and serves so little purpose.

HE: And what will you teach her, then?

I: To reason correctly, if I can. An uncommon thing in men and even rarer in women.

HE: Oh, let her be as unreasonable as she likes, so long as she is pretty, amusing and attractive.

I: Since nature has been unkind enough to give her a

delicate constitution and a sensitive soul, and expose her to the same troubles in life as if she had a robust constitution and a heart of bronze, I shall teach her, if I can, how to bear these things with fortitude.

HE: Oh, let her weep, suffer, put on affectations and nerve-storms like everybody else, so long as she's pretty, amusing and attractive. What, no dancing lessons?

I: Only what is needed for curtseying, standing up properly, having a good presence and deportment.

HE: No singing?

I: No more than you need for good enunciation.

HE: No music?

I: If there were a good teacher of harmony I would willingly send her to him for two hours a day for a year or two, but not more.

HE: And in the place of the essential things you are cutting out . . .

I: I put grammar, literature, history, geography, a bit of drawing and a great deal of ethics.

HE: How easy it would be for me to prove the uselessness of all those subjects in a world such as ours. Uselessness? I would even say danger, perhaps. But for the moment I'll stick to the one question: won't she need one or two teachers?

I: I expect so.

HE: Ah, here we are again. And you hope that these teachers will know the grammar, literature, history, geography and ethics in which they will be giving her lessons? Rubbish, my dear sir, rubbish. If they knew those things well enough to teach them they wouldn't be teaching.

I: Why not?

HE: Because they would have spent their whole life studying them. You have to be deeply versed in art or science in order to be sure of the rudiments. School textbooks can only be written by those who have grown grey in harness. It is the middle and end which throw light on the obscurities of the early stages. Ask your friend Monsieur d'Alembert, the star of mathematical science, if he thinks he is too good for the elementary work. It was only after thirty or forty years of practice that my uncle descried the first glimmerings of musical theory.

I: Oh, idiot, arch-idiot! How comes it that in that crackpot brain of yours such sound ideas are mixed up with so many absurdities?

HE: Who the devil knows? Chance chucks them at you and they stick. But still, when you don't know everything you don't know anything properly. You don't know where one thing goes or another comes from, where this or that should be fitted in, which should go first, or whether it would be better second. Can you teach properly without method? But where does method come from? For example, my dear philosopher, I've an idea physics will always be a miserable science, a drop of water taken up on a needlepoint from the vast ocean, a single particle from the chain of the Alps. And why do phenomena happen? Really, you might just as well know nothing as know so little so badly. That was exactly my position when I set up as a teacher of accompaniment and composition. But what are you dreaming about?

I: I am reflecting that everything you have said is more specious than logical. But let it go at that. You say you have taught accompaniment and composition?

HE: Yes.

I: Knowing nothing whatever about it?

HE: No, I certainly didn't, and that is why there were worse teachers than me: the ones who thought they knew something. At any rate I didn't ruin the intelligence and fingers of the children. When they went on from me to a good teacher, having learned nothing they had nothing to unlearn, and that was so much time and money saved.

I: How did you get away with it?

HE: Like they all do. I would arrive and fling myself into an arm-chair: 'What awful weather! How tiring the pavement is!' I then gossiped about various bits of news: 'Mademoiselle Lemierre was to have been a vestal in the new opera, but she is pregnant for the second time, and they don't know who will understudy her. Mademoiselle Arnould has left her Count and it is said that she is bargaining with Bertin. The Count has found the secret of Monsieur de Montamy's porcelain, though. At the last concert of the music circle there was an Italian woman who sang like an angel. As for Préville, he is a wonder. You should see him in *Le Mercure galant*; the riddle scene is priceless. Poor old Dumesnil has got beyond knowing what she is saying or doing. Now Mademoiselle, get out your music.' While Mademoiselle, in no hurry, is looking for her book which she has mislaid, while the maid is being summoned and there is a dressing-down, I go on: 'Clairon really is incomprehensible. There is talk of a very peculiar marriage, that of Mademoiselle What's-her-name, a little thing he was keeping, who has had two or three children by him and who had been kept by lots of others.' 'Now, now, Rameau, that can't be true, you are talking rubbish.' 'No I'm not; it is even said that it is an accomplished fact. Rumour has it that Voltaire is dead; that's a good thing.' 'Why a good thing?' 'Well, it means we can expect something amusing from him. He makes a habit of dying a fortnight before.' Now, what else can I tell you? I recounted a few low stories I had picked up in a house I had been in, for we are all great scandalmongers. I acted the fool and was listened to, laughed at. They exclaimed how delightful I always was. But meanwhile Mademoiselle's book had at last been found under an arm-chair where it had been dragged, chewn up and torn to pieces by a young pug-dog or by a kitten. She sat herself down at the instrument. First she strummed away on her own. Then I walked up, having made an approving sign to her mother. Mother: 'Not too bad, she only needs the will, but she won't use it. She prefers to waste her time chattering, bothering about clothes, running here and there, goodness knows what. You are no sooner gone than the book is shut and not opened again until you come back. What's more, you never find fault with her.' Well, as I had to do something, I took hold of her hands and put them into a different position. I lost my temper and shouted: 'G, G, G, Mademoiselle, it's a G!' Mother: 'Mademoiselle, have you no ears? I am not at the keyboard, and can't see over to your book, yet even I can feel it should be a G. You are giving this gentleman such a lot of trouble. I don't know how he can be so patient. You don't remember a thing he tells you. You are not making any progress at all. . . .' Thereupon I softened the blow a little, and with a toss of the head: 'Excuse me, Madame, excuse me,' I said, 'it could be much better if Mademoiselle wished and if she put in a little work, but still it is not too bad.' Mother: 'If I were you I would keep her on the same piece for a year.' 'Oh, don't you worry, she won't get away from it until she has mastered all the difficulties, and that won't be as long as you think, Madame.' Mother: 'Monsieur Rameau, you are flattering her, you are too indulgent. That's the only thing she will remember about her lesson and she will manage to trot it out again when it suits her.' The hour was going by. My pupil handed me my fee with the graceful arm movement and curtsey she had learned from her dancing-master. As I was pocketing it her mother said: 'Very nice, Mademoiselle, and if Javillier were here he would clap.' I chattered away for another minute out of politeness and then disappeared. And that is what used to be called a lesson in accompaniment.[14]

   I: And is it different nowadays?

   HE: Good Lord, I should think so. I arrive. I look solemn.

I hasten to take my hands out of my muff. I open the instrument and try the keys. I am always in a hurry, and if I am kept waiting a moment I shout as though I am being robbed. An hour from now I have to be at such and such, in two hours' time at the Duchess of So and So's. I am expected to dinner by a lovely marquise, and immediately after that there is a concert at the Baron de Bacq's in the Rue Neuve des Petits-Champs.

I: But really you aren't expected anywhere?

HE: Quite true.

I: Then why resort to all these nasty little tricks?

HE: Nasty? And for why, pray? They are customary in my profession. There is nothing degrading in doing the same as everybody else. I didn't invent them, and I should be peculiar and incompetent if I didn't conform. Of course I well know that if you start applying certain general principles of the sort of morality they all preach and nobody practises, it will work out that white is black and black white. But, Mr Philosopher, there is such a thing as a standard conscience just as there is a standard grammar, and then exceptions in every language that I think you learned people call . . . er . . . oh, what is it, er . . .

I: Idioms.

HE: Exactly. Well, then, every profession has its exceptions to the general code, and I might very well call these *trade idioms*.

I: I see. Fontenelle speaks and writes well, although his style is packed with French idioms.

HE: And sovereign, minister, financier, magistrate, soldier, writer, lawyer, attorney, merchant, banker, artisan, singing-master, dancing-master are all perfectly honest people, although their behaviour departs from the accepted code in several respects and is full of moral idioms. The longer things have been established the more the idioms; the harder times get, the more the idioms increase. The job is worth what the man is worth, and in the end vice-versa, the man is worth what the job is. So we make the job worth as much as we can.

I: All I can gather clearly from all this rigmarole is that few trades are honestly practised, or there are few men who are honest in their jobs.

HE: Quite right, there aren't any. But on the other hand not many are rascals when they are not on the job. And everything would work quite well were it not for a certain number of people of the sort called industrious, punctilious, fulfilling their duties to the letter, strict, or always on the premises, which comes to the same thing, doing their job from morn till night and doing nothing else. And they are the only ones who become wealthy and respected.

I: Through *idioms*?

HE: Quite. I see you have grasped my meaning. Well now, one *idiom* found in almost every walk of life – for some are common to all countries and times just as there are universal stupidities – one common *idiom* is to get as many customers as possible, and one common stupidity is to believe that the person with the most is the most competent. These are two exceptions to the general code which one must bow to. It is a kind of credit system – no intrinsic value, but value conferred by public opinion. It has been said that a good name is worth more than a belt of gold. Now the man with the good name has no belt of gold, but I notice that nowadays the one with the belt of gold seldom lacks the good name. So far as possible we must try to have both, and that is my object when I advertise my worth with what you style nasty tricks and shameful little deceptions. I give my lesson and I do it well – that is the general rule. I let it be known that I have more lessons to give than there are hours in the day – that is the *idiom*.

I: So you really give a good lesson?

HE: Yes, not bad, reasonably good. Dear uncle's ground

bass has simplified it all. Formerly I robbed my pupil of his money; yes, it was robbery, it really was. Now I earn it, as much as the others, anyway.

I: And did you rob without compunction?

HE: Oh yes, no compunction at all. They say that when a thief robs a thief the devil has a good laugh. The parents were rolling in money – God knows where it came from – court, high finance, commerce, banking, business of some kind. Together with a lot of others they employed, I was helping them to make restitution. In nature all the species feed on each other, and all classes prey on each other in society. We mete out justice to each other without the law taking a hand. The Deschamps female formerly, and more recently the Guimard, are the King's vengeance upon the financier, and now dressmaker, jeweller, furnisher, laundry-woman, swindler, chamber-maid, cook, harness-maker are avenging the financier upon the Deschamps.[15] In the midst of all that only the fool or the ne'er-do-well comes to any harm without hurting somebody else, and that is as it should be. Hence you observe that these exceptions to the general code, or moral *idioms* that there is so much talk about under the heading of taking one's perks, amount to nothing at all, and that, taking it all round, all that matters is keeping your eyes open.

I: Yours certainly are!

HE: Then there is poverty. The voice of conscience and honour is very hard to hear when your guts are crying out. Anyway, if I ever get rich it will be my turn to make restitution, and I am resolved to do so in all possible ways – food, gambling, wine and women.

I: But I'm afraid you won't ever get rich.

HE: I suspect as much myself.

I: But if things turned out differently, what would you do?

HE: The same as all down-and-outs who get on. I should

be the most insolent scoundrel you ever set eyes on. Then I should remember all they had made me suffer and pay them back all the humiliations I had been made to swallow. I like giving orders, and I shall give them. I like being praised, and praised I shall be. I shall have all the Villemorian[16] tribe in my pay, and I shall address them as I have been addressed: 'Come on, you scalliwags, amuse me,' and they will amuse me. 'Let decent people be pulled to pieces,' and they will be – that is if any can be found. And then we shall have women, and all be bosom friends when drunk, and drunk we shall certainly get. We'll bandy tittle-tattle and go in for all sorts of quirks and vices. It will be lovely. We shall prove that Voltaire has no brains, Buffon is always high-falutin and nothing but a windbag, Montesquieu merely a wag, D'Alembert will be relegated to his mathematics, and we shall smite hip and thigh all those little Catos like you, who despise us out of envy, whose modesty is a cloak for pride and whose sobriety is dictated by necessity. And music? Then we shall have some!

I: Judging by the worthy use you would make of wealth I see what a great pity it is that you are down and out. You would live in a way that would do the greatest honour to the human race, be most useful to your fellow citizens and most glorious for yourself.

HE: Now I think you are laughing at me, Mr Philosopher, and you don't know who it is you are up against; you seem unaware of the fact that at this moment I represent the most important part of town and Court. The opulent people we see in all walks of life may have admitted to themselves the very things I have been confiding in you, or they may not. But the fact remains that the life I should live in their place is identical with theirs. Now that is just your position: you think that happiness is the same for all. What a strange illusion! Your own brand presupposes a certain romantic turn of mind that we don't all possess, an unusual type of soul, a peculiar taste. You dignify this oddity with the name of virtue and you call it philosophy. But are virtue and philosophy made for everybody? Some can acquire them, some can keep them. Imagine the universe good and philosophical, and admit that it would be devilishly dull. So long live philosophy and long live the wisdom of Solomon – drink good wine, blow yourself out with luscious food, have a tumble with lovely women, lie on soft beds. Apart from that the rest is vanity.

I: What! fighting for one's country?

HE: Vanity! There's no such thing left. From pole to pole all I can see is tyrants and slaves.

I: Helping one's friends?

HE: Vanity! Have we got any friends? And if we had, ought we to make them ungrateful? Have a good look round and you will see that that is what you almost always get for service rendered. Gratitude is a burden, and all burdens are meant to be shaken off.

I: Having a position in society and fulfilling its duties?

HE: Vanity! What does it matter whether you have a position or not so long as you are rich, since you only take up a position in order to get rich? Fulfilling your duties, where does that land you? Into jealousy, upsets, persecution. Is that the way to get on? Butter people up, good God, butter them up, watch the great, study their tastes, fall in with their whims, pander to their vices, approve of their injustices. That's the secret.

I: Seeing to the upbringing of one's children?

HE: Vanity! That's the teacher's job.

I: But if that teacher is so imbued with your principles that he neglects his duty, who is going to be penalized for it?

HE: It won't be me, that's certain, but perhaps some day my daughter's husband or my son's wife.

I: But if they both plunge into debauchery and vice?

HE: That's their own look out.

I: If they bring dishonour upon themselves?

HE: Whatever you do, you can't bring dishonour upon yourself if you are rich.

I: And if they lose their money?

HE: That's their affair!

I: I can see that if you don't feel responsible for looking after your wife's behaviour, or your children's or your servants', you might easily neglect your own interests.

HE: Oh no, excuse me; it is difficult sometimes to raise money, and it is prudent to set about it well in advance.

I: You won't pay much attention to your wife?

HE: None at all, if you please. The best way of dealing with one's better half, I think, is to do what suits her. Don't you think society would be great fun if everybody did what appealed to him?

I: Why not? The evening is never so good for me as when I am pleased with my morning.

HE: Same with me.

I: What makes fashionable people so choosy about their amusements is their abysmal idleness.

HE: Don't you believe it. They are always on the go.

I: As they never get tired they never take a rest either.

HE: Don't you believe it. They are always knocked up.

I: Pleasure is always a business for them and never a need.

HE: All to the good. A need is always painful.

I: They wear everything out. Their souls run to seed and boredom takes over. In the midst of oppressive opulence it would be a kindness to relieve them of life. All they know of happiness is the part which cloys first. I'm not above the pleasures of the senses myself. I have a palate too, and it is tickled by a delicate dish or a rare wine. I have a heart and a pair of eyes, and enjoy looking at a pretty woman. I like to feel her firm, round bosom, press her lips with mine, drink pleasure from her eyes and die of it in her arms. I am not averse to a night out with my men friends sometimes, and even a pretty rowdy one. But I won't hide the fact that it is infinitely more pleasurable for me to have helped the unfortunate, successfully concluded some tricky bit of business, given some good advice, read something pleasant, taken a walk with a man or woman I am fond of, spent a few instructional hours with my children, written a worthwhile page, fulfilled the duties of my position, said some tender, soft words to the woman I love and made her love me. I can think of deeds I would give everything I possess to have done. *Mahomet* is a sublime work, but I would rather have restored the good name of the Calas family.[17] A man I knew had gone off to Cartagena. He was a younger son in a country where custom hands everything over to the eldest. While there he learned that his elder brother, a spoilt child, had stripped his over-indulgent parents of everything they possessed and then turned them out of the family seat, and that the poor old folk were existing in poverty in a little provincial town. What did this young man do who, harshly treated by his parents, had gone to seek his fortune in foreign parts? He sent them assistance, hastened to wind up his own business and went back a wealthy man. He restored his father and mother to their home. He found dowries for his sisters. Ah, my dear Rameau, that man looked upon this period as the happiest in his life. He told me about it with tears in his eyes, and even as I tell you the story I can feel my heart stirring with joy, and my voice fails me.

HE: What funny people you are!

I: And you are people to be pitied if you can't see that we have risen above our human condition, and that it is impossible to be unhappy with two good deeds of this kind to make one secure.

HE: That is a kind of felicity I shall find it hard to get to know, for it is not often met with. So according to you we should all be virtuous?

I: Certainly, if we want to be happy.

HE: And yet I can see countless good people who are not happy, and countless happy ones who are not good.

I: So you think.

HE: But isn't it all because of a minute's common sense and sincerity that I don't know where to turn for a meal tonight?

I: No, of course not. It's because you haven't been like that all along. Because you didn't realize early enough that you should begin by making yourself a position free from dependency.

HE: Free from dependency or no, the one I have made for myself is the most enjoyable, anyway.

I: And the least secure and the least reputable.

HE: But the one best suited to my role as an idler, fool and good-for-nothing.

I: Agreed.

HE: And since I can achieve happiness through failings natural to me which I have acquired without toil and retain without effort, which fit in with the customs of my country, appeal to the tastes of my patrons and are more in harmony with their little personal requirements than some virtues which would cramp their style by nagging away at them from morn till eve, it would be strange indeed for me to torture myself like a soul in hell so as to mutilate myself into something quite different from what I am. I should give myself a character quite foreign to me and qualities most praiseworthy (I grant you that, so as to have no argument), but which would cost a lot to acquire and land me nowhere, or worse than nowhere, because I should be continually satirizing the rich from whom poor devils like me have to make a living. People laud virtue, but they hate and avoid it, for it freezes you to death, and in this world you have to keep your feet warm. Besides, it would inevitably make me ill-tempered, for why do we so often see the virtuous so hard, tiresome and unsociable? Because they have subjected themselves to a discipline that is not in their nature. They are miserable, and when you are miserable yourself you make others miserable too. That's not my idea, nor that of my patrons: I have to be gay, adaptable, agreeable, amusing, odd. Virtue commands respect, and respect is a liability. Virtue commands admiration, and admiration is not funny. I have to deal with people who are bored, and I have to make them laugh. Now what makes people laugh is ridiculousness and silliness, so I have to be ridiculous and silly, and if nature had not made me like that it would be simplest to appear so. Fortunately I don't need to be a hypocrite – there are already so many of every hue, to say nothing of those who take in even themselves. Look at the Chevalier de la Morlière, who turns up the brim of his hat over his ear, carries his head in the air, who looks down his nose at passers-by, has a long sword rattling against his thigh and is always ready with an insult for anybody without one, and seems to be challenging all and sundry – what's he up to? He is doing everything he can to persuade himself that he is a man of courage, but he is a coward. Just flick your finger under his nose and he will take it quietly. If you want to make him lower his voice raise your own. Show him your stick or apply your foot to his backside, and in his astonishment at being a coward he will ask you who told you so and how you found out? He didn't realize it himself a moment ago, for long and continuous aping of bravery had taken him in. He had put on the appearance for so long that he thought he was the genuine article. And look at that woman who goes in for self-mortification, visits prisons, attends every charity meeting, walks with downcast eyes, would never dare look a man in the face, is for ever on guard lest she be led astray by her senses; does any of this prevent her heart from burning, sighs from bursting forth, her desires from catching fire, her lusts from obsessing her and her imagination from dwelling night and day upon scenes from the *Portier des Chartreux* or the *Postures* of Aretino?[18] And what happens to her? What does her maid make of it when she gets up in her nightgown and rushes to assist her dying mistress? Go back to bed, Justine, it is not you your mistress is calling upon in her delirium. And friend Rameau, supposing one day he began displaying scorn for fortune, women, good fare and slothful ease and went Spartan, what would he be? A hypocrite. Rameau must be what he is: a thief happy to be among wealthy thieves, and not a trumpeter of virtue or even a virtuous man gnawing his crust of bread in solitude or with a lot of down-and-outs. To put it bluntly, I have no use for your felicity or for the good life of a handful of visionaries like you.

I: I can see, my dear man, that you don't know what it is and are not even capable of learning.

HE: All the better, good God, all the better. It'd make me peg out through hunger, boredom and remorse, perhaps.

I: From what I have heard, the only advice I can give you is to get back with all speed into the house from which you so imprudently got yourself kicked out.

HE: And do what you don't object to literally, but which upsets you a bit metaphorically?

I: That's my opinion.

HE: Leaving aside that metaphor which doesn't appeal to me just at the moment, but which I shan't mind some other time....

I: How strange you are!

HE: Nothing strange about it. I am quite prepared to be abject, but not under compulsion. I am willing to give up my dignity.... But what are you laughing at?

I: Your dignity strikes me as funny.

HE: Each man has his own. I am prepared to forget
mine, but of my own free will and not on somebody else's
orders. Should people be in a position to say 'crawl', and
I have to crawl? That is the worm's method and it is mine;
we both do the same when we are left alone, but we turn
when our tails are trodden on. I have had my tail trodden
on and I shall turn. And besides, you have no idea what a
madhouse it is. Picture a doleful and dismal creature eaten
up with vapours and wrapped round in two or three thick-
nesses of dressing-gown, who finds himself pleasing, but
everything else displeasing, from whom you can scarcely
get a smile even by dislocating your body and mind in a
hundred different ways. He coldly examines the funny
contortions of my face and the even funnier ones of my
mind, for, between ourselves, that old Father Christmas
of a Benedictine who is so famed for his grimaces is, no
matter what his triumphs at Court may be, and without any
flattery to me or to him either, nothing but a wooden clown
compared with me. Struggle as I will to reach the heights of
the looney bin – nothing doing. Will he laugh? Won't he?
That's what I'm obliged to say to myself in the middle of
my contortions, and you can guess how bad this uncertainty is for one's art. Our hypochondriac, with his head
buried under a nightcap, looks like a motionless image with
a string tied to its chin and going down underneath the
chair. You wait for the string to be pulled and it isn't. Or
supposing the jaw does happen to open it is to pronounce
one devastating word, one word which shows that you
haven't been noticed and that all your monkey tricks have
been wasted. This word is the answer to a question you
asked him four days ago. Once the word has been said the
mastoid spring is released and the jaw snaps to. . . .

(Then he began to take the man off. He sat in a chair
with his head held stiff, hat down over his eyes, eyes half

71

closed, arms hanging loose, moving his jaw like an auto-
maton and saying: Yes, you are right, Mademoiselle, you
must mind how you go.)

It's His Nibs who decides, always decides, and there is
no appeal – night and morning, when he's dressing, at
dinner, at the café, at the gaming table, theatre, supper,
bed and, God forgive me, I think in his mistress's arms. I am
not in a position to hear these last decisions, but I am
hellishly sick of the others. Gloomy, inscrutable and uncompromising, like Fate – that's our boss.

Opposite him there is a straightlaced female trying to be
important. You could persuade yourself to tell her she is
pretty because she still is, in spite of some protuberances
here and there on her face and a tendency towards the
proportions of Madame Bouvillon.[19] I like flesh when it is
beautiful, but all the same too much is too much, and some
movement is so essential to matter. *Item*, she is more spiteful,
proud and stupid than a goose. *Item*, she thinks she is witty.
Item, you have to persuade her that you think she is more so
than anybody else. *Item*, the woman knows nothing and yet
makes decisions. *Item*, her decisions have to be applauded
with hands and feet, one must jump for joy, swoon with
admiration: 'How beautiful! how delicate! well put,
acutely observed, uniquely felt! Where do you women get
all this from? Without any studying, by the sheer power of
instinct, by natural reasoning alone; it really is miraculous.
And then people say that experience, study, reflection,
education all have their part to play.' And other stupidities
of the same sort, with tears of joy. Ten times per day we
bow with one knee bent forward and the other leg straight
out behind. Arms held out to the goddess, we try to read
her wishes in her eyes, hang upon her lips, wait for her
orders and dash off like lightning. Who can stoop to play
such a part except the poor wretch who by so doing two
or three times a week can find the wherewithal to soothe the

tribulation of his innards? What are we to think of others, such as Palissot, Fréron, the Poinsinets or Baculard,[20] who have some possessions and whose turpitudes cannot be excused by the rumblings of an anguished stomach?

I: I would never have thought you were so fussy.

HE: I'm not. At first I watched others at it and did likewise, and even went one better, because I am more downright impudent, a better actor, hungrier and possessed of better lungs. I suppose I must be a direct descendant of the famous Stentor.

(And to give me a correct idea of the power of this organ, he began coughing loud enough to shake the café windows and throw the chess players off their game.)

I: But what's the use of this talent of yours?

HE: Can't you guess?

I: No. I'm a bit slow in the uptake.

HE: Suppose an argument has started and the outcome is uncertain. I rise, and loosing my thunder I say: 'Yes, it is just as Mademoiselle says it is. There's judgement for you! All our great minds couldn't do it if they tried a hundred times. The expression is pure genius.' But you mustn't always gush in the same way. It would pall. You would look insincere. You would become insipid. You can't avoid that pitfall except with discrimination and versatility; you must know how to prepare and where to bring in these peremptory tones in the major key, how to seize the occasion and the moment, for example when opinion is divided and the argument has worked itself up to the highest pitch of violence, everybody is talking at once and you can't hear what they are saying. Then you must take up your position some way off in the corner of the room farthest removed from the battlefield, having prepared your explosion by a long silence, and you suddenly drop like a bomb in the middle of the contestants. Nobody has ever touched me in this art. But it is in the opposite thing that I am really

73

amazing. I have some soft notes which I accompany with a smile and an infinite variety of approving faces, with nose, mouth, eyes and brow all brought into play. I have a certain agility with my hips, a way of twisting my spine, raising or lowering my shoulders, stretching my fingers, bowing my head, shutting my eyes and being struck dumb as though I had heard an angelic, divine voice come down from heaven. That's what gets them. I wonder whether you appreciate the full power of this last attitude. Watch it. Look.

I: It certainly is unique.

HE: Do you think any somewhat vain female brain can resist it?

I: No. I must say you have taken the talent for making fools of people and bootlicking as far as it will go.

HE: They can do what they like, the whole boiling of them, but they will never reach that point. The best of them, Palissot, for example, will never be more than a good learner. But if this role is amusing at first, and you find a certain amount of pleasure in laughing up your sleeve at the stupidity of the people you are hoodwinking, it ends up by losing its point, and besides, after a certain number of inventions you are forced to repeat yourself. Ingenuity and art have their limits. Only God and one or two rare geniuses can have a career that broadens out as they go along. Bouret is one such, perhaps. Some of his tricks really strike me, yes, even me, as sublime. The little dog, the Book of Happiness, the torches along the Versailles road, these are things which leave me dumbfounded and humiliated. Enough to put you off the profession.[21]

I: What do you mean about the little dog?

HE: Where can you have dropped from? What, you don't really know how that remarkable man set about alienating from himself and attaching to the Keeper of the Seals a little dog the latter had taken a fancy to?

I: No, I confess I don't.

HE: All the better. It is one of the finest things ever conceived; the whole of Europe was thrilled by it, and there isn't a single courtier it hasn't made envious. You are not without sagacity: let's see how you would have set about it. Remember that Bouret was loved by his dog. Bear in mind that the strange attire of the Minister terrified the little creature. Think that he only had one week to overcome the difficulties. You must understand all the conditions of the problem so as to appreciate the merits of the solution. Well!

I: Well, I.have to admit that in that line the simplest things would catch me out.

HE: Listen (he said, giving me a little tap on the shoulder – he is given to taking liberties), listen and admire! He had a mask made like the face of the Keeper of the Seals, he borrowed the latter's ample robe from a footman. He put the mask over his own face. He slipped on the robe. He called the dog, caressed it and gave it a biscuit. Then, suddenly changing his attire, he was no longer the Keeper of the Seals but Bouret, and he called his dog and whipped it. In less than two or three days of this routine, carried on from morning till night, the dog learned to run away from Bouret the Farmer-General and run up to Bouret the Keeper of the Seals. But I am too good natured. You are a layman and don't deserve to be told about the miracles going on under your very nose.

I: Never mind that, what about the book and the torches, please?

HE: No, no. Ask the cobblestones and they will tell you the whole story. You must take advantage of the circumstance that has thrown us together and learn things nobody knows but me.

I: Yes, you are right.

HE: Fancy borrowing the robe and the wig (I had forgotten the wig) of the Keeper of the Seals! Having a mask made to look like him! The mask especially makes me green with envy. And what's more that man enjoys the highest esteem, and is worth millions. There are holders of the Cross of Saint Louis who haven't a bean, so why run after the medal and risk being done in instead of turning to a safe job that never fails to pay? That's what you call doing things in the grand manner. Such models are discouraging. You feel you are pitiful and get fed up. That mask! That mask! I would give one of my fingers to have thought of that mask.

I: But with this enthusiasm for fine things and this fertile genius of yours haven't you invented anything yourself?

HE: Oh, just a minute: there's that admiring way of twisting my spine that I mentioned to you, for example. I look upon that as my very own, although it may be disputed by the envious. I think it has been used before, but who realized how useful it was for having a quiet laugh at the egregious ass being admired? I have over a hundred ways of embarking upon the procuring of a young girl at her mother's side without the latter's seeing anything, and even making her an accessory. I had scarcely taken up the career before I scorned all the ordinary ways of slipping a love-letter across. I have ten ways of inducing people to snatch it away from me, and some of them, I venture to flatter myself, are quite novel. In particular I have a gift for encouraging a shy young man, and I have brought success to some who had neither wit nor looks. If it were all written down I think I should be credited with some talent.

I: And a high degree of honour?

HE: I'm quite sure of it.

I: If I were you I should put all these things into writing. It would be a shame if they were lost.

HE: Yes, that's true, but you don't suspect how little the method and the rules matter to me. The man who must have a manual won't ever go far. Geniuses read little, but do a great deal and are their own creators. Look at Caesar,

Turenne, Vauban, the Marquise de Tencin and her brother the Cardinal, and his secretary, Abbé Trublet.[22] And what about Bouret? Whoever gave lessons to Bouret? Nobody. These rare men are formed by nature. Do you suppose the story of the dog and the mask is written down anywhere?

I: But in your spare moments, when the pain in your empty stomach or the strain in your over-full one prevent you from getting to sleep. . . .

HE: I'll bear that in mind. Better to write of great things than carry out little ones. Then the soul is lifted up, the imagination is kindled, takes fire and extends, instead of being confined to sharing the Hus girl's amazement at the applause the silly public will insist on lavishing upon that simpering little Dangeville – who acts so feebly, walks across the stage bent almost double, affects to stare ceaselessly into the eyes of the person she is addressing and to underplay her part, and who takes her own grimaces for subtlety and her miserable trot for graceful movement – or upon that ranting Clairon who is scraggier, more artificial, more mannered and affected than anyone could say. The idiotic pit claps them fit to bring the house down and never seems to notice that we ourselves are a bundle of charms (it is true that the bundle is swelling a bit, but what of that?), that we have the loveliest skin, the most beautiful eyes, the daintiest mouth, no great warmth of temperament, it is true, and a walk that is not light, but neither is it as clumsy as people make out. As to intensity of feeling, on the other hand, there isn't one of them we couldn't outdo.

I: What do you mean by all this? Are you being ironical or truthful?

HE: The snag is that this remarkable feeling of ours is all inside, and not a glimmer of it penetrates to the outer world. But I who am talking to you now, I know, and know well, that she has got plenty. Or if not precisely that, well, something like it. You should see how, when the mood comes

77

over us, we can treat servants, how the maids get their ears boxed, how we can kick old Casual Parts[23] if he dares to forget the respect due to us. She's a little vixen, I tell you, and full of feeling and dignity. . . . Look here, you don't quite know what to make of all this, do you?

I: I confess I can't see whether you are talking in good faith or just out of spite. I am a plain man, so kindly deal with me straightforwardly and leave your art on one side.

HE: That is just what we tell the Hus girl about Dangeville and Clairon, with here and there a few words thrown in to put you wise. I don't mind your taking me for a scoundrel, but not for a fool, and only a fool or a man hopelessly in love could say so many outrageous things seriously.

I: But how can you bring yourself to utter such things?

HE: You can't do it all at once, but little by little it comes. *Ingenii largitor venter.*

I: You have to be forced into it by a cruel hunger.

HE: Maybe. Yet however outrageous these things may seem to you, be assured that the people they are aimed at are more used to hearing them than we are to venturing upon saying them.

I: Is there anybody there with nerve enough to be of your opinion?

HE: What do you mean by anybody? It is the sentiment and opinion of the whole of society.

I: Those among you who are not utterly worthless must be utter fools.

HE: Fools? I swear there is only one fool, and that is the chap who treats us to his hospitality in exchange for such flattering deceptions.

I: But how can anybody be so palpably taken in? After all, the superiority of the talents of Dangeville and Clairon is beyond dispute.

HE: One swallows the lie that flatters, but sips the bitter

truth drop by drop. And besides, we give the impression of so much conviction and truth!

I: And yet you must have sinned once at any rate against the rules of art, and you must have let drop accidentally some of this painful, bitter truth. For in spite of the miserable, abject, vile, abominable part you play, I think you really have great refinement of soul.

HE: I? Not at all. Devil take me if I really know what I am. As a rule my mind is as true as a sphere and my character as honest as the day: never false if I have the slightest interest in being true, never true if I have the slightest interest in being false. I say things as they come to me; if sensible, all to the good, but if outrageous, people don't take any notice. I use freedom of speech for all it's worth. I have never reflected in my life, either before speaking, during speech or after. And so I give no offence.

I: But that is just what did happen in the case of the good people with whom you were living, and who showed you so much kindness.

HE: Well, what of it? It's a pity, one of those nasty moments that you get in life. No happiness lasts. I was too well off, and it couldn't go on. You know we have the most numerous and select company. It is a school for civilized men, a renewal of the hospitality of olden times. All the fallen poets – we pick them up. We had Palissot after his *Zara*, Bret after *Le Faux Généreux*, all the unpopular musicians, unread authors, hissed actresses and booed actors, a whole lot of uncomplaining poor, of abject parasites, at the head of whom I have the honour to be, brave leader of a timorous band. When they come for the first time it is I who exhort them to eat. I am the one to ask for a drink for them. They take up so little room! A handful of ragged youngsters who don't know where to lay their heads but are good-looking, others who are criminal types who butter up the master and send him off to sleep so as to be able to have his leavings with the mistress. We look jovial, but in reality we are all foul-tempered and voracious of appetite. Wolves are not more famished, tigers no more cruel. We devour like wolves when the earth has been long under snow, like tigers we tear to pieces anything successful. Sometimes the clans of Bertins, Montsauges and Vilmoriens gather, and then there is a rare old noise in the menagerie. Never were there seen so many wretched, spiteful, malevolent and truculent creatures in one place. You hear nothing but names such as Buffon, Duclos, Montesquieu, Rousseau, Voltaire, D'Alembert, Diderot, and God knows what epithets are coupled with them. Nobody is allowed to have any brains unless he is as stupid as we are. That is where the plan for the comedy of the *Philosophes* was hatched; the scene with the pedlars was contributed by me, taken from the *Théologie en quenouille*. You are not spared in it any more than the next man.[24]

I: I'm glad to hear it. Perhaps I am being honoured beyond my deserts. I should feel humiliated if people who run down so many intelligent and worthy men were to say anything good of me.

HE: There are plenty of us, and each one has to pay his scot. When we have sacrificed the large animals we offer up the others.

I: Insulting learning and virtue for a livelihood! It seems very costly daily bread.

HE: I've told you already, we don't count. We run down everybody, but don't upset anyone. Sometimes we have with us the ponderous Abbé d'Olivet, fat Abbé Leblanc, the humbug Batteux. The fat abbé is only nasty before he is fed. Once he has had his coffee he slumps into an armchair, puts his feet up against the chimneypiece and slumbers like an old parrot on his perch. If the din becomes terrific he yawns, stretches, rubs his eyes and says: 'Well, what's up? what's up?' 'Trying to decide whether Piron[25] is more intelligent than Voltaire.' 'Let's get this clear; intelligent, you say? You are not talking about taste, for this Piron of yours hasn't a notion of what taste is.' 'Not a notion?' 'No.' And then off we go into a disquisition upon taste. Thereupon the master makes a sign for silence, for he fancies himself in the matter of taste. 'Taste,' he says ... 'er, taste is a thing ...'. Well, I don't know what he said it was, no more does he.

Sometimes we get friend Robbé.[26] He entertains us with his cynical tales, with the miracles of the Convulsionaries, of which he has been a first-hand witness, and also with a few cantos of his poem on a subject he knows through and through. I loathe his verses, but I enjoy hearing him recite. He looks like one possessed, and all the onlookers cry: 'There's a poet for you!' Between you and me this poetry is nothing but a jumble of all sorts of odd noises, the confusion of tongues of the inhabitants of the Tower of Babel.

We also have among us a certain dull and stupid-looking ninny who really has the devil's own wit and is more artful than an old monkey. He is one of those figures who invite teasing and leg-pulling and whom God made to catch out people who judge by appearances, people whose looking-glass should have taught them that it is as easy to be a man of intelligence and look silly as to conceal a fool behind a clever-looking face. It is a very common form of meanness to sacrifice a man for the amusement of others, and invariably people have a go at this particular man. He is a trap we set for newcomers, and I have scarcely known a single one who has not fallen into it.

(Sometimes I was astonished by the rightness of this clown's judgements about men and characters. I told him so.)

Well, you see (he said), you can get something out of bad company just as you can out of libertinism. You are compensated for loss of innocence by loss of prejudices. In the company of wicked people, where vice throws off the mask, you learn to recognize them. And besides, I have done some reading.

ɪ: What have you read?

ʜᴇ: I have read and I constantly re-read Theophrastus, La Bruyère and Molière.

ɪ: Excellent works.

ʜᴇ: Much better than they are thought to be, but who knows how to read them?

ɪ: Everybody, according to his intelligence.

ʜᴇ: Hardly anybody. Could you tell me what they look for in them?

ɪ: Entertainment and instruction.

ʜᴇ: But what kind of instruction, for that's the real point?

ɪ: Knowledge of one's duties, love of virtue, hatred of vice.

ʜᴇ: Well, what I find in them is everything I ought to do and everything I ought not to say. For instance, when I read *L'Avare* I say to myself: 'Be a miser if you want to, but mind you don't talk like one.' When I read *Tartuffe* I tell myself: 'Be a hypocrite, by all means, but don't talk like a hypocrite. Keep the vices that come in useful to you, but don't have either the tone or the appearance, which would expose you to ridicule.' Now in order to avoid this tone and appearance you must know what they are, and these authors have done excellent portraits of them. I am myself, and I remain myself, but I act and speak as occasion requires. I am not one of those who look down on the moralists, not I! There is much to be got from them, especially those who have shown morality in action. Evil only upsets people now and then, but the visible signs of evil hurt them from morning till night. It might be better to be a rascal than to look like one: the rascal by nature only offends now and again, but the evil-looking person offends all the time. And don't imagine that I am the only one who reads in this way. My only merit in the matter is that I have done systematically, with an accurate mind and a true aim in view, what most others have done by instinct. That is why their reading doesn't make them any better than me, and why they remain ridiculous in spite of themselves, whereas I am ridiculous only when I mean to be, and then I leave them far behind. For the same art which helps me to avoid being ridiculous on certain occasions helps me on others to achieve it in a masterly manner. At such times I recall everything others have said, everything I have read, and add everything I can get from my own resources, which in this respect are amazingly productive.

I: It's a good thing you have revealed these mysteries to me; otherwise I should have thought you inconsistent.

HE: No, I'm not. Fortunately for each single time when you must avoid being ridiculous there are a hundred when you have to be. With the great of this world there is no better part to play than that of jester. For long ages there was an official King's Jester, but at no time has there been an official King's Wise Man. I am jester to Bertin and a host of others – to you, perhaps, at this moment – or possibly you are mine. A really sensible person wouldn't have a jester. So anyone who has a jester is not sensible, and if he is not sensible he must be a jester and perhaps, if he is a king, his jester's jester. Moreover, bear in mind that in a matter as variable as behaviour there is no such thing as the absolutely, essentially, universally true or false, unless it is that one must be what self-interest dictates – good or bad, wise or foolish, serious or ridiculous, virtuous or vicious. Supposing virtue had been the road to fortune, either I should have been virtuous or I should have simulated virtue as well as the next man. But people wanted me to be ridiculous, and so I have made myself that way; as to the viciousness, nature saw to that unaided. When I say vicious, it is by way of speaking your language, for if we came to a clear understanding it might turn out that what you call vice I call virtue, and that what I call vice you call virtue.

We also have in our company the librettists of the Opéra-Comique and their actors and actresses, and more often their managers, Corbi, Moette ... all people of resource and the highest merit.

And I was forgetting the great literary critics, *L'Avant-Coureur, Les Petites-Affiches, L'Année littéraire, L'Observateur littéraire, Le Censeur hebdomadaire,* in fact all the gang of columnists.[27]

I: *L'Année littéraire! L'Observateur littéraire!* That's not possible, they are at daggers drawn.

HE: That's true. But all the down-and-outs are united in front of food. I wish the devil had taken that accursed *Observateur littéraire,* both the columnist and his columns. That little swine of a priest, the stingy, stinking usurer, is the cause of my undoing. He appeared on our horizon yesterday for the first time, at the hour which drives us all out of our dens – dinner-time. When the weather is unkind, happy the man among us who has a twenty-four sou piece in his pocket.[28] Many a man who jeered at his fellow-sponger for arriving in the morning with mud up to his middle and soaked to the skin, has got home himself at night in the same state. There was one, I forget now which, who some months ago had a violent set-to with the boot-black who has taken up his station outside our door. They were working on credit and the creditor wanted the debtor to settle the account, but the latter was not in funds. The meal is served and the abbé is given the place of honour at the head of the table. I come in and see him. 'What, are you presiding, Abbé?' say I. 'That's all right for today, but tomorrow you will go one place down, please, and the next day one more, and so on place by place either to left or right until, having started from the place I once occupied before you, and Fréron once after me, Dorat once after Fréron and Palissot once after Dorat, you come to rest beside me, a miserable bugger like yourself, *qui siedo sempre come un maestoso cazzo fra duoi coglioni.*' The abbé, who is a decent sort and takes everything in good part, began to laugh. Mademoiselle, struck by the truth of my observation and the aptness of my comparison, began to laugh, all those sitting to right and left of the abbé and whom he had sent down one place began to laugh, in fact everybody laughed except Monsieur, who went into a huff and said things to me that wouldn't have mattered had we been alone: 'Rameau, you've got a nerve.' 'Yes, I know, that's why you have me here.' 'A scamp.' 'Same as everyone else.' 'A vagabond.' 'Would I be here if I weren't?' 'I'll have you thrown out.' 'After dinner I'll go of my own accord.' 'You'd better.' So we dined, and I didn't miss a mouthful. Having eaten well and drunk copiously, because after all that wouldn't have made any difference either way, and Sir Belly is a character I have never had anything against, I made up my mind and began preparations for my departure. I had given my word in front of so many people that I couldn't avoid keeping it. I took a considerable time prowling round the rooms looking for my stick and my hat in places where they couldn't be, and still assuming that the master would burst forth into a fresh storm of abuse, that somebody would intercede and we should end by making it up because we had lost our tempers. So I went round and round, for I had nothing on my mind, but the master, more black and midnight than Homer's Apollo when he hurled his bolts against the hosts of Greece, strode up and down with his bonnet more rammed down than usual and his chin on his fist. Mademoiselle comes up to me. 'But, Mademoiselle, what is so unusual? Have I been different from myself today?' 'He must go, I insist.' 'I will go, I haven't let him down in any way.' 'Excuse me, the abbé was invited, and . . .' 'It was he who let himself down by inviting the abbé and admitting me and so many other hangers-on like myself.' 'Now, now, Rameau my dear, you must beg the abbé's pardon.' 'I've no use for his pardon.' 'Come along, come along, it'll all blow over.' I am taken by the hand and dragged over to the abbé's chair. I stretch out my arms and contemplate the abbé with a kind of wonderment, for who has ever begged his pardon? 'Abbé,' I said, 'Abbé, all this is very silly, isn't it?' And I began to laugh, and so did he. So I was forgiven in that direction, but the other one had to be faced, and what I had to say to him was quite another kettle of fish. I don't quite know how I turned my apology: 'Monsieur, look at this fool. . . .' 'He has been annoying me too long already, and I don't want to hear anything more about him.' 'Monsieur is angry!' 'Yes, I am very angry.' 'It won't happen to him again.' 'The very first rascal I . . .' I don't know whether he was having one of those moody days of his when Mademoiselle is frightened to go near him and only dare touch him with her velvet mittens, or whether he misheard what I said, or whether I put it badly, but it was worse than before. What the hell, doesn't he know me? Doesn't he know that I am like a child, and there are circumstances in which I just let the whole lot slide? And then I thought, God forgive me, that I would never have a minute off, and even a puppet made of steel would be worn out if you pulled the string from morning till night and night till morning. I have to entertain them, that is in the bargain, but I must amuse myself sometimes. In the middle of this set-out a fell thought came into my head, a thought that made me feel arrogant and filled me with pride and insolence: it was that they couldn't do without me, that I was indispensable.

I: Yes, I think you are very useful to them, but they are even more so to you. You won't find another home as good as that just when you want it, but on the other hand if they need a fool they will find a hundred.

HE: A hundred fools like me! Mr Philosopher, they are not so common. Out and out fools, I mean. Foolery is a more ticklish problem than talent or virtue. I am rare among my kind, yes, exceedingly rare. Now that they have lost me what are they doing? Getting bored stiff. I am an inexhaustible bag of tricks. At every moment I had some quip ready to make them laugh till they cried. I supplied them with a complete madhouse.

I: And that's why you had bed, board, coat, waistcoat, breeches and shoes found, plus one *pistole* per month.

HE: That's the good side, the assets, but you don't mention the liabilities. First of all, if there was talk of some new play coming on, whatever the weather I had to ferret about in all the garrets of Paris until I found the author and arranged for a reading of the work and diplomatically suggested that there was a part in it which might be beautifully acted by somebody I knew. 'And by whom, may I ask?' 'By whom? what a question! Grace, charm, subtlety. . . .' 'You are referring to Mademoiselle Dangeville? Do you know her by any chance?' 'Yes, a little, but I don't mean her.' 'Who then?' I murmured the name. 'Her!' 'Yes, her,' I repeated, a bit shamefaced, for I have my moments of modesty, and at the mention of that name you should have seen how the poet's face lengthened, and at other times how people jumped down my throat. Yes, I had to bring my man home to dinner willy-nilly, and he, afraid of getting involved, would jib and say no thank you. You should have seen how I was treated when I failed to bring it off! I was a clod, a fool, a lump, good for nothing and not worth the glass of water they gave me to drink. I was much worse when the play was put on and, bold as brass amid the boos of an audience that is quite

87

discriminating, whatever people say, I had to make my solitary claps resound, make everybody look at me, sometimes steal the hisses from the actress herself and hear them whispering round me: 'It's one of the lackeys of the chap who sleeps with her; why won't the wretch shut up?' They don't know what can make a man do such things; they think it is stupidity, but it is a motive which excuses anything.

I: Even breaking the law?

HE: In the end people got to know me, and said: 'Oh, it's Rameau!' All I could do was to pass a few sarcastic remarks in order to cover up the absurdity of my solitary applause, which they interpreted the wrong way round. You must admit that you need a powerful incentive to brave the whole assembled public in this way, and that each of these ordeals was worth more than half a crown.

I: Why didn't you get some others to help you?

HE: I did that sometimes, too, and made a bit extra on it. Before setting off for the place of execution I had to commit to memory the brilliant passages where I had to set the tone. If it happened that I forgot them or got them mixed up I was all of a tremble on my return – you've no idea what a shindy there was. And on top of that, in the house a pack of dogs to look after – it's true that like a fool I had taken that job on – and cats to superintend; I was only too honoured if Micou favoured me with a scratch that tore my cuff or my hand. Criquette is subject to the colic and I have to rub her belly. Formerly Mademoiselle used to have the vapours, nowadays it is nerves, not to mention other slight indispositions that nobody bothers about in front of me. I don't mind this; I have never wanted to make people feel awkward. I read somewhere or other that a prince known as the Great used sometimes to stand leaning upon the back of his mistress's commode. You don't have to worry in front of familiars, and I was more of a familiar than anybody. I am the apostle of familiarity and freedom, and I preached them by my example without anybody raising any objection – they just had to leave me to it. I have given you a sketch of the master. Mademoiselle is beginning to put on weight, and you should just hear the nice tales they tell about that.

I: You are not one of them?

HE: Why not?

I: Well, it is unseemly, to say the least, to poke fun at one's benefactors.

HE: But isn't it even worse to think your charities give you the right to degrade your *protégé*?

I: But if the *protégé* were not degraded in himself nothing would give the patron the right.

HE: But if the people were not ridiculous in themselves you couldn't make up good stories about them. And besides, is it my fault if once they have gone in for low company they are duped and jeered at? When they decide to live with folk like us, they must expect all sorts of dirty tricks, that is assuming that they have any common sense at all. When they take us up don't they know us for what we are, that is to say venal, vile, perfidious creatures? If they know what we are, well and good, there is a tacit agreement that they will do us good and that sooner or later we shall return evil for the good they have done us. Doesn't this understanding exist between a man and his monkey or parrot? Brun is outraged because Palissot, his friend and boon companion, has written some couplets against him. But Palissot was bound to write them and it is Brun who is in the wrong. Poinsinet is outraged because Palissot has ascribed to him the couplets he wrote himself against Brun. Palissot was bound to ascribe to Poinsinet those couplets written against Brun, and Poinsinet is in the wrong. Poor Abbé Rey is outraged because his friend Palissot snaffled his mistress when he himself introduced them. Well, he shouldn't have introduced a man like Palissot to his mistress unless he was prepared to lose her. Palissot did his duty, and Abbé Rey is in the wrong. David the publisher is outraged because his partner Palissot slept with his wife, or tried to. Publisher David's wife is outraged because Palissot let it be thought by all and sundry that he had slept with her. Whether Palissot did sleep with the publisher's wife or no is difficult to decide, since the wife was bound to deny what was true, and Palissot may have let people believe what was not true. At all events Palissot has acted in character, and David and his wife are in the wrong. Let Helvétius be outraged because Palissot puts him in a play as a crooked character while still owing him money which was lent him for medical care, food and clothes. Had he any right to expect any other treatment from a man eaten up with all sorts of infamies, who just for the fun of the thing makes his friend abjure his religion, appropriates his partner's money, who has no respect for faith, law or feeling, who is out to feather his own nest *per fas et nefas*, whose days are measured by his turpitudes and who has represented himself on the stage as one of the most dangerous rogues – a piece of impudence without, I should think, any earlier example in the past or any later in the future? No, it is not Palissot who is in the wrong, but Helvétius. If you take a young fellow just up from the provinces to the Versailles zoo and he is silly enough to put his hand through the bars of the tiger's or the panther's cage, and if the young man leaves his arm in the mouth of the wild beast, who is to blame? All that is written in the tacit agreement, and woe betide whoever doesn't know or forgets! How many people accused of wickedness could I justify by this universal and sacred pact, whereas it is oneself one should accuse of stupidity. Yes, my fat countess, you are the one to blame when you gather round you what people of your kind call characters, and these characters play low-down tricks on you and make you do the same, thus exposing you to the indignation of decent people. Decent people run true to type, but so do the characters, and you are wrong to harbour them. If Bertinhus lived quietly and peacefully with his mistress, if through the respectability of their characters they had made respectable acquaintances, if they had gathered round them men of talent, known in society for their virtue, if the hours of recreation that they snatched from the delight of being together, loving each other and telling each other so in their quiet retreat, had been devoted to a small company of choice, enlightened souls, do you think anybody would have spread tales about them, good or bad? So what has happened, then? What they deserved. They have been punished for their imprudence, and we are the ones destined by Providence from all eternity to mete out justice to the Bertins of our day, and she has destined those of our type among our descendants to do the same to the Montsauges and Bertins to come. But while we are carrying out her just decrees against stupidity, you who show us in our true colours are carrying out her just decrees against us. What would you think of us if with our scandalous behaviour we claimed to enjoy general esteem? That we were out of our minds. And people who expect honourable treatment from those born wicked, from low and depraved characters, are they sensible? Everything in this world has its just deserts. There are two Public Prosecutors: one is always in waiting, and punishes crimes against society, the other is nature. And this one knows all about the vices which escape the law. You indulge in debauchery with women: you will get the dropsy. You live a dissolute life: you will get consumption. You open your doors to a lot of rascals and consort with them: you will be tricked, laughed at, scorned. The simplest thing is to resign yourself to the equity of these judgements and tell yourself that it is reasonable, get going and either mend your ways or stay as you are, but on the above conditions.

I: You are right.

HE: After all, I don't invent any of these scandalous tales myself, I stick to the job of carrier. They say that a few days ago, at five o'clock in the morning, a furious din was heard: all the bells were jangling and there were broken and muffled cries of a man being strangled. 'Help, help! I'm suffocating, I'm dying.' These cries came from the master's room. Help arrives. That huge creature of ours, who was quite out of her mind and had lost all idea of time and place, as happens at such a moment, was still going at full speed, lifting herself up on her hands and dropping on old Casual Parts a weight of two to three hundred pounds with all the violent animation that frantic enjoyment can give. It was very difficult to extricate him. What a fantastic idea for a little hammer to put itself under a heavy anvil!

I: You are disgusting. Let us change the subject. Ever since we have been talking I have had a question on the tip of my tongue.

HE: Why keep it waiting there so long?

I: I was afraid it might be improper.

HE: After all I have revealed I don't know what secret I can hide from you.

I: You are in no doubt as to what I think of your character.

HE: None whatever. In your eyes I am an abject, despicable creature, and sometimes I am in my own eyes too, but only occasionally. I congratulate myself on my failings more often than I deplore them. You are more consistent in your scorn.

I: True, but why show me all your turpitude?

HE: First, because you know a good part of it already, and I saw more to be gained than lost by owning up to the rest.

I: How is that, pray?

HE: If it is important to be sublime in anything, it is especially so in evil. You spit on a petty thief, but you can't withhold a sort of respect from a great criminal. His courage bowls you over. His brutality makes you shudder. What you value in everything is consistency of character.

I: But you haven't got this admirable consistency of character yourself, yet. Now and again I catch you vacillating in your principles. It is not clear whether you get your wickedness from nature or from study, or whether study has taken you as far as it is possible to go.

HE: I agree, but I have done my best. Haven't I been modest enough to acknowledge that there are more perfect beings than myself? Didn't I speak of Bouret with the most profound admiration? Bouret is the greatest man in the world in my opinion.

I: But you come immediately after Bouret?

HE: No.

I: Palissot, then?

HE: Yes, Palissot, but not Palissot alone.

I: And who can be worthy of sharing second place with him?

HE: The renegade of Avignon.

I: I have never heard of this renegade of Avignon, but he must be a most astonishing man.

HE: He certainly is.

I: The history of great men has always interested me.

HE: I quite believe it. This one lived in the house of a good and virtuous descendant of the family of Abraham, promised to the father of the faithful in number equal to the stars.

I: A Jew?

HE: A Jew. First he won the Jew's sympathy, then his kindness and finally his complete confidence. And that is how it always happens. We are so sure of the effect of our

93

own acts of kindness that we rarely hide our secrets from the person on whom we have lavished our goodness. How can there fail to be ingratitude when we expose a man to the temptation of being ungrateful with impunity? This is a wise reflection which our Jew did not make. So he confided to the renegade that his conscience would not allow him to eat pork. You are about to see the advantage that a fertile brain would be able to take of this admission. Several months went by during which our renegade redoubled his attentions. When he considered that his Jew was well softened, well caught, quite convinced by his own kindnesses that he hadn't a better friend in all the tribes of Israel. . . . Just look at the circumspection of the man! No hurrying – he lets the pear ripen before shaking the branch. Too much eagerness might ruin the project. Usually greatness of character comes from a natural balance between several opposing qualities.

I: Oh, drop your reflections and go on with the story.

HE: Can't be done. There are days when I have to reflect. It's an affliction you have to let run its course. Where was I?

I: You had got to the well-established friendship between the Jew and the renegade.

HE: Well, the pear was ripe. . . . But you aren't listening. What's on your mind?

I: I was thinking how variable your style is, sometimes lofty, sometimes familiar.

HE: Can the style of an evil man have any unity? Well, one night he comes to his kind friend's house looking scared, with stammering voice and face deathly pale, shaking in every limb. 'What's the matter?' 'We are lost.' 'Lost, what do you mean?' 'Lost, I say, lost beyond recall.' 'Explain what you mean.' 'Just a minute, let me get over my fright.' 'Come along, calm yourself,' said the Jew, instead of saying: 'You are a barefaced rogue; I don't know

94

what you have to tell me, but you are a barefaced rogue and simulating terror.'

I: But why should he have spoken like that?

HE: Because the man was bogus and had gone too far. That is obvious to me, so stop interrupting. 'We are lost, lost beyond recall.' Don't you sense the affectation in those repeated 'losts'? 'Some traitor has denounced us to the Holy Inquisition, you as a Jew, I as a renegade, an unspeakable renegade.' You notice the villain unblushingly uses the most odious expressions. You need more courage than you'd think to name yourself as you should be named. You don't know what it costs to bring yourself to that pass.

I: No, I obviously don't. But to come back to this unspeakable renegade ...

HE: He is bogus, but it is a highly skilful duplicity. The Jew takes fright, tears out his beard, rolls on the ground. He sees the *sbirros* at the door already, sees himself clothed with the *san-benito*, sees his own *auto-da-fé* prepared. 'My friend, my dearest friend, my only friend, what is to be done?' 'What indeed? Be seen going about your business, affect the greatest unconcern, carry on as usual. This tribunal acts in secret, but slowly. We must take advantage of these delays and sell everything. I will go and charter a ship, or get a third party to do so – yes, a third party will be best. In it we will deposit your fortune, for that is mainly what they are after, and then you and I will sail away to another clime, there to find freedom to serve our God and live out the law of Abraham and our consciences. The important thing, in the dangerous pass to which we have come, is to do nothing imprudent.' No sooner said than done. The ship is chartered, fitted out with provisions and manned. The Jew's fortune is on board. Tomorrow, at dawn, they set sail. They can sup with good cheer and sleep in peace – tomorrow they escape from their persecutors. In the night the renegade gets up, relieves the

Jew of his wallet, his purse and his jewels, embarks and off
he goes. You think that's all? Then you haven't seen the
point! Now when I was told this story I guessed what I have
kept from you just to test your percipience. You were well
advised to be a respectable citizen, for you would only have
made a very petty thief. So far that is all the renegade is – a
despicable scamp nobody would want to resemble. The
sublimity of his wickedness comes from his having himself
informed on his good friend the Israelite, who was seized
by the Holy Inquisition as soon as he awoke and who, a few
days later, was made into a fine bonfire. And thus the
renegade became the undisputed possessor of the fortune
of that accursed descendant of those who crucified Our
Lord.

i: I don't know which strikes me as more horrible, the
villainy of your renegade or the tone in which you talk
about it.

he: That's just what I was saying to you. The enormity
of the deed carries you beyond mere contempt, and that is
the explanation of my candour. I wanted you to know how
I excelled in my art, I wanted to force you to admit that at
least I was unique in my degradation, and classify me in
your mind with the great blackguards, and then exclaim:
Vivat Mascarillus, fourbum imperator![29] Come on, join in,
Mr Philosopher, chorus: *Vivat Mascarillus, fourbum imperator!*

(Thereupon he began to execute a quite extraordinary
fugue. At one moment the theme was solemn and full of
majesty and at the next light and frolicsome, at one moment
he was imitating the bass and at the next one of the upper
parts. With outstretched arms and neck he indicated the
held notes, and both performed and composed a song of
triumph in which you could see he was better versed in
good music than in good conduct.

As for me, I didn't know whether to stay or run away,

laugh or be furious. I stayed, with the object of turning the conversation on to some other subject which would dispel the horror that filled my soul. I was beginning to find irksome the presence of a man who discussed a horrible act, an execrable crime, like a connoisseur of painting or poetry examining the beauties of a work of art, or a moralist or historian picking out and illuminating the circumstances of a heroic deed. I became preoccupied in spite of myself. He noticed it and said:)

HE: What's the matter? Do you feel ill?

I: A bit, but it will pass off.

HE: You have that worried look of a man hag-ridden by some disturbing thought.

I: That's so.

(After a moment of silence on his part and mine, during which he walked up and down whistling and singing, I tried to get him back to his own talent by saying:) What are you doing just now?

HE: Nothing.

I: Very tiring.

HE: I was silly enough as it was; I have been to hear this music by Duni and our other youngsters, and that has finished me off.[30]

I: So you approve of this style of music?

HE: Of course.

I: And you find beauty in these modern tunes?

HE: Do I find beauty? Good Lord, you bet I do! How well it is suited to the words! what realism! what expressiveness!

I: Every imitative art has its model in nature. What is the musician's model when he writes a tune?

HE: Why not go back to the beginning? What is a tune?

I: I confess the question is beyond me. That's what we are all like: in our memories we have nothing but words, and we think we understand them through the frequent use and even correct application we make of them, but in our minds we have only vague notions. When I pronounce the word 'tune' I have no clearer idea than you and most of your kind when you say 'reputation, blame, honour, vice, virtue, modesty, decency, shame, ridicule'.

HE: A tune is an imitation, by means of the sounds of a scale (invented by art or inspired by nature, as you please), either by the voice or by an instrument, of the physical sounds or accents of passion. And you see that by changing the variables the same definition would apply exactly to painting, eloquence, sculpture or poetry. Now to come to your question: what is the model for a musician or a tune? Speech, if the model is alive and thinking; noise, if the model is inanimate. Speech should be thought of as a line, and the tune as another line winding in and out of the first. The more vigorous and true the speech, which is the basis of the tune, and the more closely the tune fits it and the more points of contact it has with it, the truer that tune will be and the more beautiful. And that is what our younger musicians have seen so clearly. When you hear *Je suis un pauvre diable* you think you can tell it is a miser's plaint, for even if he didn't sing he would address the earth in the same tone when hiding his gold therein: *O terre, reçois mon trésor.*[31] And that young girl, for example, who feels her heart beating, who blushes and in confusion begs his lordship to let her go – how else could she express herself? There are all kinds of characters in these works, and an infinite variety of modes of speech. Sublime, I tell you! Go and listen to the piece when the young man, feeling himself on the point of death, cries: *Mon cœur s'en va.*[32] Listen to the air, listen to the instrumental setting, and then try and tell me the difference there is between the real behaviour of a dying man and the turn of this air. You will see whether the line of the melody doesn't coincide exactly with that of speech. I am not going into time, which is another condition of song; I am sticking to expression, and nothing is more obvious than the following passage which I have read somewhere: *Musices seminarium accentus*. Accent is the nursery-bed of melody. Hence you can tell how difficult the technique of recitative is, and how important. There is no good tune from which you cannot make a fine recitative, and no recitative from which a skilled person cannot make a fine tune. I would not like to guarantee that a good speaker will sing well, but I should be surprised if a good singer could not speak well. Believe all I say on this score, for it is the truth.

I: I should be only too willing to believe you if I were not prevented by one little difficulty.

HE: What difficulty?

I: Just this: if this kind of music is sublime, then that of the divine Lully, Campra, Destouches and Mouret, and even, between ourselves, of your dear uncle, must be a bit dull.[33]

HE (whispering into my ear): I don't want to be overheard, and there are lots of people here who know me, but it *is* dull. It's not that I care twopence about dear uncle, if 'dear' he be. He is made of stone. He would see my tongue hanging out a foot and never so much as give me a glass of water, but for all his making the hell of a hullaballoo at the octave or the seventh—la-la-la, dee-dee-dee, tum-te-tum—people who are beginning to get the hang of things and no longer take a din for music will never be content with that. There should be a police order forbidding all and sundry to have the *Stabat* of Pergolesi sung. That *Stabat* ought to have been burned by the public hangman. Lord! these confounded Bouffons, with their *Serva Padrone*, their *Tracallo*, have given us a real kick in the backside.[34] In the old days a thing like *Tancrède*, *Issé*, *L'Europe galante*, *Les Indes* and *Castor*, *Les Talents lyriques* ran for four, five or six months.[35] The performances of *Armide*[36] went on for ever. But nowadays they all fall down one after the other, like houses of cards. And Rebel and Francoeur[37] breathe fire and slaughter and declare that all is lost and they are ruined, and that, if these circus performers are going to be put up with much longer, national music will go to the devil and the Royal Academy in the cul-de-sac will have to shut up shop. And there is some truth in it, too. The old wigs who have been going there every Friday for the past thirty or forty years are getting bored and beginning to yawn, for some reason or other, instead of having a good time as they used to. And they wonder why, and can't find the answer. Why don't they ask me? Duni's prophecy will come true, and the way things are going I'll be damned if, four or five years after *Le Peintre amoureux de son modèle*, there will be as much as a cat left to skin in the celebrated Impasse. The good people have given up their own symphonies to play Italian ones, thinking they would accustom their ears to these without detriment to their vocal music, just as though orchestral music did not bear the same relationship to singing (allowances being made for the greater freedom due to range of instrument and nimbleness of finger) as singing to normal speech. As though the violin were not the mimic of the singer who in his turn will become the mimic of the violin one of these days, when technical difficulty replaces beauty. The first person to play Locatelli was the apostle of modern music. What nonsense! We shall become inured to the imitation of the accents of passion and of the phenomena of nature by melody or voice or instrument, for that is the whole extent and object of music; and shall we keep our taste for rapine, lances, glories, triumphs and victories? *Va-t-en voir s'ils viennent, Jean.*[38] They supposed they could weep or laugh at scenes from tragedy or comedy set to music, that the tones of madness, hatred, jealousy, the genuine pathos of love, the ironies and jokes of the Italian or French stage could be presented to their ears and that nevertheless they could still admire *Ragonde* and *Platée*.[39] You can bet your boots that even if they saw over and over again with what ease, flexibility and gentleness the harmony, prosody, ellipses and inversions of the Italian language suited the art, movement, expressiveness and turns of music and relative length of sounds, they would still fail to realize how stiff, dead, heavy, clumsy, pedantic and monotonous their own language is. Well, there it is. They have persuaded themselves that after having mingled their tears with those of a mother mourning the death of her son, or trembled at the decree of a tyrant ordering a murder, they won't get bored with their fairy-tales, their insipid mythology, their sugary little madrigals which show up the bad taste of the poet as clearly as they do the poverty of the art which uses them. Simple souls! It is not so, and cannot be. Truth, goodness and beauty have their claims. You may contest them, but in the end you will admire. Anything not bearing their stamp is admired for a time, but in the end you yawn. Yawn, then, gentlemen, yawn your fill, don't you worry! The reign of nature is quietly coming in, and that of my trinity, against which the gates of hell shall not prevail: truth, which is the father, begets goodness, which is the son, whence proceeds the beautiful, which is the holy ghost. The foreign god takes his place unobtrusively beside the idol of the country, but little by little he strengthens his position, and one fine day he gives his comrade a shove with his elbow and wallop! down goes the idol. That, they say, is how the Jesuits planted Christianity in China and the Indies. And the Jansenists can say what they like, this kind of politics which moves noiselessly, bloodlessly towards its goal, with no martyrs and not a single tuft of hair pulled out, seems the best to me.

I: There is a certain amount of sense in everything you have been saying.

HE: Sense! It's as well, for devil take me if I have been trying. It just comes, easy as wink. I am like those musicians in the Impasse, when my uncle arrived; if I hit the mark, well and good. A coal-heaver will always talk better about his own job than a whole Academy and all the Duhamels in the world. . . .

(And off he went, walking up and down and humming some of the tunes from *L'Ile des Fous, Le Peintre amoureux de son modèle, Le Maréchal ferrant* and *La Plaideuse*, and now and again he raised his hands and eyes to heaven and exclaimed: 'Isn't that beautiful! God, isn't it beautiful! How can anyone wear a pair of ears on his head and question it?' He began to warm up and sang, at first softly, then, as he grew more impassioned, he raised his voice and there followed gestures, grimaces and bodily contortions, and I said: 'Here we go, he's getting carried away and some new scene is working up.' And indeed off he went with a shout: *Je suis un pauvre misérable . . . Monseigneur, Monseigneur, laissez-moi partir. . . . O terre, reçois mon or, conserve bien mon trésor. . . . Mon âme, mon âme, ma vie! O terre! . . . Le voilà le petit ami, le voilà le petit ami! Aspettare e non venire. . . . A Zerbina penserete. . . . Sempre in contrasti con te si sta. . . .* He sang thirty tunes on top of each other and all mixed up: Italian, French, tragic, comic, of all sorts and descriptions, sometimes in a bass voice going down to the infernal regions, and sometimes bursting himself in a falsetto voice he would split the heavens asunder, taking off the walk, deportment and gestures of the different singing parts: in turn raging, pacified, imperious, scornful. Here we have a young girl weeping, and he mimes all her simpering ways, there a priest, king, tyrant, threatening, commanding, flying into a rage, or a slave obeying. He relents, wails, complains, laughs, never losing sight of tone, proportion, meaning of words and character of music. All the chess-players had left their boards and gathered round him. Outside, the café windows were thronged with passers-by who had stopped because of the noise. There were bursts of laughter fit to split the ceiling open. He noticed nothing, but went on, possessed by such a frenzy, an enthusiasm so near to madness that it was uncertain whether he would ever get over it, whether he should not be packed off in a cab straight to Bedlam. Singing a part of the Jomelli *Lamentations* he rendered the finest bits of each piece with incredible accuracy, truth and emotion, and the fine accompanied recitative in which the prophet depicts the desolation of Jerusalem was mingled with a flood of tears which forced all eyes to weep. Everything was there: the delicacy of the air and expressive power as well as grief. He laid stress upon the places where the composer had specially shown his great mastery, sometimes leaving the vocal line to take up the instrumental parts which he would suddenly abandon to return to the voice part, intertwining them so as to preserve the connecting links and the unity of the whole, captivating our souls and holding them in the most singular state of suspense I have ever experienced. Did I admire? Yes, I did. Was I touched with pity? Yes, I was. But a tinge of ridicule ran through these sentiments and discoloured them.

But you would have gone off into roars of laughter at the way he mimicked the various instruments. With cheeks puffed out and a hoarse, dark tone he did the horns and bassoons, a bright, nasal tone for the oboes, quickening his voice with incredible agility for the stringed instruments to which he tried to get the closest approximation; he whistled the recorders and cooed the flutes, shouting, singing and throwing himself about like a mad thing: a one-man show featuring dancers, male and female, singers of both sexes, a whole orchestra, a complete opera-house, dividing himself into twenty different stage parts, tearing up and down, stopping, like one possessed, with flashing eyes and foaming mouth. The weather was terribly hot, and the sweat running down the furrows of his brow and cheeks mingled with the powder from his hair and ran in streaks down the top of his coat. What didn't he do? He wept, laughed, sighed, his gaze was tender, soft or furious: a woman swooning with grief, a poor wretch abandoned in the depth of his despair, a temple rising into view, birds falling silent at eventide, waters murmuring in a cool, solitary place or tumbling in torrents down the mountain side, a thunderstorm, a hurricane, the shrieks of the dying mingled with the howling of the tempest and the crash of thunder; night with its shadows, darkness and silence, for even silence itself can be depicted in sound. By now he was quite beside himself. Knocked up with fatigue, like a man coming out of a deep sleep or long trance, he stood there motionless, dazed, astonished, looking about him and trying to recognize his surroundings. Waiting for his strength and memory to come back, he mechanically wiped his face. Like a person waking up to see a large number of people gathered round his bed and totally oblivious or profoundly ignorant of what he had been doing, his first impulse was to cry out 'Well, gentlemen, what's up? What are you laughing at? Why are you so surprised? What's up?' Then he went on: 'Now that's what you call music and a musician. And yet, gentlemen, you mustn't look down on some of the things in Lully. I defy anyone to better the scene *Ah, j'attendrai*, without altering the words. You mustn't look down on some parts of Campra, or my uncle's violin airs and his gavottes, his entries for soldiers, priests, sacrificers ... *Pâles flambeaux, nuit plus affreuse que les ténèbres* ... *Dieu du Tartare, Dieu de l'oubli....*'[40] At this point he raised his voice, held on to the notes, and neighbours came to their windows while we stuck our fingers in our ears. 'This,' he went on, 'is where you need lung-power, a powerful organ, plenty of wind. But soon it will be good-bye to Assumption, Lent and Epiphany have already come and gone. They don't yet know what to set to music, nor, therefore, what a musician wants. Lyric poetry has yet to be born. But they will come to it through hearing Pergolesi, the Saxon,[41] Terradoglias, Trasetta and the rest; through reading Metastasio they will have to come to it.')

I: You mean to say that Quinault, La Motte, Fontenelle didn't know anything about it?[42]

HE: Not for the modern style. There aren't six lines together in all their charming poems that you can set to music. Ingenious aphorisms, light, tender, delicate madrigals, but if you want to see how lacking all that is in material for our art, the most exacting of all, not even excepting that of Demosthenes, get someone to recite these pieces, and how cold, tired and monotonous they will sound! There is nothing in them that can serve as a basis for song. I would just as soon have to set the *Maximes* of La Rochefoucauld or the *Pensées* of Pascal to music. It is the animal cry of passion that should dictate the melodic line, and these moments should tumble out quickly one after the other, phrases must be short and the meaning self-contained, so that the musician can utilize the whole and each part, omitting one word or repeating it, adding a missing word, turning it all ways like a polyp, without destroying it. All this makes lyric poetry in French a much more difficult problem than in languages with inversions which have these natural advantages ... *Barbare, cruel, plonge ton poignard dans mon sein. Me voilà prête à recevoir le coup fatal. Frappe. Ose. . . . Ah! je languis, je meurs. . . . Un feu secret s'allume dans mes sens. . . . Cruel amour, que veux-tu de moi? . . . Laisse-moi la douce paix dont j'ai joui. . . . Rends-moi la raison. . . .* The passions must be strong and the sensibility of composer and poet must be very great. The aria is almost always the peroration of a scene. What we want is exclamations, interjections, suspensions, interruptions, affirmations, negations; we call out, invoke, shout, groan, weep or have a good laugh. No

witticisms, epigrams, none of your well-turned thoughts –
all that is far too removed from nature. And don't imagine
that the technique of stage actors and their declamation can
serve as a model. Pooh! we want something more energetic,
less stilted, truer to life. The simple language and normal
expression of emotion are all the more essential because our
language is more monotonous and less highly stressed. The
cry of animal instinct or that of a man under stress of
emotion will supply them.

(While he was saying all this the crowds round us had
melted away, either because they understood nothing he was
saying or found it uninteresting, for generally speaking a
child like a man and a man like a child would rather be
amused than instructed; everybody was back at his game
and we were left alone in our corner. Slumped on a seat
with his head against the wall, arms hanging limp and eyes
half shut, he said: 'I don't know what's the matter with
me; when I came here I was fresh and full of life and now I
am knocked up and exhausted, as though I had walked
thirty miles. It has come over me all of a sudden.')

I: Would you like a drink?

HE: I don't mind if I do. I feel hoarse. I've no go left in
me and I've a bit of a pain in my chest. I get it like this
nearly every day, I don't know why.

I: What will you have?

HE: Whatever you like. I'm not fussy. Poverty has taught
me to make do with anything.

(Beer and lemonade are brought. He fills and empties a
big glass two or three times straight off. Then, like a man
restored, he coughs hard, has a good stretch and goes on:)

But don't you think, my lord Philosopher, that it is a very
odd thing that a foreigner, an Italian, a Duni should come
and teach us how to put the stress into our own music, and
adapt our vocal music to every speed, time, interval and
kind of speech without upsetting prosody? And yet it

wouldn't have taken all that doing. Anyone who had ever heard a beggar asking for alms in the street, a man in a towering rage, a woman mad with jealousy, a despairing lover, a flatterer – yes, a flatterer lowering his voice and dwelling on each syllable in honeyed tones – in short a passion, any passion, so long as it was strong enough to act as a model for a musician, should have noticed two things: one, that syllables, whether long or short, have no fixed duration nor even a settled connexion between their durations, and the other, that passion does almost what it likes with prosody; it jumps over the widest intervals, so that a man crying out from the depths of his grief: '*Ah, malheureux que je suis!*' goes up in pitch on the exclamatory syllable to his highest and shrillest tone, and down on the others to his deepest and most solemn, spreading over an octave or even greater interval and giving each sound the quantity required by the turn of the melody without offending the ear, although the long and short syllables are not kept to the length or brevity of normal speech. What a way we have come since we used to cite the parenthesis in *Armide: Le vainqueur de Renaud* (*si quelqu'un le peut être*), or: *Obéissons sans balancer* from *Les Indes galantes* as miracles of musical declamation! Now these miracles make me shrug my shoulders with pity. The way art is advancing I don't know where it will end! Meanwhile let's have a drink.

(And he had two or three without realizing what he was doing. He would have drowned himself, just as he had exhausted himself, without noticing, had I not moved away the bottle he was absent-mindedly feeling for. Then I said:)

I: How is it that with a discrimination as delicate as yours and your remarkable sensitiveness for the beauties of musical art, you are so blind to the fine things of morality, so insensitive to the charms of virtue?

HE: Apparently because some things need a sense I don't

possess, a fibre that hasn't been vouchsafed me, or a slack one that you can tweak as much as you like but it won't vibrate; or again it may be that I have always lived with good musicians and bad people. Hence it has come about that my ear has become very sharp and my heart very deaf. Of course there was something in heredity. My father's blood and my uncle's blood are one and the same. The paternal molecule must be hard and obtuse, and this wretched first molecule has affected everything else.

I: Do you love your son?

HE: Do I love him, the little scamp? I dote on him.

I: Then won't you concern yourself seriously with checking the effect of the unfortunate paternal molecule on him?

HE: I should work to very little purpose, I think. If he is destined to become a good man I shan't do him any harm. But if the molecule meant him to become a ne'er-do-well like his father, then the trouble I should have gone to in order to make him an honest man would have been most harmful: training being continually at cross purposes with the natural bent of the molecule, he would be torn between two opposing forces and walk all crooked down life's road like a lot of them who are equally inept at good or evil and whom we call 'types', the most frightening of all epithets because it indicates mediocrity and the last stages of the contemptible. A great rogue is a great rogue, but he is not a 'type'. The boy would need a very great deal of time and waste the best years of his life before the paternal molecule had regained control and brought him to the state of total abjectness that I have reached. So I am doing nothing about it at present. I am letting him develop. I am watching him, and he is already greedy, smooth, a thief, a waster and a liar. I rather fear he will turn out a chip off the old block.

I: And will you make him a musician, to complete the resemblance?

HE: A musician! a musician! Sometimes I look at him

and grind my teeth and say: 'If you were ever to know a single note, my boy, I think I would wring your neck.'

I: And why, for goodness sake?

HE: It leads nowhere.

I: It leads everywhere.

HE: Yes, if you excel. But who can promise himself that his child will excel? You can bet ten thousand to one that he will be nothing but a miserable scraper of strings like me. Do you know, it would perhaps be easier to find a child fit to govern a realm and make a great king than a great violinist.

I: It seems to me that social talents, even if mediocre, do carry a man speedily along the road to fortune in a nation with no moral standards and given over to debauchery and luxuriousness. I myself have heard the following conversation between a sort of patron and a kind of protégé. The latter had been recommended to the former as an obliging person who might be useful to him: 'Sir, what do you know?' 'I know a certain amount of mathematics.' 'Well, Sir, if you teach mathematics you will have three or four hundred *livres* a year after ten or twelve years of dragging through the mud in the streets of Paris.' 'I have studied law, and am quite well versed in it.' 'If Puffendorf and Grotius[43] came back to the world they would die of starvation at the roadside.' 'I am very good at history and geography.' 'If there were any parents who had the good education of their children at heart your fortune would be made, but there aren't.' 'I'm not bad at music.' 'Then why didn't you say so straight away? And just to show you the benefit you can draw from this last talent, I have a daughter. Come from half past seven to nine every evening and give her a lesson, and I will pay you twenty-five *louis* a year. You can have breakfast, lunch and supper with us, and the rest of the day will be your own to make what you like of.'

HE: And what happened to this man?

I: If he had been wise he would have made a fortune, which is the only thing you are interested in.

HE: Of course. Money, money. Money is all, and the rest, without money, is nothing. And that is why, instead of stuffing his head with fine maxims that he would have to forget or else beg for bread, when I possess a *louis*, which isn't often, I take up my stand in front of him. I take the coin out of my pocket. I show it him with admiration. I roll my eyes to heaven. I kiss the *louis* in front of him. And to make him appreciate still more the importance of the sacred coin, I stammer out the names and point out with my finger all the things you can acquire with it – a nice child's frock, a nice bonnet, a lovely biscuit. Then I put the coin back into my pocket. I strut about proudly, lift my waistcoat and tap my fob pocket. In this way I make him understand that the state of self-confidence he sees me in comes from the coin in there.

I: Nothing could be better. But supposing that, deeply impressed by the value of that coin, he should one day . . .

HE: I get your meaning. We must shut our eyes to that. There is no moral principle without its drawbacks. At the worst you are in for a nasty quarter of an hour, and then it's all over.

I: But even if you hold such courageous and wise views, I still think it would be good to make him a musician. I know of no swifter way of getting into contact with the great, of pandering to their vices and turning one's own to advantage.

HE: Yes, that's true. But I have plans which work quicker and more efficaciously. Oh, if only it were a daughter! But as you don't produce what you want you have to take what comes and get the best out of it. And to that end, you mustn't stupidly give a Spartan education to a child destined to live in Paris, which is what most fathers do, and they couldn't do anything worse if they had planned a cruel fate for their children. If the education is wrong it is the fault of the customs of my nation, not mine. I don't know who is responsible, but I want my son to be happy or, what comes to the same thing, honoured, rich and powerful. I know a bit about the easiest ways of achieving this, and I shall teach them to him as early as possible. If you wise men blame me the mob (and success) will absolve me. He will have money, I can assure you, and if he has a lot, then he will lack nothing, not even your esteem and respect.

I: You might be wrong about that.

HE: All right, then he will do without, like many another.

(In all this there was much that we all think and on which we all act, but which we leave unsaid. That, indeed, was the most obvious difference between this man and most of those we meet. He owned up to the vices he had and which others have – he was no hypocrite. He was no more abominable than they, and no less. He was simply more open, more consistent, and sometimes more profound in his depravity. I trembled to think what his child would turn out like with such a teacher. Certainly with theories of teaching so exactly made to the measure of our society he would go far, unless prematurely stopped on the road.)

HE: Oh, no fear: the important point and the difficult one a good father must keep to above all, is not so much to give his child vices which will enrich him or eccentricities which will make him useful to the great – everybody does that, if not systematically, like me, at any rate by example and precept – but rather to inculcate a sense of proportion, the art of dodging disgrace, dishonour and the law. These are the dissonances in the social harmony that need skill in placing, leading in to and resolving. Nothing is so dull as a succession of common chords. There must be something arresting, to break up the beam of light and separate it into rays.

I: Very good. This comparison of yours brings me back

from morals to music, from which I had digressed in spite of myself, and I am grateful; for, to speak frankly, I like you better as a musician than as a moralist.

HE: And yet I am very second-rate in music and a much better moralist.

I: I am not so sure of that, but even if it were so, I am an honest man and your principles are not mine.

HE: More fool you. Oh, if I had your talents!

I: Never mind my talents, let's get back to yours.

HE: If only I could express myself like you. But mine is the hell of a hybrid squawking, half literary world, half fish-market.

I: I don't speak well myself. I can only speak the truth, and that doesn't always work, as you know.

HE: But it's not for telling the truth, but rather for telling lies properly that I envy your gifts. If I could write, dish up a book, turn a dedicatory epistle, make some fool really drunk with his own merit, get on with women!

I: You know all that a thousand times better than I do. I wouldn't even be fit to be your pupil.

HE: How many great qualities wasted! And you don't even realize their value!

I: I get back just as much as I put in.

HE: If that were so you wouldn't now be wearing that homespun coat, coarse waistcoat, those woollen stockings, thick shoes and that antique wig.

I: Agreed. One must be very lacking in skill if one is not rich although stopping at nothing in order to become rich. But there are people like me who don't consider wealth the most precious thing in the world – odd people.

HE: Very odd. People aren't born with that kink. It is acquired, for it isn't natural.

I: Not to men?

HE: Not to men. Every living creature, man not excepted, seeks its own well-being at the expense of whoever is in possession of it, and I am sure that if I just let the little brute go his own way and told him nothing, he would want to be expensively dressed, eat sumptuously, be popular with the men and loved by the women, in fact to gather round him all the pleasures of life.

I: If the little brute were left to himself and kept in his native ignorance, combining the undeveloped mind of a child in the cradle with the violent passions of a man of thirty, he would wring his father's neck and sleep with his mother.

HE: That proves the necessity of a good education, and who is denying it? And what is a good education if not one that leads to all kinds of enjoyment without danger or difficulty.

I: I am almost of the same opinion, but we had better not go into it.

HE: Why not?

I: Because I'm afraid we may only agree on the surface, and if we once begin going into which dangers and difficulties should be avoided we shall cease to agree.

HE: What does that matter?

I: Never mind, let it go at that. I could never teach you what I know about that subject, and you will find it easier to teach me what I don't know about music and you do. Dear Rameau, let us talk about music, and tell me how it has come about that with your gift for feeling, remembering and reproducing the finest things in the great masters, with the enthusiasm they inspire in you and that you can communicate to others, you have never done anything worth while yourself.

(Instead of answering me he scornfully tossed his head, pointed a finger to the sky and went on: 'My star! my star! When nature made Leo, Vinci, Pergolesi, Duni she smiled. She took on a solemn and imposing look when she formed dear uncle Rameau, whom people will call the great Rameau for ten years or so and soon won't ever mention again. When she botched up his nephew she made a face, and then another face and then yet another.' And while he was saying these words he made all sorts of faces – scorn, disdain, irony – and seemed to be kneading a bit of dough between his fingers and smiling at the funny shapes he made it into. Then he hurled the misshapen image away from him and said: 'That's how nature made me and then threw me down among other images, some with wrinkled, fat bellies, short necks, eyes popping apoplectically out of their heads, others with wry necks, some dried up with staring eyes and hooked nose, and they all burst out laughing at the sight of me. I held my sides and burst out laughing at the sight of them, for fools and madmen amuse each other, they seek each other out and are mutually attracted.

'If on getting there I hadn't found ready to hand the proverb which says that *the money of fools is the patrimony of those with brains*, I ought to have done. I felt that nature had put my rightful inheritance into the purses of these images, and I thought up a thousand ways of getting it back.')

I: I know those ways, you've told me about them and I have admired them. But with so many ways to choose from, why haven't you ever tried producing a work of art?

HE: What you are saying is what a man of the world said to Abbé Le Blanc. The abbé had said: 'The Marquise de Pompadour picks me up in her hand and carries me to the very doorstep of the Academy, and then takes her hand away and I fall down and break both my legs.' The man of the world replied: 'Well, Abbé, you must get up and batter the door in with your head.' The abbé answered: 'That's what I tried to do, and do you know what I got? A bump on the forehead.'

(After this anecdote my man began walking with his head down and wearing a pensive and worried look; sighing, weeping, lamenting, he lifted up his hands and eyes, beat his head with his fist hard enough to break his skull or else his fingers, and went on: 'And yet I think there is something in there, but bang and shake it as I will nothing comes out.' Then he fell to shaking his head and banging it harder than ever, and said: 'Either there is nobody at home or he won't answer.'

A moment later a look of pride came over him, he raised his head, placed his right hand on his heart, stepped forward and said: 'I feel something, yes, I do indeed.' He mimicked a man being annoyed, outraged, touched, issuing orders, supplicating, and extemporized speeches of anger, sympathy, hatred and love. He sketched the characteristics of the various passions with amazing subtlety and truth. Then he said: 'That's about it, I think. It's coming. It shows you what it means to find an *accoucheur* who knows how to stimulate and induce labour pains and deliver the baby. Left to myself I take up my pen to write. I bite my nails and rub my forehead. Nothing doing. Good night. The god is absent; I had persuaded myself I was a genius, and at the end of the first line I can read that I'm a fool, a fool, a fool. But how can anybody feel, raise his mind to higher things, think and describe vividly, if he keeps company with the sort of people one must see in order to live, in the midst of the things one says and hears said and gossip of this kind: The boulevard was ever so nice today. Have you heard the little marmot? She acts delightfully. Mr So-and-so had the most beautiful team of dappled greys you could possibly imagine. Lovely Mme Whats-it is really beginning to get beyond it. Fancy doing her hair like that at forty-five! Young Thingummy is covered with diamonds that have cost her precious little. You mean that have cost her a great deal? Oh dear no. Where did you see her? At *L'Enfant d'Arlequin perdu et retrouvé*.[44] The despair scene was played as never before. The Punch at the Fair has lung-power, but no artistic sense, no soul. Mme So-

and-so has produced two children at the same time. Each father will have his own ... And do you really think that that sort of thing, said, said again and heard every day, inspires and leads to great things?')

I: No. It would be better to retire to one's garret, live on dry bread and water and discover one's real self.

HE: That's as may be, but I haven't the courage – and then having to sacrifice one's happiness for a success that might not come off! And look at the name I bear – Rameau. Being called Rameau makes things awkward. It's not the same thing with talents as with noble blood, which can be passed on and becomes more illustrious as it descends from grandfather to father, father to son, son to grandson without the ancestor's obliging the descendant to have any merit. The old trunk branches out into an enormous bunch of fools, but who cares? It is not the same thing with talent. In order merely to be as famous as your father you must be cleverer than he was. You must have inherited the aptitude. I didn't, but my wrist got supple, the bow works and the pot boils. It may not be glory, but it's food.

I: If I were you I wouldn't take it as said and done with, but have a try.

HE: Do you think I haven't tried? Before I was fifteen I said to myself for the first time: 'What's up with you, Rameau? You're dreaming. And what are you dreaming about? That you have done or are doing something to fire the admiration of the universe. All right, all you have to do is to blow on your fingers and set them to work. Hey presto and Bob's your uncle!' In maturer years I repeated the words of my youth. I'm still repeating them now and standing round the statue of Memnon.

I: The statue of Memnon? What on earth do you mean?

HE: It seems quite clear to me. Round the statue of Memnon there were a multitude of other statues on which the sun's rays shone just the same, but Memnon's was the only one that gave forth a sound. Voltaire is one poet, and who else is there? Voltaire. And the third is Voltaire, and the fourth Voltaire. But when it comes to musicians there is Rinaldo da Capua, Hasse, Pergolesi, Alberti, Tartini, Locatelli, Terradoglias, my uncle, that chap Duni who looks quite nondescript, but he has feeling, by God, and plenty of melody and expression. The others round this small company of Memnons are just so many pairs of ears stuck on the end of so many poles. And so we are just beggars, and beggars with a vengeance. Ah, Mr Philosopher, poverty is a terrible thing. I see her crouching with open mouth trying to catch a few drops of the icy water falling from the cask of the Danaides. I don't know whether she sharpens the wits of the philosopher, but she certainly cools the poet's head like the devil. You can't sing well under that cask. You are only too fortunate if you can get under it at all. I was once, but I couldn't stay there. I had already done that silly trick once before. I've travelled in Bohemia, Germany, Switzerland, Holland, Flanders and God knows where.

I: Under the leaking cask?

HE: Under the leaking cask. There was a wealthy and open-handed Jew who liked my music and my jokes. I made music as God meant me to, acted the fool and had all I wanted. My Jew was a man who knew his law and observed it to the last detail, sometimes with his friends, but always with strangers. He got himself into a bad scrape which I must tell you about because it is amusing. There lived in Utrecht a charming whore. He fell for this Christian woman, and sent a special messenger with a pretty large letter of credit. The strange creature turned down this offer. He was in despair. The messenger said: 'Why take it so badly? You want to sleep with a pretty woman – nothing simpler, and even a prettier one than the one you are running after. It's my wife, and I will let you have her at the same price.' Signed and settled. The messenger pockets the letter of credit and the Jew sleeps with the wife. The expiry date of the letter comes round. The Jew lets it be protested and disputes its validity. Lawsuit. The Jew says to himself: 'Never will this man dare say how he came into possession of my letter, and I won't honour it.' At the trial he interrogates the messenger. 'How did you come by this letter of credit?' 'I had it from you.' 'In respect of a loan?' 'No.' 'For goods supplied?' 'No.' 'Services rendered?' 'No, but that's not the point. I am in possession, you signed it and you are going to pay up.' 'I did not sign it.' 'So I am a forger?' 'You or somebody you are acting for.' 'I am a coward, but you are a rogue. Look, don't push me too far or I shall out with the lot. I mean it. I shall dishonour myself, but I shall ruin you.' The Jew ignored the threat and at the next hearing the messenger revealed the whole business. They were both reprimanded and the Jew was sentenced to honour the letter of credit and the whole sum was given to the poor. At that I left him and came back here. What could I do? Either I had to do something or die of poverty. All sorts of plans went through my head. One day I decided to go off on the morrow and join a company of strolling players, in which I would be equally good or bad on the stage or in the orchestra; the next day I thought of having one of those pictures painted that they stick on a pole and set up at a cross-road, and there I should have bawled at the top of my voice: 'Here is the town where he was born, here he is saying good-bye to his father the apothecary, here he is arriving in the capital and looking for his uncle's house, here he is begging before his uncle who is turning him away, here he is with a Jew, etc, etc.' The day after that I got up resolved to throw in my lot with the street singers, and I might have done much worse, for we might have gone and performed under dear uncle's windows and he would have pegged out with fury. But I decided on something else.

(He stopped at that point and went successively through the attitudes of a man holding a violin, tuning it furiously, of a poor devil knocked up with fatigue, at the end of his tether and with his legs giving way, on the point of expiring unless somebody throws him a bit of bread. He indicated his desperate plight by pointing with one finger at his half-open mouth, then went on: 'So you see, they threw me the loaf and we three or four starvelings fought over it. And then have lofty thoughts, create noble things in the middle of distress like that!')

I: Not easy, certainly.

HE: Tumbling from one damn thing to another I had come down to this job. And I was living snug as a bug in a rug! Well, I walked out of it, and once again I shall have to scrape the catgut and come back to the finger pointing at the gaping mouth. Nothing lasts in this world. Today the top, tomorrow the bottom of the wheel. Bloody circumstances take us along, and take us very badly.

(Thereupon, draining a drop left in the bottom of the bottle, he addressed his neighbour: 'Sir, just a little pinch of snuff if you would be so kind. That's a lovely box you've got. You are not a musician? No. Good for you, for they're a lot of poor buggers and very much to be pitied. Fate decreed that I should be one, while in a mill in Montmartre there may well be a miller or a miller's boy who will never hear anything but the click of a ratchet and who might have composed the loveliest tunes. Rameau, get to the mill, the mill! That's the place for you.')

I: Whatever a man takes up, nature intended him for it.

HE: Then she makes some strange blunders. For my part I don't look down from that height from which everything looks the same – the man pruning a tree with shears, the caterpillar gnawing one of its leaves, look like two different insects, each doing its own job. Go and perch on the epicycle of Mercury,[45] and from there, if it appeals to you, like Réaumur[46] while he classifies flies into tailors, surveyors and harvesters, you can divide men into cabinet-makers, carpenters, runners, dancers, singers. It's your business, and I'm not interested. I am in this world, and here I stay. But if it is in nature to have an appetite – and I always come back to hunger, the sensation I am always conscious of – I think that it is not in the right order of things to have to go without food sometimes. What a bloody awful economy: some men bursting with everything, while others, with stomachs just as clamorous and a hunger just as unremitting, have nothing to get their teeth into. The worst thing is the subservient posture in which you are kept by need. The necessitous man doesn't walk like anybody else, he jumps, crawls, twists himself up, creeps along. He spends his life taking up positions and carrying them out?

I: What are positions?

HE: Go and ask Noverre.[47] Society offers many more than his art can imitate.

I: So you also, to use your own expression, or rather that of Montaigne, are *perched on the epicycle of Mercury*, contemplating the various pantomimes of the human species.

HE: No, no, I tell you. I am too heavy to soar so high. I leave such misty realms to the cranes. I am of the earth, earthy. I look about me and take up my positions or find fun in watching the positions taken up by others. I am an excellent mimic, as you are about to see.

(Then, smiling as he did so, he began impersonating the admiring man, the supplicating man, the complaisant man, right foot forward, left foot behind, back bent, head up, looking fixedly into somebody else's eyes, lips parted, arms held out towards something, waiting for a command, receiving it, off like an arrow, back again with it done, reporting it. He is attentive to everything, picks up what has been dropped, adjusts a pillow or puts a stool under someone's feet, holds a saucer, pushes forward a chair, opens a door, shuts a window, pulls curtains, keeps his eyes on the master and mistress, stands motionless, arms at his side and legs straight, listening, trying to read people's expressions. And he goes on: 'That is my act, about the same as that of flatterers, courtiers, flunkeys and beggars.'

This man's antics, like the tales of Abbé Galiani[48] and the extravaganzas of Rabelais, have sometimes given me furiously to think. They are three storehouses which have provided me with absurd masks which I fit on to the faces of the most pompous individuals, and I can see a Pantaloon in a prelate, a satyr in a judge, a porker in a monk, an ostrich in a minister of the crown and a goose in his first secretary.)

I: But by your reckoning there are lots of beggars in this world, and I can't think of anybody who doesn't know a few steps of your dance.

HE: You are right. There is only one man in the whole of a realm who walks, and that is the sovereign. Everybody else takes up positions.

I: The sovereign? But even then isn't there something else to be said? Do you think he doesn't find himself from time to time in the vicinity of a dainty foot, a little lock of hair, a little nose that makes him put on a bit of an act? Whoever needs somebody else is necessitous and so takes up a position. The king takes up a position with his mistress and with God; he performs his pantomime step. The minister executes the movements of courtier, flatterer, flunkey or beggar in front of his king. The mob of place-seekers dance your steps in a hundred ways, each more vile than the one before, in front of the minister. The abbé of noble birth puts on bands and long cassock at least once a week when he calls on the keeper of the list of benefices.

Good heavens, what you call the beggars' pantomime is what makes the whole world go round. Every man has his little Hus and his Bertin.

HE: That cheers me no end.

(But while I had been talking he had been mimicking in a killing way the positions of the types as I mentioned them. For example, for the little abbé he held his hat under his arm and his breviary in his left hand, while with his right he held up the skirt of his cassock, advanced with head a bit on one side, eyes downcast, taking off the hypocrite so perfectly that I thought I could see the author of the *Réfutations* before the bishop of Orléans. When it came to the flatterers and place-hunters he crawled on his belly. In fact, exactly Bouret at the Treasury.)

I: Beautifully done. And yet there is one person free to do without pantomime, and that is the philosopher who has nothing and asks for nothing.

HE: Where does that animal exist? If he has nothing he suffers. If he asks for nothing he won't get anything, and he will go on suffering.

I: Diogenes laughed at his needs.

HE: But you must have clothes.

I: No, he went about quite naked.

HE: But it was cold in Athens sometimes.

I: Less than here.

HE: But they had to eat.

I: No doubt.

HE: At whose expense?

I: Nature's. To what does the savage turn? To the earth, animals, fish, trees, plants, roots, streams.

HE: A nasty diet.

I: But copious.

HE: And badly served.

I: Yet it is from that table we take things to eat at our own.

HE: But you will surely admit that the skill of our cooks, pastrycooks, eating-house keepers, caterers and confectioners does contribute something. Your Diogenes could not have had very recalcitrant organs with that austere diet of his.

I: You are wrong there. The Cynic's habit was the same as a monk's and with the same virtue. The Cynics were the Carmelites and Cordeliers of Athens.

HE: I get your meaning. So Diogenes danced the pantomime too, if not before Pericles then at any rate in front of Laïs or Phryne.

I: You are wrong there too. Others paid a great deal of money to the courtesan who gave herself to him just for the pleasure.

HE: But supposing the courtesan was busy and he was in a hurry?

I: He went back into his barrel and managed without.

HE: And you advise me to do the same?

I: I'll be hanged if that wouldn't be better than crawling, cringing and prostituting myself.

HE: But I must have a good bed, good food, warm clothes in the winter and cool ones in summer, leisure, money and lots of other things, and I would rather owe them to charity than have to work for them.

I: Then you are an idler, greedy, cowardly and with a soul of dirt.

HE: I believe I've told you that already.

I: The good things of this life have their worth, no doubt, but you have no idea of the price you are paying to get them. You are dancing, you have danced, and you will go on dancing this vile pantomime.

HE: Quite true, but it hasn't cost me much and doesn't cost me any more because of all that. And that is why I should be ill advised to adopt any other means of locomotion which I should find painful and wouldn't be able to keep up. But from what you say I can see that my poor little wife was a philosopher of sorts. She had the courage of a lion. At times we had no bread and were penniless. We had sold almost all our clothes. I would throw myself down across the bed racking my brains to think of someone who would lend us a crown that I wouldn't have to pay back. But she, gay as a lark, would sit down at the keyboard and sing to her own accompaniment. She had the throat of a nightingale, and I am sorry you never heard her. When I was playing at some concert I took her with me, and on the way I said: 'Now come along, Madame, make them all admire you, show off your talent and your charms. Up you go! Then back!' We arrived, she sang, up she went, and then back. Alas, I lost her, poor little dear! Apart from her talent, she had a mouth you could hardly get your little finger into, teeth – a row of pearls – eyes, feet, skin, cheeks, breasts, the legs of a gazelle, thighs and buttocks fit for a sculptor. Sooner or later she would have got a farmer-general at the very least. She had a walk and haunches! Oh, God, what haunches!

(And off he went miming his wife's walk: little steps, head held high, he played with a fan, wriggled his behind, in fact a most amusing and ridiculous caricature of some of our little tarts.

Then, taking up the thread of his discourse again:)

I used to take her everywhere, to the Tuileries, the Palais-Royal and the Boulevards. It was not possible that she should stay with me. When she crossed the street in the morning, hatless and with a short skirt, you would have stopped to look at her, and you could have held her waist between the fingers of your two hands without squeezing her. Men following her and watching her mincing along on her tiny feet, gauging with their eyes those lovely hips outlined through her thin petticoats, quickened their step; she let them catch up and then suddenly swivelled round at them her two great, dark, shining eyes which stopped them short, for the right side of the medal came fully up to the reverse. But alas, I have lost her, and with her all my hopes of fortune have vanished into air. I had only married her for that, and I had confided all my schemes to her, and she was too intelligent not to see how infallible they were and too wise not to approve of them.

(And, sobbing and weeping, he went on:)
No, no, I shall never get over it. Since then I have taken to bands and a skull cap.

I: Out of grief?

HE: If you like, but the real reason is so as to wear my basin on my head. But will you see what the time is, for I have to go to the opera.

I: What's on?

HE: Something of Dauvergne's. There are some quite nice things in his music; the pity of it is that he wasn't the first to write them. There are always some of the dead who plague the living. Can't be helped. *Quisque suos non patimur manes.* But it is half past five. I can hear the bell ringing for vespers for Abbé de Canaye and for me. Good-bye, Mr Philosopher. Isn't it true that I am always the same?[49]

I: Alas, yes, unfortunately.

HE: So long as I have that misfortune for another forty years! He laughs best who laughs last.

NOTES ON *RAMEAU'S NEPHEW*

1. The Allée d'Argenson was the name given to the avenue of trees on the east, or Rue de Valois, side of the garden, and the Allée de Foy was the corresponding one on the west, or Rue de Richelieu, side. The garden is virtually unchanged today and is the loveliest oasis in central Paris, probably more beautiful and peaceful than ever before owing to the disappearance of some doubtful shops from the arcades and a thorough cleaning of the stonework.

2. The Café de la Régence was in the Place du Palais-Royal, and the proprietor's name was Rey.

3. Jean-Baptiste Lully, or Lulli (1632–87) was of Florentine origin, but his career was wholly French. Favourite composer of Louis XIV, he was the founder of French opera, and his influence upon French music was immense, as in the following century Handel's was to be upon English.

4. Mlle Clairon (1723–1803), one of the most famous actresses of the age, created many of the parts in Voltaire's tragedies. Her art is discussed in Diderot's *Paradoxe sur le comédien*. For an account of her colourful life see J. Christopher Herold, *Love in Five Temperaments*, London, Hamish Hamilton, 1961, pp. 223–79.

5. Briasson, of the Rue Saint-Jacques, one of the group of publishers behind the *Encyclopédie*. Barbier was a silk-merchant.

6. Charles Duclos (1704–72), novelist, historian and essayist. His most important work was the *Considérations sur les mœurs de ce siècle* (1750). In 1755 he became secretary of the Académie française. Although sympathetic towards the Encyclopaedists he was a moderate man and thought Diderot a violent fanatic, and used his influence to keep him out of the Academy. Hence Diderot's resentment.

   The Abbé Trublet (1697–1770) was a deadly enemy of Voltaire and a sarcastic, unpleasant person.

   The Abbé d'Olivet (1682–1768), historian of the Académie française, had a reputation for hypocrisy and dissimulation. Diderot is therefore ironically praising this trio for the opposite virtues to their known vices.

7. Voltaire's *Mahomet* dated from 1742, but the parliamentary reforms of Maupeou in 1771, though widely disapproved, were praised by Voltaire. This passage shows that Diderot was still revising the dialogue as late as 1772.

8. By Philippe Rameau.

9. Palissot (1730–1814), arch-enemy of the movement, caricatured Diderot and his associates in the comedy *Les Philosophes* (1760). There were two Poinsinets, cousins, one of whom, Henri Poinsinet (1735–69), known as the younger, attacked the Encyclopaedists in his comedy *Le Petit Philosophe* (1760). The elder Fréron (1719–76), the great enemy of Voltaire, waged an anti-philosophic warfare in his *Année littéraire*. His son was born in 1754, which again dates this part of the work well into the 1770s. *Les Trois siècles de la littérature française*, 3 vols, 1772, by Sabatier des Castres, Palissot and others, a sort of history of French literature, was violently biased and hostile to Voltaire and the Enlightenment. This reference is yet another factor in the dating of the final version of the work.

10. Mlle Hus (1734–1805), actress of the *Comédie française*, where she was for a time chief rival of Clairon. Mistress of Bertin until he was supplanted in her favours by Vieillard in September 1761 (another dating factor), it was at their establishment that Rameau the nephew led his sycophantic existence until he was thrown out for his ill-advised candour.

11. Samuel Bernard (1651–1739), great financier, was banker to both Louis XIV and Louis XV.

12. In the garden of the Luxembourg. At this point the conversation refers to Diderot's difficult early years in Paris.

13. Diderot's daughter Angélique, later Madame de Vandeul, was born in September 1753. This is another of the conflicting dating factors, and suggests 1761 as the date of composition.

14. The gossip in this burlesque version of how to be a teacher contains mostly names of notorious operatic and theatrical personalities. Lemierre and Arnould were singers, Montamy an expert on porcelain enamel, Préville a famous character actor, one of whose successes was in *Le Mercure galant*, the famous seventeenth-century comedy by Boursault, in which he played several parts, Dumesnil an actress noted for the wild abandon of her acting (see *Le Paradoxe sur le comédien*), Javillier a male dancer.

15. Deschamps and Guimar, ballet dancers, whose rapacity is here likened to divine chastisement upon their victims.

16. Adjective from Villemorien, a Farmer-General, nephew of Bouret (see note 21).

17. Refers to the Affaire Calas, Voltaire's campaign in defence of the Calas family, Huguenot victims of religious persecution, the noblest fight for justice in Voltaire's career. Another dating factor (see Introduction).

18. Obscene books.

19. Madame Bouvillon, enormously fat character in Scarron's *Roman comique*.

20. Baculard D'Arnaud (1718–1805), novelist of some importance and interest, but a sponger on the wealthy.

21. Bouret (1710–77). Farmer-General and sycophantic careerist. The references are to excessively flattering attentions on the occasion of a visit by the king. The little dog story is explained later.

22. Madame de Tencin and her brother the cardinal. See Introduction to *D'Alembert's Dream*, also J. Christopher Herold, *Love in Five Temperaments*, pp. 3–51.

23. Bertin.

24. This speech is a sustained piece of invective against enemies of the Encyclopaedic movement, whether wealthy people with vested interests in ignorance and reaction or their abject tools, the army of unsuccessful writers and professional scandalmongers (today we might call them gossip columnists).

25. Alexis Piron (1689–1773), whose comedy *La Métromanie* (1738) was one of the great comedies of the eighteenth century.

26. Robbé, a poet who specialized in the pornographic.

27. Anti-Encyclopaedic periodicals.

28. The standard fare for a cab.

29. From Molière: *L'Etourdi*, Act II, scene 8. 'Long live Mascarille, Emperor of the Rogues!'.

30. Duni (1709–75), Italian operatic composer, settled in Paris in 1757 and after that date composed some twenty operas of a 'light' type.

31. Airs from Duni's *L'Isle des Fous* (1760).

32. From *Le Maréchal ferrant*, by Philidor (1761).

33. Musicians of the 'French' school, from Lully to Philippe Rameau.

34. Operas by Pergolesi. The term *Bouffons*, applied to these Italian composers in the famous *Guerre des Bouffons* in the fifties of the eighteenth century in Paris, was derived from the Italian *buffi*.

35. *Tancrède* by Campra, *Issé* by Destouches, *L'Europe galante* by Campra, *Les Indes galantes, Castor et Pollux, Les Talents lyriques*, musico-dramatic works of Rameau.

36. *Armide* (1686), opera by Lully to libretto by Quinault, the dramatic poet with whom Lully had a long and fruitful collaboration.

37. Directors of the Paris opera, threatened by the Italian vogue.

38. Refrain of a popular song.

39. Operatic works by Mouret and Rameau respectively.

40. From *Castor et Pollux* by Rameau.

41. 'The Saxon' in this list of Italian composers may be Hasse or Handel.

42. Quinault, La Motte, Fontenelle all wrote operatic libretti. Fontenelle (1657–1757) was, of course, also an important literary figure in other fields, particularly as a popularizer of scientific ideas and the great champion of the Moderns in the Quarrel of the Ancients and Moderns in the last years of the seventeenth century.

43. Puffendorf (1632–94) and Grotius (1583–1645), the two great legal writers.

44. A French adaptation of the work of Goldoni, played at the Comédie Italienne in Paris, 1761.

45. Allusion to Montaigne, Essays, II, 17, *On Presumption*. J. M. Cohen's rendering of the relevant passage in the Penguin Classics translation (1958) reads: 'Those people who bestraddle the epicycle of Mercury and see so far into the heavens make me grind my teeth.'

46. Réaumur (1683–1757), the great scientist and naturalist.

47. Noverre, a French dancer and author of a book on the technique of dancing: *Lettres sur la danse et les ballets* (1759). Hence the play on the meaning of the words 'taking up positions'.

48. Galiani (1728–87), Italian writer and diplomat, posted in Paris and a great friend of Diderot and his circle, was famous for his amusing stories. Hence his name's being coupled with that of Rabelais.

49. Performances at the Opera, situated in those days hard by the Palais-Royal, began regularly at six o'clock. A bell was rung half an hour earlier in the garden of the Palais-Royal to warn the denizens of the various cafés. The Abbé de Canaye, a great friend of Diderot, greatly preferred music to his ecclesiastical duties, hence this almost proverbial expression for his regular attendance at the opera. The implication that the whole of this conversation and the pantomime-interludes, which had begun 'at about five', could only have lasted about half an hour strains the reader's credulity.

D'ALEMBERT'S DREAM

(LE RÊVE DE D'ALEMBERT)

INTRODUCTION TO *D'ALEMBERT'S DREAM*

I

DIDEROT's lifelong interest in science was as keen as that of a boy in his hobby, though not to the exclusion of anything else. But not for him the abstract sciences, pure mathematics, or indeed anything having no obvious immediate bearing upon our individual and social behaviour. These were to him luxury articles; for those who live in this world science should be the study of what can be demonstrated and verified by experiment in the material universe of which we are a part. All his life Diderot was a humanist in the sense that human life, the activities of real people, were more important than theoretical speculation. And since he was a convinced materialist, that meant the working of our bodies and belief in the purely bodily origin of so-called intellectual and spiritual manifestations. Hence his passion for physiology and medicine. As early as 1749, in the *Lettre sur les aveugles*, he had shown how a man's ideas, character and even moral and religious position are determined by the purely material state of his body, in this case blindness from birth; so that, to take a simple example, he will not *naturally* have any conception of 'modesty' or 'indecency' in the matter of nakedness or performing the necessary bodily functions in public. To him the moral and spiritual universe is a different thing from what it is to the sighted. The horrifying implications of all this from the point of view of orthodox religion and morality earned Diderot a sojourn in the prison of Vincennes. In 1754, in the *Pensées sur l'interprétation de la nature*, Diderot had renewed the call for purely experimental and practical science as opposed to a Cartesian type of theoretical reasoning, and had skirmished with such problems as the living, organic nature of matter, the origin of life, evolution and natural selection. He had ended that essay on natural science with fifteen points, or questions, which summarized his perplexities in the face of the mysteries of nature. If natural phenomena are linked, as they demonstrably are, there is progress or evolution. But that would suppose some sense of direction which, in its turn, would suggest some guiding intelligence, which would bring back the religious belief he was trying to eliminate. There seems to be no answer to the question: why does anything exist and to what end? A tentative answer might be that the material universe consists of living and dead matter, and that the one can pass across to the other, but that still does not explain *why* living matter. Then for about fifteen years, as though all his other activities, Encyclopaedic, artistic, dramatic or critical, were not enough, he had turned these speculations over in his mind and kept abreast of current research in anatomy, physiology and medicine.

2

At last, in the summer of 1769, he found himself alone and relatively free for two or three months in his house in the Rue Taranne (since swallowed up by the Boulevard Saint-Germain), his wife and daughter being away at Sèvres, and most of his intimates, such as F. M. Grimm, having left Paris. In a letter to his friend and confidante Sophie Volland, dated 2 September, he wrote:

I think I told you that I have written a dialogue between D'Alembert and myself. On re-reading it I was moved to write a second one, and it is now done. The speakers are D'Alembert (dreaming), Bordeu and D'Alembert's friend Mlle d'Espinasse [*sic*]. It is entitled *D'Alembert's Dream* and is as profound and as extravagant as can be. I have tacked on to the end of that five or six pages capable of making that sentimental lady's hair stand on end, so she won't ever see them. . . .

That is to say that Diderot dashed off in two or three weeks the conclusions he had reached after many years of physiological and medical reading and discussion with friends, and a tentative answer to the questions raised in the *Interprétation de la nature*.

The history of the text is only slightly less complicated than that of *Rameau's Nephew*, and nearly as exciting as an adventure story. Here, in the barest outline, are the facts, or what the researches of the most recent serious student of the text, M. Paul Vernière, suggest are the facts:

Grimm, Diderot's closest literary friend, did not return to Paris from Germany until mid-October, when Diderot read the dialogues over to him. The two friends realized that such scandalous matter, put into the mouths of very well-known people, a famous mathematician, a famous literary hostess and a distinguished physician, meant not only that publication was out of the question but also that the fewer people in the secret the better. Diderot entrusted the manuscript to Grimm so that the latter's copyist could make a fair copy. The dialogue was read to one or two close friends, and inevitably, in such a small society, most of whose members spent their evenings in one of the great cafés, such as the Procope, or at one or other of the great salons, of which the most advanced and influential was that of Mademoiselle de L'Espinasse herself, the secret leaked out. Mademoiselle de L'Espinasse was horrified at reports, probably from Suard, of outrageous opinions put into her mouth by a casual acquaintance, the former colleague of her intimate friend D'Alembert. On her behalf, as well as on his own, for he was a timid man who preferred his quiet mathematical researches to hurly-burly and unpleasantness, D'Alembert insisted that the manuscript be destroyed, and Diderot, always tender-hearted, regretfully yielded to an old friend.

And there the matter might have ended. But Grimm was editor of the *Correspondance littéraire* and, with an eye to possible future publication in this organ, he had had a second copy of the dialogues taken. In 1782 Grimm's successor as editor of the *Correspondance* suggested to Diderot that the three dialogues, a copy of which had 'miraculously' reappeared, be copied and circulated to subscribers. Mademoiselle de L'Espinasse had died in 1776, D'Alembert, a broken man after her death, had retired into misanthropic isolation, while Diderot himself was old and tired. Permission was given and the text appeared in four successive numbers from August to November of that year. But that was not publication; it was only clandestine circulation. After Diderot's own death in 1784 his daughter Madame de Vandeul loyally fulfilled the conditions whereby Catherine the Great of Russia had helped Diderot financially on the understanding that his library and copies of his papers be sent to her after his death. A copy of these dialogues was accordingly sent to St Petersburg. From this manuscript, which has remained in Leningrad ever since, succeeding editions of varying accuracy have been made from 1830, the first printed edition, down to the Second World War.

It is at this point that the story, like that of so many Diderot texts, begins to vie with tales of mystery and adventure. A *Correspondance littéraire* copy of 1782, preserved in the Bibliothèque Nationale, differs materially from those texts springing from Catherine's copy. Then what text did Madame de Vandeul use when she had this copy made? Only since the Vandeul papers have been made available, that is to say since 1949 (see Introduction to *Rameau's Nephew*), has a perfect manuscript been accessible, a manuscript in writing identical with Diderot's own fair copy of *Rameau's Nephew* (the Monval text) which he must have made towards the end of his life. The Leningrad manuscript is a hasty and faulty copy of this, Madame de Vandeul having understandably preferred to send the Empress a copy rather than an original in her father's most careful hand. It is this Vandeul manuscript which has been utilized by Paul Vernière in his critical edition (*Société des Textes Français Modernes*, Paris, Didier, 1951) and subsequently in his Classiques Garnier edition of the *Œuvres philosophiques*, from which this translation has been made.

3

The fictional framework of the dialogues forms a kind of play in three acts:

Act I. The scene is presumably Diderot's house, or some café, and the action opens in the middle of an argument in which Diderot has stated a purely materialistic and consequently atheistic view of the universe. D'Alembert, who thinks himself a sceptic, neither believing nor disbelieving anything on principle, feeling that elimination of God, and therefore of thought and purpose behind nature, raises more questions than it answers, challenges his friend to prove his point. The dialogue which follows seeks to get round these difficulties, and in particular that of the origin of life and the nature of animal reproduction, by showing that all matter is sensitive in greater or lesser degree, active or inert, and that the passage from inert or potential to active sensitivity can be explained in purely physical and mechanical terms.

Act II. The following morning, presumably at D'Alembert's apartment in the Rue de Bellechasse, or perhaps Diderot might have been thinking of that visit he paid to D'Alembert's sick-bed when he had found Mademoiselle de L'Espinasse devotedly nursing him. Mademoiselle de L'Espinasse has been up all night watching at D'Alembert's bedside. He had returned late the previous evening in a very agitated state and pouring forth bits of the evening's argument in a raging delirium. She has summoned Bordeu, the distinguished doctor and a personal friend, and while D'Alembert is still in an exhausted sleep behind a screen she tells the doctor what she has gathered from her friend's ravings, including some notes she has jotted down. Bordeu, a materialist like Diderot, develops and explains, with examples and analogies – Diderot's characteristic method of reasoning. The conversation is punctuated by interruptions from D'Alembert himself, who wakes up, begins to dress and pops in and out from behind the screen, and eventually goes out. Bordeu must go and visit another patient, but Mademoiselle de L'Espinasse makes him promise to come back to lunch with her at two o'clock. This dialogue, by far the most substantial of the three, develops and meditates upon three main themes: (1) animal reproduction is purely mechanical and subject to breakdowns and mutations, hence some discussion leading to a tentative theory of evolution; (2) the mechanical structure of the body which Diderot likens to a spider (= the nerve-centre in the brain) and its web (= the nervous system running from it all over the body), and this analogy is considered at some length, with examples intended to show that monsters, freaks, exceptions in nature are due simply to physical damage to the web or network through threads having become tangled, crushed or broken; (3) hence our psychological or moral behaviour is also explicable in terms of physiology (the trepanning case, speculations about Siamese twins, etc.).

Act III. After lunch Mademoiselle de L'Espinasse and Bordeu hold an inquest, not without its frivolous and prurient moments, into some of the physical implications of the discussion in Act II and in particular into possibilities of cross-breeding and deliberate eugenic experiments, but most important of all into the moral and psychological ones. There are some physical acts which have nothing to do with morality. The only relevant question that should be asked about such acts is: is this act harmful to the individual, to another human being or to society? If the answer is no, and especially if the act gives pleasure to the individual, then it is no concern of morality, which is a social thing. By this standard the conventional moral code in sexual matters is radically changed, for solitary or homosexual behaviour is clearly to be preferred to selfish, unreciprocated or violent 'normal' acts which may imperil the happiness, health and possibly even life of another, to say nothing of unwanted children and their sufferings. In this, as in so many other respects, Diderot is uncannily modern. Little wonder that Mademoiselle de L'Espinasse and D'Alembert, hearing that their names were associated with such horrifying notions, took fright and made Diderot destroy what they hoped, and at that moment Diderot probably feared, was the only copy of the text in existence.

4

Apart from their personal, scientific and moral significance these dialogues have a certain literary interest. Whereas Diderot altered and in some respects confused the form and matter of *Rameau's Nephew* over a long period of years, *D'Alembert's Dream* was slowly incubating in Diderot's mind for many years, but was produced at white heat in a few days. Some of the matter may appear to have been regurgitated before being wholly digested – this bit comes from Buffon, that from Haller, and so on – but the form is homogeneous. It is repetitive, there may be a surfeit of examples and analogies, but they can be justified by the fictional framework, for in order to explain difficult and unfamiliar physiological and biological theories to an intelligent woman quite without scientific training, or indeed to D'Alembert himself who, after all, was a mathematician and not a biological scientist, there must be pauses for assimilation, recapitulations, the same thing must be put another way, simple examples must be thought of. Similarly, though where possible Diderot uses technical words, there must also be non-scientific words and metaphors to make things clear – swarms of bees, spiders, cobwebs, threads, networks, musical instruments capable of repeating and memorizing tunes they play. Of course scientific language was not yet precise and standardized in 1769, and Diderot is imprecise even in his use of such words as *molecule* or *atom*.

But it is questionable whether his main object was as much to expound a system of physiology as to sound a trumpet-blast for materialistic determinism against the forces of metaphysics, conventional morality, belief in the supernatural and obscurantism used as pretexts for man's interference with his fellow-men. He may have had a boyish enthusiasm for the wonders of science, and a somewhat ghoulish interest in the kinds of monstrosities and freaks of nature one sees exhibited at a fair, but he was above all a moralist concerned with man and the foundations of his behaviour as an individual and as a social animal.

We cannot tell whether Mademoiselle de L'Espinasse and D'Alembert ever saw the text as we know it or whether they were given by Suard, or whoever it was, a very detailed account of it. But apart altogether from moral considerations Mademoiselle de L'Espinasse was well advised to insist on its suppression. Perhaps she realized that although Diderot did not know her very intimately there were in these dialogues one or two penetrating judgements on her character, and also that, for the sake of light relief and human interest as well as out of didacticism, Diderot does make her appear unnecessarily obtuse at times, and at others coquettish, sniggeringly prurient and in fact not a very pleasing personality. The truth was, as all those who knew her at all well agreed, that her personal charm matched her intelligence, and indeed had it not been so she would never have succeeded, with very little money and few material resources, in attracting to her modest *salon* some of the finest brains in Europe. Most of us, faced by a situation of this kind, would rather appear shameless or even downright wicked than look just silly.

BIOGRAPHICAL NOTE ON THE
CHARACTERS

JEAN LE ROND D'ALEMBERT (1717–83) was the illegitimate child of Madame de Tencin by the Chevalier
Destouches (called La Touche in this dialogue), an artillery
officer. Madame de Tencin, a remarkable woman even by
eighteenth-century French standards, extremely intelligent
and quite unprincipled, broke her vows as a nun and became
mistress of many influential men who might be useful to
her. Fontenelle, Bolingbroke, Matthew Prior, the Regent,
the Duc de Richelieu are well authenticated lovers, Cardinal Dubois probably was, and it was alleged that she had
unnatural relations with her own brother who, through her
untiring efforts, became Cardinal de Tencin. Other activities included political intrigues, being hostess of a famous
Parisian salon – Marivaux was her devoted protégé – and
writing highly sentimental novels. She regarded her baby's
birth as a tiresome accident, had the child exposed on the
steps of the church of Saint-Jean-le-Rond, whence his name,
and then had nothing more to do with him, even when he
became famous. But the father, unlike most 'natural'
fathers, acknowledged the baby, rescued him from an
orphanage as soon as he returned from active service, and
put him in the care of a foster-mother, Madame Rousseau,
a glazier's wife, whom the boy was to love as a mother, and
at whose house he was to live until he was nearly fifty. The
father paid for the best available education, which soon
brought out the boy's unusual intellectual gifts. He became
one of the greatest mathematicians of his day, member of
most learned societies in Europe, including the Académie
des Sciences and the Académie française. Co-editor with

Diderot of the *Encyclopédie*, his *Discours préliminaire* at the head of Volume I in 1751 was the great manifesto of positivism in the eighteenth century, though D'Alembert himself was not a militant atheist but a true sceptic, unable to accept the uncompromising claims of belief or unbelief. The uproar which greeted his article on Geneva in Volume VII of the *Encyclopédie* (1757), and unleashed Jean-Jacques Rousseau's diatribe, the *Lettre à D'Alembert*, discouraged D'Alembert and caused him to resign from the editorship and seek peace and quiet in his researches, for he was the typical bachelor scholar, and he left Diderot to carry on alone. A lovable, amusing man, he was the greatest ornament of the salon of Madame du Deffand, whence he followed Mademoiselle de L'Espinasse to her new home in the Rue de Bellechasse, and they lived there together in an almost certainly platonic relationship of intimate friendship. After her death he discovered in her papers evidence of her passionate love-affairs which he alone had not suspected, and heartbroken he withdrew into a misanthropic retirement for the rest of his life.

Julie de L'Espinasse (1732–76) was, like D'Alembert, an illegitimate child, but unlike him in her youth she went through all the humiliations of bastardy. Her family tree was extremely twisted. Illegitimate daughter of the Comtesse d'Albon by the Comtesse's cousin Comte Gaspard de Vichy, she was brought up by her mother with the latter's two legitimate children, a girl of sixteen and a boy of eight. When Julie was seven there occurred an event unusual even in such circles at that period. Her father Gaspard de Vichy married Diane d'Albon, his discarded mistress's daughter and Julie's half-sister. When she was sixteen her mother died and the girl, virtually penniless, had to go and live with the Vichys at the château of Chambron, in the Lyonnais. No cruelty is so deadly as family cruelty, especially to a poor female relation and an illegitimate one at that. Julie, at sixteen, found herself nursemaid, governess and victim in a household of which the father, now aged fifty-three, was her own father as well as being her brother-in-law, the mother her sister as well as stepmother and employer, the children her nephews and nieces as well as her brothers and sisters. Small wonder that the extremely intelligent and meanly exploited girl should develop an insatiable longing for understanding and affection. When she was twenty-one Julie was rescued from this intolerable position by her aunt, Gaspard's sister Madame du Deffand, hostess of one of the most celebrated *salons* in Europe. Madame du Deffand's sumptuous *appartement* occupied two floors of the convent of Saint Joseph in the Rue Saint-Dominique, on the site of the present Ministry of War. The convent had been founded in the seventeenth century by Madame de Montespan as a comfortable place to retire to when age and a spreading figure put an end to her reign as mistress of Louis XIV, and that was the measure of its holiness as a religious house. To the evenings at the Rue Saint-Dominique came most of the great social and literary figures of the age: Voltaire, Montesquieu, Turgot, Marmontel, Condorcet, La Harpe, and Jean-Jacques Rousseau until he went off in a huff, as he did sooner or later with everybody. But the great man of her *salon*, to whom she was devoted, was D'Alembert, who was delightful company and apparently very clever and amusing as a mimic of the more pompous personages of the town.

In 1753 the threat of blindness, soon to be fulfilled, forced Madame du Deffand to take a rest at the home of her brother Gaspard de Vichy, where she met her niece and was at once charmed by her character and brains; she saw in her the ideal companion and helper who might be indispensable to her in the days of blindness about to come, who could act as a kind of assistant hostess in the famous *salon*, for she had no intention of allowing blindness to put an end to her own social reign. Julie lived in the Rue Saint-Dominique for ten years from 1754, was immensely successful in that intricate world of social and intellectual intercourse with some of the greatest in the land, and for some years there was a genuine affection between the two women. But inevitably relations became strained – indeed it would have been remarkable had they not done so between an old, blind woman and her young and extremely popular assistant. And Madame du Deffand had grounds for her suspicions, for very soon there developed between Julie and D'Alembert a close friendship in which the two lonely souls found in each other the end of their search for affection and understanding. With the sixth sense of the blind, Madame du Deffand perceived that Julie was more popular than she deemed desirable, and the explosion came in 1764, when she discovered that before officially presenting themselves in her *salon* a select few of her male guests would assemble for informal talk in Julie's room. Foolishly Madame du Deffand made a scene and attempted a trial of strength. Julie of course had to go at once, and D'Alembert was forced to choose between the two women. His choice was a foregone conclusion. Julie was brilliant, thirty-two years old and universally admired for her charm and intelligence; Madame du Deffand, for all her prestige, was a vain, crotchety old lady of seventy, blind and with the most devastating tongue in Paris. So D'Alembert went, and neither he nor Julie was ever forgiven. Madame du Deffand found a new outlet for her maternal possessiveness in Horace Walpole.

Many of the other habitués of Madame du Deffand's *salon* followed the outgoing young queen, and Mademoiselle de L'Espinasse set up in a modest *appartement* in the Rue de Bellechasse, only a few yards away. She had very little money of her own, and was helped by many friends, including the ever-generous Madame Geoffrin, who by giving

Julie an allowance expressed her very real affection and admiration for her, and at the same time settled an old score with her long-standing rival Madame du Deffand. Soon D'Alembert left the home of the good Madame Rousseau, the foster-mother with whom he had lived all his life, and moved to the floor immediately above Julie's *appartement*. Henceforth they kept house in common. The *salon* of Mademoiselle de L'Espinasse became the most informal, but also intellectually the freest and most advanced in Paris, the very centre of the Enlightenment.

But all the time Julie was leading a double life. Intensely sensitive and emotional, easily moved to tears by music or the theatre, her soul and body longed for a love and passion of which the gentle and devoted D'Alembert was temperamentally incapable, whatever the truth may have been about his physical condition. By 1766 she was passionately in love with a handsome and romantic young Spaniard, Jose de Mora, whose lingering death from consumption and frequent absences in search of health only inflamed her passion the more. He died hundreds of miles away from her, but already in her distracted state she had given herself to the conceited lady-killer Guibert, when she was over forty and he under thirty, knowing full well what he was, despising herself yet unable to stop her headlong rush to self-destruction. She died in May 1776, and only when clearing up her papers did D'Alembert discover how deeply she had been deceiving him. He loyally destroyed Mora's letters unread, as Julie had requested on her deathbed, and returned some of Guibert's with a covering letter, of which I translate a few lines:

Pity me, Monsieur, pity my loneliness, my misery, the awful emptiness I can see before me for the rest of my life. I loved her with an affection that will now make love indispensable to me; I have never had the first place in her heart. I have lost sixteen years of my life, and I am now sixty. . . . Alas, she died believing that her death would be a relief to me, she told me so two days before her death. . . . Everything is finished for me, and I have nothing left but to die.

But Madame du Deffand wrote on the day after Julie's death:

Mademoiselle de L'Espinasse died this morning at two o'clock. Once upon a time this would have been quite an event for me; today it means nothing whatever.

Guibert did not destroy his letters from Julie; he was the sort of man who collects trophies of that kind. Some thirty years later they were published by his widow. These are the *Letters of Mademoiselle de L'Espinasse*, of which no less an authority than Sainte-Beuve has said that as immortal expressions of tragic passion there are only two other texts in modern French with which they can be compared, *Phèdre* and *Manon Lescaut*.

When Diderot wrote his dialogues he had of course known D'Alembert intimately for years, but apparently he did not know Julie de L'Espinasse at all well, for his own social life since the break with D'Alembert over the editorship of the *Encyclopédie* was lived largely elsewhere, although the two men remained good friends. Diderot seems to have met Julie for the first time in 1765, before D'Alembert joined her in the Rue de Bellechasse, when he went to visit his friend who was seriously ill. In a letter to Sophie Volland dated 28 July 1765 Diderot refers to this visit to D'Alembert's bedside where he saw 'a Mademoiselle d'Espinas [*sic*] who takes up her position there at eight in the morning and only goes at midnight'. Of course in 1769 he could know nothing of her hidden life, yet his portrayal of this woman shows a remarkable insight into the passionate potentialities of her nature and her lively intelligence. At the same time it shows either obtuseness or bad taste in its suggestion of a certain arch flirtatiousness and mixture of the prurient giggle and the prudish blush difficult to reconcile with all that we know of her.

Théophile de Bordeu (1722–76), a distinguished doctor, had contributed to the *Encyclopédie* and in 1756 had published researches into the behaviour of the pulse, in which he discussed the significance of the pulse in diagnosis. In this dialogue there are a few obvious references to his known interests and belief in letting nature do her own remedial work whenever possible, but clearly he is mainly a mouthpiece for Diderot's arguments. See Introduction to Vernière edition.

CONVERSATION BETWEEN D'ALEMBERT AND DIDEROT

D'ALEMBERT: I grant you that a Being who exists somewhere but corresponds to no one point in space, a Being with no dimensions yet occupying space, who is complete in himself at every point in this space, who differs in essence from matter but is one with matter, who is moved by matter and moves matter but never moves himself, who acts upon matter yet undergoes all its changes, a Being of whom I have no conception whatever, so contradictory is he by nature, is difficult to accept. But other difficulties lie in wait for anyone who rejects him, for after all, if this sensitivity that you substitute for him is a general and essential property of nature, then stone must feel.[1]

DIDEROT: Why not?

D'ALEMBERT: That takes a bit of swallowing.

DIDEROT: Yes, for the person who cuts it, carves it, crushes it yet doesn't hear it crying out.

D'ALEMBERT: I wish you would tell me what difference you think there is between a man and a statue, between marble and flesh.

DIDEROT: Not very much. You can make marble out of flesh and flesh out of marble.

D'ALEMBERT: But still the one is not the other.

DIDEROT: Just as what you call actual energy is not potential energy.

D'ALEMBERT: I don't follow you.

DIDEROT: Let me explain. When a thing is moved from one place to another that is not motion, but only its effect. Motion is inherent in the thing itself, whether it is moved or remains stationary.

D'ALEMBERT: That is a novel way of looking at it.

DIDEROT: But none the less true. Take away the obstacle resisting that particular movement of the motionless body and it will move. If by a sudden rarefaction you take away the air surrounding the trunk of that huge oak, the water it contains will suddenly expand and blow it into a hundred thousand splinters. And I say the same thing about your own body.

D'ALEMBERT: All right. But what relationship is there between motion and sensitivity? Could it possibly be that you take cognizance of active and latent sensitivity as of actual and potential energy? Actual energy manifests itself by motion and potential energy by pressure. In the same way there is an active sensitivity which is characterized by certain reactions observable in animals and perhaps plants, and a latent sensitivity, the existence of which can only be verified when it changes into active sensitivity.

DIDEROT: That's exactly it. You have hit the nail on the head.

D'ALEMBERT: Thus the statue has only latent sensitivity while man, the animal world and perhaps even plants, are vouchsafed active sensitivity.

DIDEROT: There is of course this difference between the block of marble and the living tissue of flesh, but you realize, don't you, that it is not the only one?

D'ALEMBERT: Yes, of course. Whatever resemblance there may be between the external forms of the man and the statue, there is no relationship between their internal organizations. The chisel of the most skilful sculptor can't even make an epiderm. But whereas there is a very simple method for making potential energy turn into actual energy (it is an experiment being repeated before our eyes a hundred times a day), I don't quite see how you can make a body pass from a state of latent sensitivity into one of active sensitivity.

DIDEROT: That's because you don't want to see. It is an equally common phenomenon.

D'ALEMBERT: And what is this equally common phenomenon, may I ask?

DIDEROT: I'm about to tell you, since you don't mind having to be told. It happens every time you eat.

D'ALEMBERT: Every time I eat!

DIDEROT: Yes, for what do you do when you eat? You remove the obstacles which were resisting the active sensitivity of the food. You assimilate the food with yourself, you turn it into flesh, you animalize it, make it capable of feeling. What you do to that food I will do to marble, and whenever I like.

D'ALEMBERT: How?

DIDEROT: How? By making it eatable.

D'ALEMBERT: Make marble eatable . . . doesn't sound very easy to me.

DIDEROT: It's my business to show you how it is done. I take this statue you can see, put it into a mortar, and with some hard bangs with a pestle. . . .

D'ALEMBERT: Mind how you go, please. It is Falconet's masterpiece. If it were merely something by Huez or somebody . . .[2]

DIDEROT: It doesn't make any difference to Falconet; the statue has been paid for, and Falconet cares very little about his present reputation and not at all about it in the future.

D'ALEMBERT: All right, pulverize away, then.

DIDEROT: When the marble block is reduced to the finest powder I mix this powder with humus or compost, work them well together, water the mixture, let it rot for a year, two years, a century, for I am not concerned with time. When the whole has turned into a more or less homogeneous substance – into humus – do you know what I do?

D'ALEMBERT: I am sure you don't eat it.

DIDEROT: No, but there is a way of uniting that humus with myself, of appropriating it, a *latus*, as the chemists would call it.

D'ALEMBERT: And this *latus* is plant life?

DIDEROT: Precisely. I sow peas, beans, cabbages and other leguminous plants. The plants feed on the earth and I feed on the plants.

D'ALEMBERT: It may be true or it may not, but I like this transition from marble to humus, from humus to vegetable matter and from vegetable matter to animal, to flesh.

DIDEROT: So I can make flesh, or soul as my daughter calls it, that is to say an actively sensitive substance. And if I don't solve the problem you have put to me, at least I get quite near to the solution, for you will admit that it is much more of a far cry from a piece of marble to a being who can feel than from a sentient being to a thinking one.

D'ALEMBERT: Agreed. Nevertheless the sentient being is not quite the same thing as the thinking one.

DIDEROT: Before taking another step forward, let me tell you the story of one of the greatest mathematicians in Europe. What was this wondrous being in the beginning? Nothing.

D'ALEMBERT: Nothing! How do you mean? Nothing can come from nothing.

DIDEROT: You are taking words too literally. What I mean is that before his mother, the beautiful and scandalous Madame de Tencin, had reached the age of puberty, and before the soldier La Touche had reached adolescence, the molecules which were to form the first rudiments of our mathematician were scattered about in the young and undeveloped organs of each, were being filtered with the lymph and circulated in the blood until they finally settled in the vessels ordained for their union, namely the sex glands of his mother and father. Lo and behold, this rare seed takes form; it is carried, as is generally believed, along the Fallopian tubes and into the womb. It is attached thereto by a long pedicle, it grows in stages and advances to the state of foetus. The moment for its emergence from its dark prison has come: the new-born boy is abandoned on the steps of Saint-Jean-le-Rond, which gave him his name, taken away from the Foundling Institution and put to the breast of the good glazier's wife, Madame Rousseau; suckled by her he develops in body and mind and becomes a writer, a physicist and a mathematician. How did all this come about? Through eating and other purely mechanical operations. Here is the general formula in a few words: eat, digest, distil *in vasi licito et fiat homo secundum artem*. And anyone lecturing to the Academy on the stages in the formation of a man or animal need refer only to material factors, the successive stages of which would be an inert body, a sentient being, a thinking being and then a being who can resolve the problem of the precession of the equinoxes, a sublime being, a miraculous being, one who ages, grows infirm, dies, decomposes and returns to humus.[3]

D'ALEMBERT: So you don't believe in pre-existent germs?[4]

DIDEROT: No.

D'ALEMBERT: Oh, how glad I am!

DIDEROT: It is contrary to experience and reason: contrary to experience which would search in vain for such germs in the egg and in most animals under a certain age, and to reason which teaches us that in nature there is a limit to the divisibility of matter – even if there is none in our theoretical reasoning – and which jibs at imagining a fully formed elephant inside an atom, and within that another fully formed elephant, and so on *ad infinitum*.

D'ALEMBERT: But without these pre-existent germs the original genesis of animal life is inconceivable.

DIDEROT: If you are bothered about the question of the priority of the egg over the hen or of the hen over the egg, it is because you assume that animals were in the beginning what they are at present. How absurd! We have no more idea of what they have been in the past than we have of what they will become. The imperceptible worm wriggling in the mire is probably on its way to becoming a large animal; the huge beast whose size terrifies us is perhaps on its way to becoming a worm. Perhaps they are each a momentary production of this planet and peculiar to it.

D'ALEMBERT: What did you mean by that?

DIDEROT: I was saying . . . but that will take us away from our original discussion . . .

D'ALEMBERT: What does that matter? We shall come back to it, or else we shan't.

DIDEROT: Will you let me travel forward some thousands of years in time?

D'ALEMBERT: Why not? Time doesn't mean anything to nature.

DIDEROT: You agree to my extinguishing our sun?

D'ALEMBERT: All the more willingly since it won't be the first sun to be extinguished.

DIDEROT: If the sun is extinguished, what will happen? The plants will perish, the animals will perish, and you will have a deserted and silent earth. Light up that heavenly body again and at once you restore the indispensable cause of countless new forms of life; I wouldn't care to guarantee that as the ages roll on our present-day plants and animals will or will not recur among them.

D'ALEMBERT: And why, if the same scattered elements come together, shouldn't they produce the same results again?

DIDEROT: Because in nature everything depends on everything else, and therefore anyone who postulates a quite new phenomenon or brings back a moment from the past is creating a fresh world.

D'ALEMBERT: Anyone who thought deeply about

things would have to grant that. But, to get back to man, since the general order of things has brought him into being, remember that you left me midway between a sentient being and a thinking one.

DIDEROT: I remember perfectly.

D'ALEMBERT: Frankly you would greatly oblige me if you would rescue me from there. I am rather anxious to begin thinking.

DIDEROT: But even if I didn't manage that where would it lead us in the face of a series of incontestable facts?

D'ALEMBERT: Nowhere, except that we should have stopped dead at that point.

DIDEROT: So as to get a bit farther, should we be justified in inventing an agency with contradictory attributes, a word devoid of meaning, unintelligible?

D'ALEMBERT: No.

DIDEROT: Could you tell me what the existence of a sentient being means to that being himself?

D'ALEMBERT: Consciousness of having been himself from the first instant he reflected until the present moment.

DIDEROT: But what is this consciousness founded on?

D'ALEMBERT: The memory of his own actions.

DIDEROT: And without that memory?

D'ALEMBERT: Without that memory there would be no 'he', because, if he only felt his existence at the moment of receiving an impression, he would have no connected story of his life. His life would be a broken sequence of isolated sensations.

DIDEROT: All right. Now what is memory? Where does that come from?

D'ALEMBERT: From something organic which waxes and wanes, and sometimes disappears altogether.

DIDEROT: Therefore if a sentient being who is endowed with this organization necessary for memory links together the impressions he receives, and constructs from this a story, that of his life, and so acquires consciousness of himself, he can deny, affirm, conclude, think.

D'ALEMBERT: That's how it seems to me. I have only one more difficulty left.

DIDEROT: You are mistaken there. You have a lot left.

D'ALEMBERT: But one main one; it is that it seems to me that we can think of only one thing at a time, and in order to construct, I don't say vast chains of reasoning of the kind that range over thousands of ideas, but just one simple proposition, it would seem that at least two things would have to be present: the object which one would say remains under the scrutiny of the intellect while the intellect is concerning itself with affirming or denying certain qualities of the object.

DIDEROT: That's what I think, and it has sometimes led me to compare the fibres of our organs with sensitive vibrating strings. A sensitive vibrating string goes on vibrating and sounding a note long after it has been plucked. It is this oscillation, a kind of necessary resonance, which keeps the object present while the understanding is free to consider whichever of the object's qualities it wishes. But vibrating strings have yet another property, that of making others vibrate, and it is in this way that one idea calls up a second, and the two together a third, and all three a fourth, and so on; you can't set a limit to the ideas called up and linked together by a philosopher meditating or communing with himself in silence and darkness. This instrument can make astonishing leaps, and one idea called up will sometimes start an harmonic at an incomprehensible interval. If this phenomenon can be observed between resonant strings which are inert and separate, why should it not take place between living and connected points, continuous and sensitive fibres?[5]

D'ALEMBERT: If all that isn't true it certainly is very

ingenious. But one might be tempted to think that you are falling, without realizing it, into the very difficulty you were trying to avoid.

DIDEROT: What difficulty?

D'ALEMBERT: You are opposed to the distinction between the two substances.[6]

DIDEROT: I make no secret of that.

D'ALEMBERT: But if you examine carefully what you have just said, you make the philosopher's understanding an entity distinct from the instrument: a kind of musician listening to vibrating strings and making pronouncements about their harmony or dissonance.

DIDEROT: I may have laid myself open to that objection, but perhaps you would not have raised it if you had considered the difference between the instrument called philosopher and the instrument called clavichord. The philosopher-instrument is sensitive, being at one and the same time player and instrument. As a sensitive being he has momentary consciousness of the sound he is producing, as an animal he remembers it. This organic faculty, by linking together the sounds in his own mind, makes a melody out of them and preserves it. Assume that the clavichord has both sensitivity and memory, and then tell me whether it won't know and repeat on its own the tunes you will play on its keys. We are instruments possessed of sensitivity and memory. Our senses are so many keys which are struck by things in nature around us, and often strike themselves. And in my opinion this is all that happens in a clavichord organized like you and me. There is an impression which has its cause within the instrument or outside it, and from this impression is born a sensation, and this sensation has duration, for it is impossible to imagine that it is both made and destroyed in a single, indivisible instant. Another impression succeeds the first which also has its cause both inside and outside the animal, then a second sensation, and tones which describe them in natural or conventional sounds.

D'ALEMBERT: I see. Thus if this sensitive and animated clavichord were endowed with the further powers of feeding and reproducing itself, it would be a living creature and engender from itself, or with its female, little clavichords, alive and resonant.

DIDEROT: No doubt. What else do you suppose a finch is, or a nightingale, or a musician, or a man? And what other difference do you think there is between a canary and a bird-organ? Look at this egg: with it you can overthrow all the schools of theology and all the churches in the world. What is this egg? An insensitive mass before the germ is put into it, and after the germ is in it what is it then? Still an insensitive mass, for the germ itself is merely inert and thick fluid. How does this mass evolve into a new organization, into sensitivity, into life? Through heat. What will generate heat in it? Motion. What will the successive effects of motion be? Instead of answering me, sit down and let us follow out these effects with our eyes from one moment to the next. First there is a speck which moves about, a thread growing and taking colour, flesh being formed, a beak, wing-tips, eyes, feet coming into view, a yellowish substance which unwinds and turns into intestines – and you have a living creature. This creature stirs, moves about, makes a noise – I can hear it cheeping through the shell – it takes on a downy covering, it can see. The weight of its wagging head keeps on banging the beak against the inner wall of its prison. Now the wall is breached and the bird emerges, walks, flies, feels pain, runs away, comes back again, complains, suffers, loves, desires, enjoys, it experiences all your affections and does all the things you do. And will you maintain, with Descartes, that it is an imitating machine pure and simple? Why, even little children will laugh at you, and philosophers will answer that if it is a machine you are one too! If, however, you admit that the only difference between you and an animal is one of organization, you will be showing sense and reason and be acting in good faith; but then it will be concluded, contrary to what you had said, that from an inert substance arranged in a certain way and impregnated by another inert substance, subjected to heat and motion, you will get sensitivity, life, memory, consciousness, passions, thought. Only one of these two lines of argument is left: either to suppose that within the inert mass of that egg there was a hidden element waiting for the egg's development before revealing its presence, or to assume that this imperceptible element had found its way through the shell at some particular moment in the process. But what was this element? Did it occupy any space or not? How did it get in or out without moving? Where was it? What was it doing there or elsewhere? Was it only created when the need for it arose? Or did it exist already, waiting for somewhere to go? Was it of the same nature as this 'somewhere' or not? If of the same nature it must have been matter, if not it is impossible to understand its inertia before the hatching or its energy in the fully developed bird. Just listen to your own arguments and you will feel how pitiful they are. You will come to feel that by refusing to entertain a simple hypothesis that explains everything – sensitivity as a property common to all matter or as a result of the organization of matter – you are flying in the face of common sense and plunging into a chasm of mysteries, contradictions and absurdities.[7]

D'ALEMBERT: Hypothesis! Call it that if you want to. But suppose it were a property essentially incompatible with matter?

DIDEROT: And how do you know that sensitivity is essentially incompatible with matter, since you don't know what the essence of anything is, whether it be matter or sensitivity? Do you understand the nature of motion any the more, its existence in a body, or its communication from one body to another?

D'ALEMBERT: While not understanding the nature of sensitivity or matter, I can see that sensitivity is a simple quality, one and indivisible, and incompatible with any divisible object or *suppositum*.

DIDEROT: Sheer metaphysico-theological balderdash! What, don't you see that all the properties and all the appreciable forms with which matter is endowed are essentially indivisible? There cannot be more or less impenetrability. There is half of a round body, but not half of roundness. There is more or less motion, but you must either have motion or not. There is no such thing as a half, a third, or a quarter of a head, an ear or a finger, any more than there is a half, a third or a quarter of a thought. Since not a single molecule in the universe is exactly like any other and there is no atom within a molecule just like another, you must admit that the atom itself has an indivisible form and quality. You must allow that division is incompatible with the essence of all forms because it destroys them. Be a good scientist and admit that an effect has indeed happened when you have seen it happen even though you cannot explain the relationship between cause and effect. Be a good logician and don't substitute for a cause which does exist and which explains everything some other cause which defies the understanding, whose connexion with the effect is even more inconceivable, and which gives rise to innumerable difficulties without solving any of them.

D'ALEMBERT: Well, supposing I give up this cause?

DIDEROT: That leaves only one substance in the universe, in man, in animals. The bird-organ is made of wood, man is made of flesh. A canary is flesh, a musician is flesh differently organized, but they have one and the same origin, formation, functions and end.

D'ALEMBERT: And how do your two keyboard instruments arrange a conventional system of sounds?

DIDEROT: Assuming each animal to be a sensitive instrument, exactly similar to every other, made to the same pattern, fitted with the same strings and plucked in the same way by joy, sorrow, hunger, thirst, anger, admiration and fright, then it cannot make anything but the same sounds, whether it be at the Pole or the Equator. That is why you will find the interjections more or less the same in all languages, dead or living. You have to explain the origin of conventional sounds by need and proximity. The sensitive instrument (or animal) found by experience that if it made a given sound there followed a certain effect outside itself, and that other sensitive instruments (or animals) like itself came up, went away, asked for something, offered something, hurt or caressed it. And these effects became associated in its memory and that of the others with the formation of these sounds. Notice, moreover, that all human intercourse consists solely of noises and actions. And to give my system its full weight, notice also that it is open to the same insurmountable objection that Berkeley raised against the real existence of material bodies. Thus there can come a moment of madness when a sensitive clavichord imagines that it is the only one that has ever existed in the world, and that all the harmony in the universe is being produced by it alone.

D'ALEMBERT: A great deal could be said on that subject.

DIDEROT: That's true.

D'ALEMBERT: For example, it is not too clear from your system how we form syllogisms and draw conclusions.

DIDEROT: As a matter of fact we don't: they are all drawn by nature. All we do is describe connected phenomena, the connexion between which is either necessary or contingent, and these phenomena are known through experience. They are necessary in mathematics, physics and other exact sciences, contingent in ethics, politics and other speculative sciences.

D'ALEMBERT: But is the connexion between phenomena any less necessary in one case than in the other?

DIDEROT: No, but the cause is subject to too many peculiar vicissitudes which we fail to perceive, and so we cannot count infallibly upon the effect that will result. Our certainty that a violent man will lose his temper when insulted is not of the same kind as the certainty that if two bodies collide the larger will cause the smaller to move.

D'ALEMBERT: And what about analogy?

DIDEROT: Analogy, even in the most complex cases, boils down to a rule-of-three progression working itself out in the sensitive instrument. If a certain known phenomenon in nature is followed by a certain other phenomenon also known in nature, what fourth phenomenon will be consequent on a third one either found in nature or conceived in imitation of nature? If the lance of an ordinary soldier is ten feet long, how long is the lance of Ajax? If I can throw a stone weighing four pounds, Diomedes should be able to move a chunk of rock. The strides of the gods and the leaps of their steeds will be in the same ratio as the gods are deemed to bear to men. It is a fourth harmonic string. It is a fourth harmonic string proportional to the three others and from which an animal is always ready to hear a sympathetic resonance set up within itself, though it does not occur in nature. It matters little to the poet, but it is true nonetheless. But for the philosopher it is another matter; he must set to work and interrogate nature, which often presents him with a quite different phenomenon from the one he had been counting on. And then he realizes that analogy has been playing tricks on him.

D'ALEMBERT: Well, so long, my friend, good night and sleep well.

DIDEROT: Laugh if you like, but you will dream about

this talk when your head is on your pillow, and if it doesn't make sense, it will be too bad, for then you will be obliged to entertain some even more ridiculous hypotheses.

D'ALEMBERT: Don't you believe it; sceptic I shall go to bed and sceptic I shall get up.

DIDEROT: Sceptic! Can anybody be a sceptic?

D'ALEMBERT: Aha, this is something new! Aren't you by way of maintaining that I am not a sceptic? Who knows better than I do?

DIDEROT: Just a minute.

D'ALEMBERT: Well, don't be long, for I am anxious to get to sleep.

DIDEROT: I shall be brief. Do you think there is a single question ever argued on which a man can be for and against with an exactly equal amount of reason?

D'ALEMBERT: No, that would be like Buridan's ass.[8]

DIDEROT: Then in that case there is no such thing as a sceptic, since, with the exception of mathematics, where there cannot be the slightest uncertainty, there is a for and against in everything. So the scales are never exactly balanced, and it is impossible for them not to go down on the side which seems to us more probable.

D'ALEMBERT: But in the morning I see probability on my right, and by afternoon it is on my left.

DIDEROT: That is to say that you are dogmatically for in the morning and dogmatically against in the afternoon.

D'ALEMBERT: And by evening, recalling the rapid changeableness of my judgements, I don't believe anything, either the morning's opinion or the afternoon's.

DIDEROT: In other words, you no longer remember clearly the reasons why one of the two opinions between which you wavered eventually prevailed, and this preponderance now seems too slight to be a foundation for a stable opinion. So you decide to give up worrying about such problematical subjects, to leave others to discuss them and stop arguing yourself.

D'ALEMBERT: Perhaps.

DIDEROT: But if someone took you to one side and asked you in a friendly way to say quite frankly which of the two sides seemed to raise fewer difficulties, would you honestly be embarrassed about answering? Would you go through the act of Buridan's ass?

D'ALEMBERT: No, I don't think I would.

DIDEROT: Now look, my friend, if you come to think it out you will find that in all things our real opinion is not the one from which we have never wavered, but the one to which we have most regularly returned.

D'ALEMBERT: I think you are right.

DIDEROT: And so do I. Good night, my friend and *memento quia pulvis es, et in pulverem reverteris.*

D'ALEMBERT: That's depressing.

DIDEROT: But unavoidable. Vouchsafe a man, I don't say immortality, but only twice his normal span, and see what will happen!

D'ALEMBERT: What do you expect to happen? But what do I care? Let it happen, whatever it is. I want to go to sleep. Good night.

D'ALEMBERT'S DREAM

SPEAKERS: D'Alembert, Mademoiselle de L'Espinasse, Doctor Bordeu.

BORDEU: Well, what's happened now? Is he ill?

MADEMOISELLE DE L'ESPINASSE: I'm afraid so; he has had a most disturbed night.

BORDEU: Is he awake?

MADEMOISELLE DE L'ESPINASSE: Not yet.

BORDEU (having gone over to D'Alembert's bed and felt his pulse and skin): It won't be anything.

MADEMOISELLE DE L'ESPINASSE: You don't think so?

BORDEU: Take my word for it. Pulse all right . . . a bit weak . . . skin moist . . . breathing easy.

MADEMOISELLE DE L'ESPINASSE: Nothing we ought to do for him?

BORDEU: No, nothing.

MADEMOISELLE DE L'ESPINASSE: I'm glad of that; he hates taking medicine.

BORDEU: So do I. What did he eat for supper?

MADEMOISELLE DE L'ESPINASSE: He wouldn't eat anything. I don't know where he spent the evening, but he came back with something on his mind.

BORDEU: It's only a bit of a temperature and there won't be any after-effects.

MADEMOISELLE DE L'ESPINASSE: As soon as he came in he changed into his dressing-gown, put on his night-cap, threw himself into an arm-chair and dropped off to sleep.

BORDEU: Sleep is beneficial wherever it happens, but he would have been better off in bed.

MADEMOISELLE DE L'ESPINASSE: He lost his temper with Antoine for saying so, and we had to keep on at him for half an hour before we could get him to bed.

BORDEU: That happens to me every day although I am perfectly fit.

MADEMOISELLE DE L'ESPINASSE: When he had been got to bed he didn't settle down in his usual way, for he normally sleeps like a child, but began tossing and turning, throwing his arms about, pushing back the bedclothes and talking out loud.

BORDEU: Talking about what? Geometry?

MADEMOISELLE DE L'ESPINASSE: No, it was just as though he were delirious. At first some gibberish about vibrating strings and sensitive fibres. It seemed so crazy to me that, having decided to sit up with him all night and not knowing what to do with myself, I moved a little table to the foot of his bed and set about writing down whatever I could catch of his wanderings.

BORDEU: Good idea – and quite typical of you. Can I see it?

MADEMOISELLE DE L'ESPINASSE: By all means. But I'll bet my life you won't make head or tail of it.

BORDEU: You never know.

MADEMOISELLE DE L'ESPINASSE: Are you ready, doctor?

BORDEU: Yes.

MADEMOISELLE DE L'ESPINASSE: Listen: 'A living point.... No, that's wrong. Nothing at all to begin with, and then a living point. This living point is joined by another, and then another, and from these successive joinings there results a unified being, for I am a unity, of that I am certain.... (As he said this he felt himself all over.) But how did this unity come about?' 'Now, my dear,' I said, 'what does it matter? go to sleep.' He fell silent, but after a moment he went on as though speaking

to somebody: 'Now listen, Mr Philosopher, I can understand an aggregate, a tissue of tiny sensitive bodies, but an
animal! . . . A whole, a system that is a unit, an individual,
conscious of its own unity! I can't see it, no, I can't see it.'
Doctor, can you make any sense out of that?[9]

BORDEU: Yes, perfect sense.

MADEMOISELLE DE L'ESPINASSE: Then you are lucky.
'My difficulty may come from a false notion. . . .'

BORDEU: Is this you speaking?

MADEMOISELLE DE L'ESPINASSE: No, this is what he
said in his dream.

BORDEU: All right, go on.

MADEMOISELLE DE L'ESPINASSE: Well, he went on,
addressing himself: 'Friend D'Alembert, mind how you go,
you are assuming that there is only contiguity, whereas there
is continuity. . . . Yes, he is artful enough to say that. . . .
And how is this continuity formed? He'll find no trouble
about that. . . . Just as a globule of mercury joins up with
another globule of mercury, so a sensitive, living molecule
joins up with another sensitive and living molecule. First
there were two globules, but after contact there is only
one. The same sensitivity is common to the whole mass.
And why not? I can mentally divide the length of an
animal fibre into as many distinct parts as I like, but in
fact that fibre will be continuous, all of a piece, yes, all of a
piece. Contact between two homogeneous molecules – perfectly homogeneous – gives the continuity, and this applies
to the most complete union, cohesion, combination or
identity imaginable. . . . Yes, Mr Philosopher, all very well
if these molecules are simple and elementary, but suppose
they themselves are aggregates, compounds. . . . The combination will still take place, and consequently there will be
identity and continuity. . . . And then the usual actions and
reactions. . . . It is certain that contact between two living
molecules is quite a different thing from mere contiguity of

two inert masses. . . . Never mind, never mind, some holes could no doubt be picked in all this, but I don't care; I never pick holes for the sake of it, so let's go on. A wire of pure gold is one comparison I remember his making, a homogeneous network into the interstices of which others fit to form, perhaps, a second network, a tissue of sensitive matter which is in contact with the first and which assimilates active sensitivity here and inactive there and passes it on like movement. And then there is the fact, as he has clearly stated, that there must be some difference between the contact of two molecules that are sensitive and two that are not. And what can that difference be? The usual action and reaction . . . but of a special character. . . . So everything works together to produce a sort of unity which is only found in the animal world. . . . Really, if that isn't what you call truth it is very like it. . . .' But you are laughing, doctor. Can you see any kind of sense in all this?

BORDEU: Quite a lot.

MADEMOISELLE DE L'ESPINASSE: He is not out of his mind, then?

BORDEU: Certainly not.

MADEMOISELLE DE L'ESPINASSE: After this preamble he started shouting: 'Mademoiselle de L'Espinasse! Mademoiselle de L'Espinasse!' 'Well, what is it?' 'Have you ever seen a swarm of bees leaving their hive? . . . The world, or the general mass of matter, is the great hive. . . . Have you seen them fly away and form at the tip of a branch a long cluster of little winged creatures, all clinging to each other by their feet? This cluster is a being, an individual, a kind of living creature. . . . But these clusters should be all alike. . . . Yes, if he admitted the existence of only one homogeneous substance. . . . Have you seen them?' 'Yes, I have.' 'You have?' 'Yes, dear, I'm telling you so.' 'If one of those bees decides to pinch in some way the bee it is hanging on to, what do you think will happen? Tell me.'

'I've no idea.' 'Tell me all the same. . . . So you don't know, but the Philosopher does. If ever you see him, and you are bound to see him sooner or later, for he has promised you will, he will tell you that this second bee will pinch its neighbour, and that throughout the cluster as many individual sensations will be provoked as there are little creatures, and that the whole cluster will stir, move, change position and shape, that a noise will be heard, the sound of their little cries, and that a person who had never seen such a cluster form would be tempted to take it for a single creature with five or six hundred heads and a thousand or twelve hundred wings.' Well, doctor?

BORDEU: Well, do you know that that is a most beautiful vision and that you did well to write it down.

MADEMOISELLE DE L'ESPINASSE: Are you dreaming, too?

BORDEU: Far from dreaming, I would almost undertake to tell you what comes next.

MADEMOISELLE DE L'ESPINASSE: I bet you can't.

BORDEU: You bet me?

MADEMOISELLE DE L'ESPINASSE: Yes.

BORDEU: And if I hit on the right answer?

MADEMOISELLE DE L'ESPINASSE: If you hit on the right answer I promise . . . I promise to consider you the biggest madman in the world.

BORDEU: Look at your notes and listen: 'A man who took that cluster for an animal would be making a mistake.' But, Mademoiselle, I presume he went on addressing you. 'Do you want him to give a more balanced opinion? Do you want to change the cluster of bees into one individual animal? Soften the feet with which they cling to each other, that is to say make them continuous instead of contiguous. Obviously there is a marked difference between this new condition of the cluster and the preceding one, and what can this difference be if not that it is now a whole, one and the same animal, whereas before it was a collection of animals? . . . All our organs –'

MADEMOISELLE DE L'ESPINASSE: *All* our organs!

BORDEU: '– for anybody who has practised medicine and made a few observations . . .'

MADEMOISELLE DE L'ESPINASSE: What next?

BORDEU: What next? '. . . are only distinct animals kept by the law of continuity in a state of general sympathy, unity, identity.'

MADEMOISELLE DE L'ESPINASSE: I really am amazed; that's what he said, almost word for word. I can now proclaim to all the world that there is no difference at all between a doctor awake and a philosopher dreaming.

BORDEU: That has been suspected already. Is that all he said?

MADEMOISELLE DE L'ESPINASSE: Oh dear no. You'd never guess. After that gibberish of yours – or his – he said: 'Mademoiselle?' 'Here I am, my dear.' 'Come nearer, nearer still, there's something I'd like you to do for me.' 'What?' 'Take this cluster of bees, there, you see it over there, and let us do an experiment.' 'How?' 'Take your scissors; are they sharp?' 'They cut beautifully.' 'Now carefully, very carefully, bring your scissors to bear on these bees and cut them apart, but mind you don't cut through the middle of their bodies, cut exactly where their feet have grown together. Don't be afraid, you will hurt them a little, but you won't kill them. Good – your touch is as delicate as a fairy's. Do you observe how they fly off in different directions, one by one, two by two, three by three? What a lot there are! Now if you have followed me. . . . You have?' 'Perfectly.' 'Then suppose . . . suppose . . .!' Really, doctor, I took in so little of what I was writing; he spoke so softly, and this part of my notes is so scrawled that I can't make it out.

BORDEU: I'll supply what is missing, if you like.

MADEMOISELLE DE L'ESPINASSE: If you can!

BORDEU: Nothing simpler. 'Suppose that these bees are so tiny that the thick blade of your scissors always missed their bodies, in fact that you can cut them up as small as you like without ever killing one, and that the whole mass, composed of bees too small to be seen, will be a real polyp that can be destroyed only by crushing. The difference between the cluster of continuous bees and the cluster of contiguous ones is precisely the same as that between ordinary animals, such as ourselves or fish, and worms, serpents and polypous creatures. And what is more, with a few modifications –'

(At this point Mademoiselle de L'Espinasse jumps up and goes and pulls the bell-rope.)

Mind how you go, Mademoiselle, you will wake him up, and he needs sleep.

MADEMOISELLE DE L'ESPINASSE: I forgot. I am so stunned. (To the servant who comes in:) Which of you went to fetch the doctor?

SERVANT: I did, Mademoiselle.

MADEMOISELLE DE L'ESPINASSE: A long time ago?

SERVANT: I haven't been back an hour.

MADEMOISELLE DE L'ESPINASSE: Did you take anything to him?

SERVANT: No, nothing.

MADEMOISELLE DE L'ESPINASSE: No papers?

SERVANT: No.

MADEMOISELLE DE L'ESPINASSE: All right, you can go. . . . I can't get over it. You see, doctor, I suspected one of them of having passed my scribblings on to you.

BORDEU: I can assure you there has been nothing of the kind.

MADEMOISELLE DE L'ESPINASSE: Doctor, now that I know how clever you are, you can be very useful to me in social life. His dream did not stop at that point.

BORDEU: I'm very glad.

MADEMOISELLE DE L'ESPINASSE: You don't see anything disturbing in all this?

BORDEU: Not in the least.

MADEMOISELLE DE L'ESPINASSE: He went on: 'Well, Mr Philosopher, so you think there are polyps of all kinds, even human ones? But we don't find any in nature.'

BORDEU: He obviously hadn't heard of the two girls who were connected by the head, shoulders, back, buttocks and thighs, and lived in that condition, stuck together, up to the age of twenty-two, and then died within a few minutes of each other. What did he say next?

MADEMOISELLE DE L'ESPINASSE: The sort of nonsense you only hear in the madhouse. He said: 'That is past or to come. And besides, who knows the state of affairs on other planets?'

BORDEU: There's probably no need to go so far afield.

MADEMOISELLE DE L'ESPINASSE: 'Human polyps in Jupiter or Saturn! Males splitting up into males and females into females – that's a funny idea. . . . (At that he went off into bellows of laughter which frightened me.) Man splitting up into myriads of men the size of atoms which could be kept between sheets of paper like insect-eggs, which spin their own cocoons, stay for some time in the chrysalis stage, then cut through their cocoons and emerge like butterflies, in fact a ready-made human society, a whole province populated by the fragments of one individual, that's fascinating to think about. . . . (More bursts of laughter.) If there is a place where man can divide himself up into myriads of microscopic men, people there should be less reluctant to die, for the loss of one man can so easily be made up that it must give rise to little regret.'

BORDEU: This extravaganza is almost the true history of all existing and future animal species. Man may not divide up into myriads of men, but at any rate he does break up into myriads of minute creatures whose metamorphoses and future and final state are impossible to foresee. Who knows whether this is not the breeding-ground of another generation of beings separated from this one by an inconceivable interval of successive centuries and modifications?

MADEMOISELLE DE L'ESPINASSE: What are you muttering about now, doctor?

BORDEU: Nothing, nothing. I was having my dream, too. Go on with your reading, Mademoiselle.

MADEMOISELLE DE L'ESPINASSE: 'All things considered, however, I prefer our present method of renewing the population,' he went on. 'Mr Philosopher, you know what is going on here or elsewhere, so tell me this: doesn't the splitting up of different parts of a man produce men of as many different kinds? The brain, the heart, chest, feet, hands, testicles. . . . Oh how this simplifies morality! A man born a . . . A woman who had come from . . . (Doctor, will you let me skip this bit?) . . . a warm room, lined with little phials, each one bearing a label: warriors, magistrates, philosophers, poets – bottle for courtiers, bottle for prostitutes, bottle for kings.'

BORDEU: All very amusing and idiotic. This is only a dream, yet it is a vision that reminds me of some rather curious phenomena.

MADEMOISELLE DE L'ESPINASSE: Then he began mumbling something or other about seeds, bits of flesh pounded up in water, different races of animals he saw coming into being and perishing one after the other. He was holding his right hand to make it look like the tube of a microscope, and his left, I think, represented the mouth of some receptacle. He looked down the tube into the receptacle and said: 'That Voltaire can joke as much as he likes, but the Eelmonger is right;[10] I believe my own eyes, and I can see them, and what a lot of them there are darting

to and fro and wriggling about!' He compared the receptacle, in which he could see so many instantaneous births,
to the universe, and in a drop of water he could see the
history of the world. This idea struck him as sublime, and
he thought it quite consistent with good scientific method,
which finds out about large bodies by studying small ones.
Then he went on: 'In Needham's drop of water everything
begins and ends in the twinkling of an eye. In the real world
the same phenomenon lasts somewhat longer, but what is
the duration of our time compared with eternity? Less
than the drop I have taken up on a needle-point compared
with the limitless space surrounding me. Just as there is an
infinite succession of animalculae in one fermenting speck of
matter, so there is the same infinite succession of animalculae in the speck called Earth. Who knows what animal
species preceded us? Who knows what will follow our
present ones? Everything changes and passes away, only the
whole remains unchanged. The world is ceaselessly beginning and ending; at every moment it is at its beginning and
its end. There has never been any other world, and never
will be.

'In this vast ocean of matter not a single molecule
resembles any other, not a single molecule remains for a
moment just like itself: *Rerum novus nascitur ordo*, that is its
unvarying device. . . .' Then he added with a sigh: 'Oh,
vanity of human thought! oh, poverty of all our glory and
labours! oh, how pitiful, oh, how limited is our vision!
There is nothing real except eating, drinking, living, making
love and sleeping. . . . Mademoiselle de L'Espinasse, where
are you?' 'Here.' Then his face became flushed. I wanted
to feel his pulse, but he had hidden his hand somewhere.
He seemed to be going through some kind of convulsion.
His mouth was gaping, his breath gasping, he fetched a
deep sigh, then a gentler one and still gentler, turned his
head over on the pillow and fell asleep. I was watching him

very attentively, and felt deeply moved without knowing why; my heart was beating fast, but not with fear. A few moments later I saw a little smile flicker round his lips, and he whispered: 'On a planet where men reproduced like fish, where a man's spawn was simply spread over that of a woman . . . I should have fewer regrets. . . . Nothing must be lost if it might be useful. Mademoiselle, if that stuff could be collected into a phial and sent first thing in the morning to Needham. . . .' Doctor, don't you call this sheer raving?

BORDEU: In your presence, I suppose so.

MADEMOISELLE DE L'ESPINASSE: In my presence or not, it's all the same, and you don't know what you are talking about. I had hoped that the rest of the night would be undisturbed.

BORDEU: It usually does work out like that.

MADEMOISELLE DE L'ESPINASSE: It was nothing of the kind. At about two in the morning back he came to his drop of water, which he called, er, a mi . . . cro . . .

BORDEU: A microcosm.

MADEMOISELLE DE L'ESPINASSE: Yes, that was the word. He admired the sagacity of the ancient philosophers. He said, or put into his Philosopher's mouth, I forget which: 'If Epicurus, when he affirmed that the earth contained the germs of everything and that the animal world was the product of fermentation, had proposed to show a small-scale picture of what had happened on a large scale at the beginning of time, what answer could have been given to him? . . . And now you have this same picture before your eyes and are learning nothing from it. Who can tell whether the fermentation with its products is not still going on? Who can tell what stage in the sequence of these animal generations we have now reached? Who knows whether that shapeless biped a mere four feet in height, which is still called a man in polar regions, but which would very soon lose that name if it went just a little more misshapen, is not an example of a disappearing species? Who knows whether this is not the case with all animal species? Who knows whether everything is not tending to degenerate into the same great, inert, motionless sediment? And who knows how long this inertia will last? Who knows what new species may once again evolve from such a huge mass of sensitive and living particles? Why not just one kind of animal? What was the elephant at its inception? Perhaps the enormous animal as we now know it or perhaps one single atom, for each possibility exists equally, they merely depend upon the motion and various properties of matter.... The elephant, that huge and highly organized mass, a sudden product of fermentation? And why not? The ratio between the great quadruped and the womb in which it was formed is less than that of the mite to the particle of flour which produces it, but the mite is only a mite.... I mean that the smallness which conceals its complex organization also deprives it of its wonder. The real wonder is life itself, sensitivity, and this miracle is one no longer. Once I have seen inert matter change into something sensitive there is nothing left to marvel at. What a striking comparison it is between a small number of elements fermenting in the hollow of my hand and the measureless reserves of different elements in the bowels of the earth and on its surface, in the depths of the seas and in the wastes of the air!... And yet, since the same causes are still in existence, why have the effects ceased? Why do we no longer see the bull pushing his horns through the soil as with feet pressing the ground he strains to free his heavy body therefrom?...[11] Let the present species of animals pass away, let the great, inert sediment go on working for millions more ages. It may well be that in order to renew species ten times longer is needed than their actual duration. Take care, don't make hasty pronouncements about the functioning of nature. You have two great phenomena: the transition from a state of inertia to one of sensitivity, and spontaneous generation; let them satisfy you, and draw correct conclusions from them and in a natural order, where nothing is great or small, permanent or variable in the absolute. Beware of the fallacy of the ephemeral....' Doctor, what is the fallacy of the ephemeral?

BORDEU: That of a transient being who believes in the immutability of things.

MADEMOISELLE DE L'ESPINASSE: Like Fontenelle's rose, who declared that no gardener had ever been known to die? [12]

BORDEU: Exactly. That is both graceful and profound.

MADEMOISELLE DE L'ESPINASSE: Why can't these philosophers of yours express themselves as gracefully as Fontenelle? We should understand them then.

BORDEU: Frankly I'm not sure whether such a frivolous tone is suitable for serious subjects.

MADEMOISELLE DE L'ESPINASSE: What do you call a serious subject?

BORDEU: Well, universal sensitivity, the formation of a sentient being, its unity, the origin of animal life, its duration and all the questions these matters raise.

MADEMOISELLE DE L'ESPINASSE: For my part I call all these things a lot of nonsense, something that I admit we can dream of when we are asleep, but which a reasonable man will not bother about in his waking hours.

BORDEU: And why, please?

MADEMOISELLE DE L'ESPINASSE: Because some of them are so obvious that it is pointless to look for an explanation, but others so obscure that you can't make head or tail of them, and all of them are absolutely useless.

BORDEU: Do you think, Mademoiselle, that it doesn't matter whether you accept or deny the existence of a Supreme Intelligence?

MADEMOISELLE DE L'ESPINASSE: No.

BORDEU: Do you think one can make up one's mind about Supreme Intelligence without knowing exactly where one stands on the indestructibility of matter and its properties, the distinction between mind and matter, the nature of man and the reproduction of animal life?

MADEMOISELLE DE L'ESPINASSE: No.

BORDEU: Then these questions are not as pointless as you suggest.

MADEMOISELLE DE L'ESPINASSE: But what has their importance to do with me if I can't possibly understand them?

BORDEU: How can you if you don't go into them? But might I ask you which questions you find so obvious that there is no need to examine them?

MADEMOISELLE DE L'ESPINASSE: Well, for example, there is the matter of my unity, my identity. Good Lord, it seems to me that there is no need for a lot of verbiage in order to know that I am myself, always have been and will never be anyone else.

BORDEU: That fact may be clear, but the reason for it isn't by any means, especially if you adopt the hypothesis that there is only one kind of matter, and that man, and animal life in general, is formed simply by juxtaposition of several sensitive molecules. Now each sensitive molecule had its own identity before the juxtaposition, but how has it lost it, and how have all these losses added up to the conscious individuality of the whole?

MADEMOISELLE DE L'ESPINASSE: I imagine that contact alone would be enough. There is an experiment I have done a hundred times . . . but just a minute . . . I must have a look at what is going on behind those curtains . . . he's asleep. . . . When I put my hand on my thigh I can feel perfectly well at first that my hand is not my thigh, but after some time, when each is at the same temperature,

I can't tell which is which, where one begins and the other ends, and they are as one.

BORDEU: Yes, until somebody sticks a pin into one or the other, and then back comes the distinction. Therefore there is something within you which knows whether it was your hand or thigh which was pricked, and that something is not your foot, nor even your pricked hand. The hand hurts, but it is something else that knows about it without itself feeling the pain.

MADEMOISELLE DE L'ESPINASSE: Well, I suppose it's my head!

BORDEU: *All* your head?

MADEMOISELLE DE L'ESPINASSE: Of course not. Look, doctor, I will explain by means of a parable. Most of the reasoning of women and poets is done in parables. Now think of a spider. . . .[13]

D'ALEMBERT: Who's that? Is that you, Mademoiselle de L'Espinasse?

MADEMOISELLE DE L'ESPINASSE: Sh . . . sh . . .

(Mademoiselle de L'Espinasse and the doctor remain silent for a little while, then Mademoiselle de L'Espinasse says softly:) I think he's dropped off again.

BORDEU: No, I think I can hear something.

MADEMOISELLE DE L'ESPINASSE: You are right. Is he going on with his dream, do you think?

BORDEU: Listen.

D'ALEMBERT: Why am I what I am? Because I had to be as I am. Yes, in this particular place, no doubt, but elsewhere? At the Pole? On the Equator? Or on Saturn? If a distance of a few thousand leagues can change me into another species, what about a distance of several thousand times the earth's diameter? And if everything is in a state of flux, as the spectacle of the universe shows everywhere, what might not be the result here and elsewhere of several million years of changes? Who can tell what a thinking and sentient being on Saturn is like? But do thought and feeling exist on Saturn? Why not? Has the thinking and sentient being on Saturn more senses than I have? If that is the case how unhappy that Saturnian must be! Without senses there would be no more needs.

BORDEU: He is right; the organs produce the needs, and conversely the needs produce the organs.

MADEMOISELLE DE L'ESPINASSE: Doctor, are you seeing visions as well?

BORDEU: Why not? I have seen two stumps finish by turning into two arms.

MADEMOISELLE DE L'ESPINASSE: That is not true.

BORDEU: I know it isn't, but when the arms were missing I have seen two shoulder-blades grow longer, develop into pincers and become a pair of stumps.

MADEMOISELLE DE L'ESPINASSE: How ridiculous!

BORDEU: It's a fact. Let us assume a long succession of armless generations, and at the same time unremitting efforts, and you would see the two members of these pincers get longer and longer, cross each other at the back and come round to the front again, possibly develop fingers at the extremities and so make new arms and hands. The original shape of a creature degenerates or perfects itself through necessity and habitual functioning. We walk so little, work so little, but think so much that I wouldn't rule out that man might end by being nothing but a head.

MADEMOISELLE DE L'ESPINASSE: Nothing but a head! a head! that's not much use. For my part I was hoping that with unlimited love-making ... What awful ideas you are putting into my head!

BORDEU: Now, now!

D'ALEMBERT: So I am what I am because it was inevitable that I should be. Change the whole and of necessity you change me. But the whole is constantly changing. . . . Man is merely a frequent effect, a monstrosity is a rare one, but both are equally natural, equally inevitable, equally part of the universal and general order. And what is strange about that? All creatures are involved in the life of all others, consequently every species . . . all nature is in a perpetual state of flux. Every animal is more or less a human being, every mineral more or less a plant, every plant more or less an animal. . . . There is nothing clearly defined in nature. . . . It's a case of Father Castel's ribbon. . . .[14] Yes, Father Castel, it's your ribbon, that's all it is. Any given thing is a specific thing only in greater or lesser degree, more or less earth, more or less water, more or less air, more or less fire, more or less in one classification or another . . . so nothing is of the essence of a particular being. . . . No, presumably because there is no quality which any given being does not share with some other, and it is the greater or less proportion of that quality which makes us attribute it to one being to the exclusion of another. . . . And then you talk of individuals, you poor philosophers! Stop thinking about your individuals and answer me this: Is there in nature any one atom exactly similar to another? No. . . . Don't you agree that in nature everything is bound up with everything else, and that there cannot be a gap in the chain? Then what are you talking about with your individuals? There is no such thing; no, no such thing. There is but one great individual, and that is the whole. In this whole, as in any machine or animal, there is a part which you may call such and such, but when you apply the term individual to this part of a whole you are employing as false a concept as though you applied the term individual to a bird's wing or to a single feather of that wing. You poor philosophers, and you talk about essences! Drop your idea of essences. Consider the general mass, or if your imagination is too limited to take it all in, consider your own origin and your final state. Oh Architas, you who measured the globe, what are you now? A little dust. . . . What is a being? The sum of a certain number of tendencies. . . . Can I be anything more than a tendency? . . . No, I am moving towards a certain end. . . . And what of species? Species are merely tendencies towards a common end peculiar to them. . . . And life? A series of actions and reactions. . . . Alive, I act and react as a mass . . . dead, I act and react as separate molecules. . . . Don't I die, then? Well, not in that sense, neither I nor anything else. . . . To be born, to live and to die is merely to change forms. . . . And what does one form matter any more than another? . . . Each form has its own sort of happiness and unhappiness. From the elephant down to the flea . . . from the flea down to the sensitive and living molecule which is the origin of all, there is not a speck in the whole of nature that does not feel pain or pleasure.

MADEMOISELLE DE L'ESPINASSE: He has stopped.

BORDEU: Yes, and he has made a very fine disquisition. That's what you call lofty philosophy. Although at present it is theoretical I think that the more man's knowledge progresses the more it will be verified.

MADEMOISELLE DE L'ESPINASSE: Well now, where had we got to?

BORDEU: As a matter of fact, I don't remember. He reminded me of so many things while I was listening!

MADEMOISELLE DE L'ESPINASSE: Let me see. . . . I was talking about my spider.

BORDEU: Yes, yes.

MADEMOISELLE DE L'ESPINASSE: Doctor, come nearer. Imagine a spider at the centre of its web. Disturb a thread and you will see the creature rush up on the alert. Now suppose that those threads that the insect draws from its own body and draws in again at will were a sensitive part of itself.

BORDEU: I follow you. You are assuming the existence

inside yourself, in some part of the brain, for example the part we call the meninges, of one or more points to which are signalled all the sensations produced anywhere along the threads.

MADEMOISELLE DE L'ESPINASSE: That's it.

BORDEU: Your idea is as sound as it could be, but don't you see that it is roughly the same thing as a certain swarm of bees?

MADEMOISELLE DE L'ESPINASSE: Ah, so it is. I have been speaking prose without realizing it!

BORDEU: And very good prose, too, as you are about to see. Anyone who only knows man in the form he presents at birth doesn't know anything about him at all. Man's head, feet, hands, all his limbs, his viscera, his organs, nose, eyes, ears, heart, lungs, intestines, muscles, bones, nerves, membranes are really nothing more than crude extensions of a network which takes form, grows, extends and throws out a multitude of imperceptible threads.

MADEMOISELLE DE L'ESPINASSE: Back to my web; and the starting-point of all those threads is my spider.

BORDEU: Exactly.

MADEMOISELLE DE L'ESPINASSE: Where are the threads? And where does the spider live?

BORDEU: The threads are everywhere; there isn't a single point on the surface of your body that is not the terminus of one of them, and the spider lurks in a part of your brain I have already mentioned, the meninges, which can scarcely be touched without reducing the whole organism to unconsciousness.

MADEMOISELLE DE L'ESPINASSE: But if the smallest speck of matter makes one thread of the web vibrate, the spider is alerted, excited and darts here or there. At the centre she is conscious of what is going on at any point in the huge mansion she has woven. Why don't I know what is going on in my own system or in the world at large, since

I am a bundle of sensitive particles and everything is touching me and I am touching everything else?

BORDEU: Because messages weaken in proportion to the distance they come from.

MADEMOISELLE DE L'ESPINASSE: Yet if there is the very gentlest tap on the end of a long rod I can hear it if my ear is applied to the other end. Even if that rod had one end on earth and the other on Sirius, the same phenomenon would be produced. If everything were interconnected and contiguous, as in the rod if it really existed, why can't I hear whatever is going on in the limitless spaces around me – especially if I listen attentively?

BORDEU: And who has suggested that you can't, to a greater or lesser degree? But the distance is so great, the initial impression so weak and so confused on its way by others, and you are surrounded and deafened by so much violent and varied din. In particular, between Saturn and you there are only contiguous bodies, and not continuous, as there should be.

MADEMOISELLE DE L'ESPINASSE: That seems a pity.

BORDEU: True. Were it otherwise you would be God. Through your oneness with all the beings in nature you would know everything that is going on, and thanks to your memory you would know everything that has been.

MADEMOISELLE DE L'ESPINASSE: And will be?

BORDEU: As for the future, you would make some very shrewd guesses, but they would be subject to correction. It is just as if you were trying to guess what is going to happen inside you, or at the extremity of your foot or hand.

MADEMOISELLE DE L'ESPINASSE: But how do you know that the whole world hasn't its meninges, or that there isn't a big or little spider living in some corner of space with threads extending everywhere?

BORDEU: Nobody knows, but still less does anybody

know whether there ever has been one or will be one in the future.

MADEMOISELLE DE L'ESPINASSE: But how could a God like that –

BORDEU: The only conceivable kind of God –

MADEMOISELLE DE L'ESPINASSE: – have existed, or have come into being and ceased to exist?

BORDEU: Quite, but since he would be part of a material universe and so subject to change, he would grow old and die.

MADEMOISELLE DE L'ESPINASSE: But that brings another fantastic idea into my mind.

BORDEU: No need to tell me, I know what it is.

MADEMOISELLE DE L'ESPINASSE: Well, what is it then?

BORDEU: You notice that intelligence is part and parcel of very energetic portions of matter, hence the possibility of all kinds of marvels one can imagine. That has been thought of before.

MADEMOISELLE DE L'ESPINASSE: You have guessed right, but it doesn't add to my respect for you. It simply shows that you have a wonderful partiality for the fantastic.

BORDEU: That may well be, but what is so alarming about that? There would be an epidemic of good and evil geniuses, the most constant laws of nature would be suspended by quite natural agencies, our understanding of general physical laws would be made more difficult, but no miracle would be involved.

MADEMOISELLE DE L'ESPINASSE: It certainly behoves us to be very circumspect about what we affirm or deny.

BORDEU: To be sure, anyone telling you about a phenomenon like that would be taken for a great liar. But let us drop all these imaginary beings, including your spider with its infinite network. Let us come back to yourself considered as a network, and that network's formation.

MADEMOISELLE DE L'ESPINASSE: All right.

D'ALEMBERT: Mademoiselle, there is somebody there with you. Who is talking to you?

MADEMOISELLE DE L'ESPINASSE: It's the doctor.

D'ALEMBERT: Good morning, doctor. Why are you here so early?

BORDEU: You'll know later, go back to sleep.

D'ALEMBERT: Good Lord, I certainly need it. I don't think I've ever had such a disturbed night. Don't go away before I'm up.

BORDEU: No, I won't. Now, Mademoiselle, I'll guarantee that you have been thinking that, as at the age of twelve you were a woman half the size you are now, and at four half as small again, at the foetal stage a miniature woman and in your mother's ovaries a minute woman, you were always a woman with the same form as you have now, so that only the successive stages of growth you have been through have made the difference between you at your origin and you as you are now.[15]

MADEMOISELLE DE L'ESPINASSE: Yes, I admit that's true.

BORDEU: Yet nothing is more false than that notion. First of all, you were nothing. In the beginning you were an imperceptible speck, made of even smaller particles dispersed in the blood and lymph of your father and mother. This speck became a fine thread, then a bundle of threads. So far not the slightest suggestion of the attractive form you now have: your eyes, those lovely eyes, were no more like eyes than the tip of a sea-anemone's claw is like an anemone. Each thread in the bundle evolved, simply by being fed and because of its special structure, into a particular organ – except those organs formed by a complete metamorphosis of certain threads in the bundle. This bundle is a system capable of feeling sensations, and nothing more. If it continued to be just that it would be sensitive to any impression affecting sensitivity alone, such as heat, cold, smoothness, roughness. This sequence of impressions, varying in intensity and differing from each other, might perhaps produce memory, consciousness of self and a limited kind of intelligence. But this sensitivity pure and simple, which is nothing but touch, becomes modified in character in organs developed from different threads: one forms an ear and gives rise to a kind of touch that registers noise or sound; another forms the palate and gives rise to a second kind of touch that we call taste; a third, forming the nose and its lining membrane, gives rise to a third kind of touch that we call sense of smell; a fourth, forming an eye, gives rise to a fourth kind of touch we call awareness of colour.

MADEMOISELLE DE L'ESPINASSE: But if I have understood you aright, people who deny the possibility of a sixth sense, or a true hermaphrodite, are just silly. How do they know that nature couldn't form a bundle with a peculiar thread in it which could give rise to some organ we don't know about?

BORDEU: Or with the threads characteristic of both sexes? You are right. It is a pleasure to talk to you: not only do you follow what is said, but you draw conclusions therefrom which amaze me by their rightness.

MADEMOISELLE DE L'ESPINASSE: You are trying to be encouraging, doctor.

BORDEU: No, honestly I say what I think.

MADEMOISELLE DE L'ESPINASSE: I quite understand the function of some of the threads in the bundle, but what happens to the rest?

BORDEU: And do you honestly believe that anyone but you would have thought of that question?

MADEMOISELLE DE L'ESPINASSE: Of course I do.

BORDEU: You certainly aren't conceited. The rest of the threads go to form as many other varieties of touch as there are differences between the organs and parts of the body.

MADEMOISELLE DE L'ESPINASSE: What are they called? I have never heard of them.

BORDEU: They have no names.

MADEMOISELLE DE L'ESPINASSE: Why not?

BORDEU: Because there is not as much differentiation between the sensations they excite as there is between the sensations excited by the other organs.

MADEMOISELLE DE L'ESPINASSE: You seriously think that the foot, hand, thighs, belly, stomach, chest, lungs and heart each have their peculiar kinds of sensation?

BORDEU: Yes, I do. If I dared I would ask you whether, among those nameless sensations. . .

MADEMOISELLE DE L'ESPINASSE: Enough said. No, that one is the only one of its kind, and more's the pity. But what reason can you think up for the multiplicity of sensations, more painful than pleasant, that you are pleased to bestow on us?

BORDEU: Reason? Simply that we are aware of most of them. If this great diversity of tactile sensations did not exist, we should know we were feeling pleasure or pain, but should have no idea what to relate them to. We should have to rely on sight, and that would no longer be a matter of sensation, but of experience and observation.

MADEMOISELLE DE L'ESPINASSE: Supposing, for example, that I said that my finger hurt, then if I were asked why I affirmed that the pain was in my finger, I should have to answer not that I felt it, but that I felt a pain and saw that there was something wrong with my finger?

BORDEU: That's right. Come and let me give you a kiss.

MADEMOISELLE DE L'ESPINASSE: With great pleasure.

D'ALEMBERT: Doctor, you are kissing Mademoiselle. A very good idea on your part.

BORDEU: I have given the matter a good deal of thought, and it seems to me that in order to make an instantaneous decision the thing at the centre of the network needs to know more than just the direction from which a blow comes and the spot where it strikes.

MADEMOISELLE DE L'ESPINASSE: I couldn't possibly say.

BORDEU: I am glad you are sceptical. It is such a common thing for people to take natural qualities for acquired habits nearly as old as mankind.

MADEMOISELLE DE L'ESPINASSE: And vice-versa.

BORDEU: Anyhow, you can see that where the early stages of the development of an animal are concerned, it is beginning at the wrong end to observe and study the mature animal. You must go back to its rudimentary state, and it is relevant to strip yourself of your present bodily organization and return for a moment to the time when you were simply a soft, fibrous, shapeless, vermicular substance, more comparable to a bulb or root than to an animal.

MADEMOISELLE DE L'ESPINASSE: If it became customary to go out into the street stark naked I should not be the first nor the last to conform. So treat me just as you like, so long as I can learn. You said that each thread in that bundle went to form a particular organ, for example that one forms the eyes. What proof have you got?

BORDEU: Do mentally what nature sometimes does in reality: cut away one of the threads in the bundle, for example the one that forms the eyes. What do you think happens?

MADEMOISELLE DE L'ESPINASSE: The animal won't have any eyes, I suppose.

BORDEU: Or will have only one in the middle of its forehead.

MADEMOISELLE DE L'ESPINASSE: It will be a Cyclops.

BORDEU: Yes, a Cyclops.

MADEMOISELLE DE L'ESPINASSE: So a Cyclops might not be a mythical creature after all?

BORDEU: Quite likely not – in fact I'll show you one if you like.

MADEMOISELLE DE L'ESPINASSE: And is the cause of this abnormality known?

BORDEU: Yes. The scientist who dissected this particular monstrosity found it had only one optic thread. Now do mentally what nature sometimes does in reality. Take another thread away from the bundle – the one destined to form the nose – and the creature will be noseless. Take away the one that should form the ear and it will have no ears or only one ear, and the anatomist in his dissection won't find either the olfactory or auditory threads, or will only find one of the latter instead of two. Go on taking away threads and the creature will be headless, footless, handless. It won't live long, but nevertheless it will have lived.

MADEMOISELLE DE L'ESPINASSE: Are there any examples of this?

BORDEU: Oh yes. And that isn't all. Duplicate some of the threads in the bundle, and the animal will have two heads, four eyes, four ears, three testicles, three feet, four arms, six fingers to each hand. Jumble up the threads in the bundle and the organs will be displaced: the head will be in the middle of the body, the lungs on the left, the heart on the right. Stick two threads together and the organs will run into each other: the arms will be stuck to the body, the thighs, legs and feet will be all in one piece. In short, you will have every imaginable kind of monstrosity.

MADEMOISELLE DE L'ESPINASSE: But it seems to me that a machine as complicated as an animal, a machine originating in a single particle, in churned-up fluid, or perhaps two fluids mingled by pure chance (for at such times we don't quite know what we are doing), a machine which evolves towards perfection through countless successive stages, a machine whose regular or irregular formation depends upon a collection of fine, slender, flexible threads, a sort of skein the smallest threads of which cannot be broken, smashed, displaced or missing without serious damage to the whole, such a machine would be bound to get caught up and tangled in its formative stages even more often than my silks on their spindle.

BORDEU: Indeed this machine is damaged much more often than you would think. There is not enough dissection being done, and our knowledge about ante-natal development is very far from accurate.

MADEMOISELLE DE L'ESPINASSE: Are there any remarkable cases of these pre-natal malformations, apart from hunchbacks and cripples, whose deformity might be attributed to some hereditary defect?

BORDEU: Oh, yes, innumerable cases. Quite recently there died of pneumonia in the Charity Hospital in Paris a carpenter named Jean-Baptiste Macé, aged twenty-five and a native of Troyes, the positions of whose internal organs in the chest and abdomen were reversed: his heart was on the right just as yours is on the left, his liver on the left, the stomach, spleen and pancreas by the right hypochondrium, the main artery was in the same relation to the left side of the liver as it normally is to the right when the liver is on the right. There was the same transposition along the intestinal tract, and the kidneys, back to back near the lumbar vertebrae, formed a horseshoe. And then after all that they prate about *final causes*!

MADEMOISELLE DE L'ESPINASSE: Most odd!

BORDEU: If Jean-Baptiste Macé had been married and had had children. . . .

MADEMOISELLE DE L'ESPINASSE: Well, doctor, what about the children?

BORDEU: They would have been quite normal, but some child of their children, after a century or so, for these irregularities go in leap-frog jumps, would hark back to the strange anatomy of his ancestor.

MADEMOISELLE DE L'ESPINASSE: What is the reason for these leaps?

BORDEU: Who knows? It takes two to make a baby, as you know. It may be that one of the parties counteracts the defect of the other and that the defective system only returns when the descendant of the abnormal strain predominates and governs the pattern of the network. The original differences between all species of animals come from the arrangement of the bundle of threads, hence variations in bundles within the same species account for any freakish monstrosities in that species.

(After a long silence MADEMOISELLE DE L'ESPINASSE emerged from her reverie and roused the doctor from his with the following remark:)

I have just had a very silly idea.

BORDEU: What?

MADEMOISELLE DE L'ESPINASSE: That perhaps man is merely a woman with freakish malformations, or woman a freakish man.

BORDEU: This idea would have occurred to you even sooner had you realized that a woman possesses all the parts of a man and that the only real difference is that between a pouch hanging outside or a pouch reversed to go inside the body; that a female foetus is indistinguishable from a male foetus. The part which gives rise to the mistake diminishes in size in the female foetus as the internal pouch grows, but it never disappears to the extent of losing its original shape, which it keeps in miniature, together with the ability to behave in a similar way, and it is also the seat of pleasurable sensations. This part has its glans and prepuce, and at its extremity can be seen a dot which might have been the orifice of a urinary canal now blocked. And there is in a man, between the anus and the scrotum, the space called the perineum, and from the scrotum to the tip of the penis a seam which looks like a vulva that has been sewn up. Furthermore, women with an excessively large clitoris develop a beard; eunuchs do not, but their thighs become fleshy, the hips broaden and the knees become rounded – in fact, while losing the characteristic formation of one sex they seem to revert to that of the other. Arabs who have been castrated by continual horse-riding lose their beards, develop a high-pitched voice, dress like women, sit with them in the wagons, crouch down to piss and put on women's manners and behaviour. . . . But we have strayed a long way from our subject. Let us get back to our bundle of living, animated threads.

D'ALEMBERT: I think you are talking smut to Mademoiselle de L'Espinasse.

BORDEU: When you talk science you have to use technical terms.

D'ALEMBERT: You are right; in that way they lose the string of associated ideas which might make them objectionable. Go on, doctor. You were telling her that the uterus is nothing but a scrotum turned inside, and that during this process the testicles were thrown out from the envelope containing them and distributed to left and right of the abdominal cavity; that the clitoris is a miniature male organ, that this male organ in the female gets smaller and smaller as the uterus, or reversed scrotum, gets bigger, and that –

MADEMOISELLE DE L'ESPINASSE: Yes, yes, but keep quiet and don't interfere with our business.

BORDEU: So you see, Mademoiselle, that in this matter of our sensations in general, which are all simply variations of the sense of touch, we must ignore the successive forms taken on later by the network, and concentrate on the original network alone.

MADEMOISELLE DE L'ESPINASSE: Each thread of the sensitive network can be hurt or tickled at any point along its entire length. Pleasure or pain is in this place or that,

at one point or other of one of the long legs of my spider –
for I always come back to my spider example. The spider is
at the central junction of all the legs, and notes that the
pleasure or pain is at such and such a place without itself
feeling it.

BORDEU: It is the constant, invariable relationship
between all impressions and the common centre which
constitutes the individuality of an animal.

MADEMOISELLE DE L'ESPINASSE: It is the recollection
of all these successive impressions which makes up the story
of each animal's life and its consciousness of self.

BORDEU: And memory and comparison, which necessarily follow from all these impressions, are the basis of
thought and reasoning power.

MADEMOISELLE DE L'ESPINASSE: But where does this
comparison take place?

BORDEU: At the centre of the network.[16]

MADEMOISELLE DE L'ESPINASSE: And the network
itself?

BORDEU: Has at its centre no sense that is its own: it
cannot see, hear, feel pain. It comes into being and is
nourished; it emanates from a soft, insensitive, inert substance, which acts as a cushion on which it is enthroned,
hears cases, considers its judgement and pronounces
verdicts.

MADEMOISELLE DE L'ESPINASSE: It feels no pain?

BORDEU: No. The slightest pressure makes the judge
suspend his sitting and the animal falls into a deathlike
trance. Remove the pressure and he resumes his functions
and the animal comes back to life.

MADEMOISELLE DE L'ESPINASSE: But how do you
know this? Has anybody ever made a man die and come
back to life at will?

BORDEU: Yes.

MADEMOISELLE DE L'ESPINASSE: But how?

BORDEU: I'll tell you; it is a curious case. La Peyronie,[17] whom you may have known, was summoned to see a patient who had had a violent blow on the head. The man felt a throbbing sensation which convinced the surgeon that an abscess had formed on the brain, and that there was not a moment to lose. He shaved the man and trepanned. The point of the instrument struck at the very centre of the abscess. It was full of pus; he drained off the pus and cleaned the abscess with a syringe. As soon as he directed the jet into the abscess the patient closed his eyes and his limbs went stiff and motionless, with no sign of life. When he sucked back the injected fluid and thus took the weight and pressure off the centre of the network, the patient opened his eyes again, moved, spoke, could feel and came back to life.

MADEMOISELLE DE L'ESPINASSE: Very strange; and did the patient recover?

BORDEU: Yes, he recovered, and when he was quite well again he reflected, thought, reasoned, had the same amount of wit, common sense and shrewdness as before, and that minus a fair portion of his brain.

MADEMOISELLE DE L'ESPINASSE: That judge you were taking about is a most remarkable being.

BORDEU: He sometimes makes mistakes, though; he tends to be biased out of force of habit: for example people feel pain in an amputated limb. What's more, you can deceive him when you like: cross two of your fingers and touch a little ball, and he will declare there are two.

MADEMOISELLE DE L'ESPINASSE: That is to say he is like all judges in the world and needs experience, without which he will be capable of mistaking the feel of ice for that of fire.

BORDEU: He can do a great deal more: he can give almost infinite space to the individual or reduce him almost to vanishing point.

MADEMOISELLE DE L'ESPINASSE: I'm afraid I don't understand.

BORDEU: What really sets a limit to the space you feel you occupy? I mean the real sphere of your sensations?

MADEMOISELLE DE L'ESPINASSE: My sight and touch.

BORDEU: Yes, by day, but at night, in the dark, when you are dreaming about something abstract, or even by day when your mind is preoccupied?

MADEMOISELLE DE L'ESPINASSE: There are no limits at all. I seem to exist as a single point, I almost cease to be material and am only conscious of thought. I have lost the sense of position, motion, body, distance and space. The universe is reduced to nothing and I am nothing to the universe.

BORDEU: That is the extreme limit of concentration of your existence, but its theoretical expansion knows no limit. Once the true limit of your physical sensitivity has been passed, whether by retreating and so to speak condensing yourself, or by extending outwards, there is no knowing where it might lead.

MADEMOISELLE DE L'ESPINASSE: Yes, doctor, you are right. I have often felt in dreams –

BORDEU: – and it happens to those with gout –

MADEMOISELLE DE L'ESPINASSE: – that I was becoming enormous –

BORDEU: – whose foot seems to be touching the canopy of the bed.

MADEMOISELLE DE L'ESPINASSE: – and that my arms and legs were lengthening for ever and ever and the rest of my body was swelling in the same proportion, that Enceladus of the fable was but a pigmy, that Ovid's Amphitrite, whose long arms could make a girdle round the earth, was a mere dwarf beside me, and that I was scaling the very heavens or embracing both hemispheres.

BORDEU: Quite. And I once knew a woman in whom the phenomenon worked the other way round.

MADEMOISELLE DE L'ESPINASSE: What! she got smaller and smaller and shrank into herself?

BORDEU: Yes, to the point of feeling herself as fine as a needle. She could see, hear, reason and come to logical decisions, but she had a mortal dread of getting lost, she shuddered when the tiniest objects came near her, and dared not stir from one place.

MADEMOISELLE DE L'ESPINASSE: That's a very odd delusion to have, and most annoying and inconvenient.

BORDEU: It wasn't a delusion at all, it was one of the things that happen at the change of life.

MADEMOISELLE DE L'ESPINASSE: And did she go on thinking she was a minute, imperceptible being for long?

BORDEU: It lasted an hour or two, after which she would gradually return to her normal size.

MADEMOISELLE DE L'ESPINASSE: And why these strange sensations?

BORDEU: In their natural, undisturbed state the threads in the bundle are under a certain tension; they have a tone, a normal energy which governs the real or imaginary extent of the body. I say real or imaginary because as the tension, tone or energy are variable our bodies are not always of the same volume in any case.

MADEMOISELLE DE L'ESPINASSE: So in physical as well as moral things we are by way of thinking ourselves bigger than we really are?

BORDEU: Cold makes us shrink, and heat expand, and a given person may go through life under the impression that he is smaller or bigger than he really is. If it happens that the whole of the bundle goes into a state of violent erethism, so that the separate fibres are distended and the extremities push out beyond their normal limits, the head, feet and other parts, in fact every point on the surface of the body, will seem to be a huge distance away and the individual will feel gigantic. The opposite will happen if insensitivity, apathy and inertia work their way from the ends of the fibres towards the centre.

MADEMOISELLE DE L'ESPINASSE: I quite see that this expansion cannot be measured and, moreover, that this insensitivity or numbness might progress and ultimately become permanent.

BORDEU: That's what happened to La Condamine:[18] then the person feels as though he is walking on balloons.

MADEMOISELLE DE L'ESPINASSE: He exists beyond the limits of his sensory impressions and if this apathy overtook him in a general way I suppose we should see a tiny man living inside a dead one.

BORDEU: From which you might conclude that an animal which in the beginning was only a single point still doesn't know whether he is really anything more. But let us get back to the subject.

MADEMOISELLE DE L'ESPINASSE: What subject?

BORDEU: Why, La Peyronie's trepanned patient. That's what you asked for, wasn't it? An example of a man living and dying alternately. But I can go one better than that.

MADEMOISELLE DE L'ESPINASSE: Whatever can it be?

BORDEU: The fable of Castor and Pollux in real life. Two children, the life of one of whom caused the immediate death of the other, and the return to life of that one meant the death of the first.

MADEMOISELLE DE L'ESPINASSE: That's a likely tale! Did this go on for long?

BORDEU: Their existence lasted for two days, which they shared equally turn and turn about, so that each one's share was one day of life and one of death.

MADEMOISELLE DE L'ESPINASSE: I fear, doctor, that you are taking advantage of my credulity. Mind what you do; if you deceive me once I shall never believe you again.

BORDEU: Do you ever read the *Gazette de France*?

MADEMOISELLE DE L'ESPINASSE: Never, although it is the masterpiece of two intelligent men.

BORDEU: Get somebody to lend you the number for the 4th of September, and you will see that at Rabastens, in the diocese of Albi, two girls were born back to back, joined by their lowest lumbar vertebrae, the buttocks and the hypo-gastric region. The one could only be kept upright if the other was upside-down. Lying down they could look at each other; their thighs were bent up between their bodies and their legs pointed upwards. Half way round the circular line where their bodies were joined in the hypogastric region you could just see their sex, and between the right thigh of the one and the corresponding left thigh of her sister there was a tiny anus from which came meconium.[19]

MADEMOISELLE DE L'ESPINASSE: A very extraordinary case.

BORDEU: They took milk from a spoon. They lived for twelve hours as I told you, one falling unconscious when the other revived, one dead while the other lived. The first collapse of one and revival of the other lasted four hours, the alternate collapses and recoveries which followed were of shorter duration, and they expired at the same moment. It was also observed that their navels followed the same rhythm of expansion and contraction, depressed in the one who was unconscious and protruding in the one recovering.

MADEMOISELLE DE L'ESPINASSE: What do you make of these alternations of life and death?

BORDEU: Nothing of value, probably, but as we all see everything through the spectacles of our own pet systems, and as I don't want to be an exception to that rule, I should say that it is La Peyronie's trepanning case duplicated in two individuals joined together. In these two children the two networks were so inextricably mixed together that they acted and reacted upon each other. When the centre of the network of the one was in the ascendant it took over the other one's system, and she immediately collapsed; and the opposite happened when it was the turn of the second one to dominate the common system. In La Peyronie's trepanning case pressure was exerted downwards by the weight of the liquid; in the twin girls of Rabastens it was exerted from below upwards by a tightening of some of the threads in the network. And this theory is corroborated by the alternate in and out movement of the navels, out in the one returning to life, in in the one losing it.

MADEMOISELLE DE L'ESPINASSE: A case of twin souls indeed!

BORDEU: One animal with a double sensory system and two centres of consciousness.

MADEMOISELLE DE L'ESPINASSE: Yet only experiencing one at any given moment. But what might have happened if this creature had lived?

BORDEU: What sort of communication might have been established between two brains by the experiences of every moment in life and the strongest imaginable force of habit?

MADEMOISELLE DE L'ESPINASSE: Double senses, a double memory, a double imagination and a double faculty for paying attention. Half a being observing, reading, meditating, while the other half takes its rest, and the second half taking over the same functions when its companion is tired. In fact the double life of a double creature.

BORDEU: Quite possible, and since, given time, nature brings about everything that is possible, she will sooner or later produce some such strange composite.

MADEMOISELLE DE L'ESPINASSE: How badly off we should seem to be in comparison with such a creature!

BORDEU: Does that follow? Already there are so many uncertainties, contradictions and follies in one simple intelligence that I don't know what it would be like with a double one. . . . But it is ten-thirty, and I can hear a patient calling for me right across the town!

MADEMOISELLE DE L'ESPINASSE: Would he be in any danger if you didn't go and see him?

BORDEU: Probably less than if I saw him. If nature can't do the job without me we shall have our work cut out to do it together, and for sure I can't do it without her.

MADEMOISELLE DE L'ESPINASSE: Then stay here.

D'ALEMBERT: Doctor, just one more word and I'll let you go to your patient. Taking into account all the changes I have undergone in the course of my life, and in view of the fact that at present I probably haven't a single one of the molecules I brought with me when I was born, how have I kept my own personality for myself as well as for others?

BORDEU: You told me how during your dream.

D'ALEMBERT: Have I been dreaming?

MADEMOISELLE DE L'ESPINASSE: All night long, and it sounded so much like delirium that I sent for the doctor this morning.

D'ALEMBERT: In order to talk about spider's legs acting on their own, keeping the spider on the alert and making the creature speak? And what did the creature say?

BORDEU: That it remained itself both for others and for itself thanks to memory. And I would add because of the gradualness of change. If you had passed from childhood to decrepitude in the twinkling of an eye you would have found yourself thrown into the present world as you were at the first moment of birth, and you would not have been a real person to others or to yourself, and the others would not have been themselves to you either. All relationships would have been nullified and the whole story of your life as I know it, and of mine as you do, would have been a jumble. How could you have known that that old chap, bent over his stick, with eyes dim and scarcely dragging himself along, and even more a stranger to himself within than without, was the same man who only yesterday was walking so springily, handling heavy loads, was capable of undertaking the most abstruse thinking, the most delicate as well as the most violent physical acts? You wouldn't have understood your own writings or recognized yourself or anybody else and nobody would have recognized you; the whole set-up of the world would have changed. And moreover bear in mind that there was less difference between yourself as a new-born baby and yourself as a young man than there would be between you as a young man and you suddenly decrepit. Bear in mind also that although our birth and young manhood were linked by an uninterrupted series of sensory impressions, the first three years of your life have never been part of your conscious life-story. What would the period of your youth have meant to you if it had borne no relationship at all to this moment of your decrepitude? D'Alembert as a decrepit old man wouldn't have the faintest recollection of the young D'Alembert.

MADEMOISELLE DE L'ESPINASSE: In fact it would be like the swarm of bees in which no bee had had time to learn about its membership of the swarm.

D'ALEMBERT: What's all this you're saying?

MADEMOISELLE DE L'ESPINASSE: I am saying that the corporate spirit of a monastery keeps its character because the monastery replaces its membership only gradually, and when a new monk arrives he finds a hundred old ones who influence him to feel and think like them. One bee goes away, but another replaces it in the swarm, and he soon knows what's what.

D'ALEMBERT: Get along with you and your tales about monks, bees, swarm and monastery.

BORDEU: She's not as silly as you might think. There may be only one centre of consciousness in an animal, but there are countless impulses, for each organ has its own.

D'ALEMBERT: What do you mean by that?

BORDEU: I mean, for example, that the stomach wants some food, but the palate doesn't, and the difference between the palate and stomach on the one hand and the complete animal on the other is that the animal knows that it wants something whereas the stomach or palate want something without knowing it. Stomach or palate is to the complete being much as the brute beast is to man. Bees lose their individual consciousness but keep their appetites or impulses. An animal fibre is a simple animal, man is a composite one, but let us leave that subject for another time. There is no need for anything as wholesale as sudden decrepitude in order to take away a man's consciousness of self. A man at the point of death receives the sacraments with deep religious feeling, confesses his sins, begs his wife's forgiveness, embraces his children, sends for his friends, talks to his doctor, issues orders to his servants, dictates his last wishes, puts his affairs in order, and he does all these things with the most balanced judgement and complete presence of mind. He recovers, is convalescent, and hasn't the slightest idea what he said or did when he was ill. That interlude, and sometimes it can be quite long, has vanished from his life. There are even examples of people having gone on with a conversation or action which the sudden illness had interrupted.

D'ALEMBERT: I recall how, during a public disputation, a university pedant, puffed up with his own omniscience, was completely floored, as they say, by a Capuchin he had despised. Completely floored – him? And by whom? By a Capuchin! And on what question? The contingent future! The *scientia media* which he had been studying all his life! And in what circumstances? In front of a vast audience, nay, in front of his own students! Behold him utterly disgraced. His head churned these ideas over so much that he fell into a lethargic condition which blotted out all the knowledge he had acquired.

MADEMOISELLE DE L'ESPINASSE: But it was a merciful deliverance.

D'ALEMBERT: You are certainly right. He still kept his native intelligence but he had suffered total loss of memory. He was taught to speak and read again, and died just as he was beginning to spell quite well. This man was no fool; he was considered rather good as a public speaker.

MADEMOISELLE DE L'ESPINASSE: As the doctor has listened to your story he will have to hear mine as well. A young man of eighteen or twenty, whose name I don't remember. . . .

BORDEÜ: It was one M. de Schellemberg of Winterthur, and he was only fifteen or sixteen.

MADEMOISELLE DE L'ESPINASSE: Well, this young man had a fall and he suffered very bad concussion.

BORDEU: What do you mean by very bad concussion? He fell off the top of a barn, his skull was smashed and he was unconscious for six weeks.

MADEMOISELLE DE L'ESPINASSE: Well, anyway, do you know what the sequel to the accident was? The same as with your pedant: he forgot everything he knew and reverted to his babyhood, and then went through a second childhood which lasted a long time. He was timid and frightened, and played with toys. If he had been naughty and was scolded he ran away and sulked in a corner. He asked if he could do Number One and Number Two. They did teach him to read and write, but I forgot to mention that he had to be taught to walk all over again. He did finally become a man again, and a very clever one, and left a book on natural history.

BORDEU: That is to say engravings, illustrations to the work of M. Sulzer on insects, classified according to Linnaeus. I was acquainted with this case because it happened in the canton of Zürich, in Switzerland, and there are a number of similar examples. Upset the centre of the web and you change the nature of the whole creature whose entire being seems to be concentrated there, sometimes dominating outlying threads, sometimes being dominated by them.

MADEMOISELLE DE L'ESPINASSE: So that the animal is either ruled by a despotism or in a state of anarchy?

BORDEU: Despotism is the right word. The centre of the network issues the orders and all the rest obeys. Then the animal is master of itself, *mentis compos.*

MADEMOISELLE DE L'ESPINASSE: But it is anarchy if all the threads of the web are in rebellion against their ruler, and there ceases to be any central authority.

BORDEU: Exactly. In fits of strong passion, in delirium or at times of imminent danger, if the master throws all the forces under his command towards a single objective, then even the weakest animal develops incredible strength.

MADEMOISELLE DE L'ESPINASSE: In cases of the vapours there is a sort of anarchy peculiar to women.

BORDEU: It is the epitome of a weak political administration in which each one usurps the authority of the ruler. There is only one way of curing this that I know of; it is hard, but sure. It is for the centre of the sensitive network, the part which constitutes the self, to be given some powerful motive for regaining its authority.

MADEMOISELLE DE L'ESPINASSE: And what happens then?

BORDEU: Either it recovers its authority in fact, or the animal perishes. If I had the time I would tell you two strange things about that.

MADEMOISELLE DE L'ESPINASSE: But, doctor, the time for your visit has gone by long ago, and your patient won't be expecting you now.

BORDEU: Really, I should only come here when I've nothing else to do, for I can never get away.

MADEMOISELLE DE L'ESPINASSE: Now you have had a nice little outburst of temper, what about your stories?

BORDEU: For today you must be satisfied with this one. A woman who was getting over childbirth fell into a terrible attack of the vapours. She couldn't stop laughing and crying, she had fits of suffocation and convulsions, her bosom swelled, she went in for sulky silences or piercing shrieks – all the worst symptoms – and this went on for several years. She was passionately in love, and she thought she could see that her lover was getting tired of her illness and beginning to cool off. So she resolved to get better or die in the attempt. There broke out in her a civil war in which sometimes the ruler won and sometimes the subjects. If the action of the threads of the network and the reaction of the central authority happened to reach a stalemate, she fell into a dead faint and was carried to her bed where she stayed for hours on end, motionless and almost lifeless, while at other times she had no more than lassitude or general exhaustion, but again sometimes unconsciousness which seemed as though it must be the end. She went on for six months in this state of warfare, in which the rebellion always began in the separate threads, and she could feel it coming on. At the first sign she stood up, ran about, went in for the most violent exertion, ran up and down the stairs, sawed timber, dug the ground. The seat of her will-power in the centre of the network was stiffening its resistance; she said to herself, victory or death. After a prodigious number of victories and defeats the ruler won the contest and the subjects became so submissive that there has never been any question of vapours from that time on, and this despite domestic difficulties of all kinds and various illnesses she has gone through.

MADEMOISELLE DE L'ESPINASSE: Bravo! but I think I would have done the same thing myself.

BORDEU: Yes, because if you fell in love you would love with your whole being, and you have a strong character.[20]

MADEMOISELLE DE L'ESPINASSE: I think I see why.

A person has a strong character if, because of education, habit or the way he is made, the centre of the network dominates the threads, but a weak one if it is the other way round.

BORDEU: Many other conclusions could be drawn from that.

MADEMOISELLE DE L'ESPINASSE: You can draw them afterwards; let's have your other story first.

BORDEU: A young woman had gone in for several affairs. One day she decided to cut it all out and eschew sensual pleasure. So she found herself alone, and on came melancholia and vapours. She sent for me. I advised her to dress like a peasant, till the soil all day long, sleep on straw and eat dry bread. The prescription did not appeal to her. Very well, travel then, I said. She embarked on a tour of Europe, and recovered her health on the highways.

MADEMOISELLE DE L'ESPINASSE: That is not what you were going to say, but never mind, let us come to your conclusions.

BORDEU: It would be an endless job.

MADEMOISELLE DE L'ESPINASSE: All the better. Fire away then.

BORDEU: I daren't.

MADEMOISELLE DE L'ESPINASSE: Why not?

BORDEU: Because at the rate we are going one can only skim the surface of everything and not go into anything properly.

MADEMOISELLE DE L'ESPINASSE: What does that matter? We are not composing a major work, we are just talking.

BORDEU: For example, if the centre of the network absorbs all the strength of a person into itself, if the whole system works so to speak from the inside outwards, as I believe happens to a man lost in deep meditation, a visionary who sees the heavens open, a savage singing amid the flames, or in cases of ecstasy or insanity, whether self-induced or involuntary . . .

MADEMOISELLE DE L'ESPINASSE: Well?

BORDEU: Well, the creature becomes impervious to feeling – it only exists at one point. I have not seen that priest of Calamos, mentioned by St Augustine, who could induce a state of self-alienation to the point of no longer feeling live coals; I have not seen those savages, stretched on the rack, who smile at their torturers, insult them and urge them to use even more exquisite forms of torture than those being inflicted upon them; I have not seen those dying gladiators in the arena who remember all the graceful movements of their gymnastic lessons, but I believe all these facts because I have seen with my own eyes a performance every bit as amazing as any of these.

MADEMOISELLE DE L'ESPINASSE: Tell me, doctor. I am like a child, I love tales of wonder, and when they do honour to the human race I don't often dispute their truth.

BORDEU: In the little town of Langres, in Champagne, there lived a worthy priest named Le Moni, or De Moni, a man utterly convinced of the truth of religion. He suffered from the stone and had to have an operation. The date was fixed, and the surgeon, with his assistants and me, went to his house. He welcomed us with a serene face, undressed, lay down on the bed. They offered to tie him down, but he refused. 'Just put me in the right position,' he said, and was put. Then he asked for a big crucifix, which was at the foot of the bed; it was given to him and he held it in his arms and pressed it to his lips. They operated, he remained motionless and never a tear or a sigh escaped him, and he didn't even know that they had taken the stone out.

MADEMOISELLE DE L'ESPINASSE: That is sublime, and after that how can you doubt that a man in the very course of having his ribs crushed by boulders witnessed the heavens open before his eyes?

BORDEU: Do you know what earache is like?

MADEMOISELLE DE L'ESPINASSE: No.

BORDEU: You have been lucky. It is the most horrible pain there is.

MADEMOISELLE DE L'ESPINASSE: Worse than toothache, which I unfortunately do know?

BORDEU: Incomparably worse. A philosopher friend of yours had a fortnight's torment with it, and one morning he said to his wife: 'I don't know how I am going to get through the day. . . .' He hit on the idea that the only way out would be to play tricks on the pain. By degrees he got himself so engrossed in some question of metaphysics or geometry that he forgot all about his ear. Dinner was served, and he ate it absent-mindedly; he reached bedtime without having felt anything. The horrible pain only came on again when the mental strain was relieved, but then it was with redoubled fury. Of course it might really have been that fatigue had aggravated the trouble, or his tired state had made it harder to bear.

MADEMOISELLE DE L'ESPINASSE: After such an experience one must really be quite knocked up. That is what sometimes happens to this man here.

BORDEU: It is dangerous; he ought to be careful.

MADEMOISELLE DE L'ESPINASSE: I am always telling him so, but he takes no notice.

BORDEU: He can't help it; it's his way of life, and it will be the death of him in the end.

MADEMOISELLE DE L'ESPINASSE: That is a frightening statement.

BORDEU: What does this exhaustion and lassitude prove? That the threads in the bundle have not remained idle, but that the whole system has been in a state of extreme tension towards the common centre.

MADEMOISELLE DE L'ESPINASSE: What if such tension goes on and on and becomes habitual?

BORDEU: Then the centre of the network develops a mannerism and the animal goes mad, almost hopelessly so.

MADEMOISELLE DE L'ESPINASSE: Why?

BORDEU: Because it is a very different thing to have something wrong with the nerve-centre from having it just in one of the nerves. The head can command the feet, but not the feet the head. The centre can command one of the threads, but not the thread the centre.

MADEMOISELLE DE L'ESPINASSE: And what is the difference, please? Why don't I think everywhere? It's a question I should have thought of earlier.

BORDEU: Because there is only one centre of consciousness.

MADEMOISELLE DE L'ESPINASSE: That's very easy to say.

BORDEU: It can only be at one place, at the common centre of all the sensations, where memory resides and comparisons are made. Each individual thread is only capable of registering a certain number of impressions, that is to say sensations one after the other, isolated and not remembered. But the centre is sensitive to all of them; it is the register, it keeps them in mind or holds a sustained impression, and any animal is bound, from its embryonic stage, to relate itself to this centre, attach its whole life to it, exist in it.

MADEMOISELLE DE L'ESPINASSE: Supposing my finger could remember?

BORDEU: Then your finger would be capable of thought.

MADEMOISELLE DE L'ESPINASSE: Well, what exactly is memory?

BORDEU: The property of the centre, the specific sense of the centre of the network, as sight is the property of the eye, and it is no more surprising that memory is not in the eye than that sight is not in the ear.

MADEMOISELLE DE L'ESPINASSE: Doctor, you are dodging my questions instead of answering them.

BORDEU: No, I'm not dodging anything. I'm telling you what I know, and I would be able to tell you more about it if I knew as much about the organization of the centre of the network as I do about the threads, and if I had found it as easy to observe. But if I am not very strong on specific details I am good on general manifestations.

MADEMOISELLE DE L'ESPINASSE: And what might these be?

BORDEU: Reason, judgement, imagination, madness, imbecility, ferocity, instinct.

MADEMOISELLE DE L'ESPINASSE: Yes; all these things are only products of the original or habitually acquired relationship between the centre of the network and its ramifications.

BORDEU: Precisely. If the nerve-centre or trunk is too vigorous in relation to the branches we find poets, artists, people of imagination, cowards, fanatics, madmen. If it is too weak we get what we call louts or wild beasts. If the whole system is flaccid, soft, devoid of energy, then idiots. On the other hand, if it is energetic, well balanced and in good order the outcome is the great thinkers, philosophers, sages.

MADEMOISELLE DE L'ESPINASSE: And according to which branch dominates the rest we see various specialized instincts in animals and special aptitudes in men: a sense of smell in the dog, of hearing in fish, of sight in the eagle. D'Alembert is a mathematician, Vaucanson a mechanical genius, Grétry a musician, Voltaire a poet – all diverse effects of some one thread of the bundle being more vigorous in them than any other and than the corresponding one in other people of their kind.

BORDEU: And then there is force of habit which can get the better of people, such as the old man who still runs after women, or Voltaire still turning out tragedies.

(Here the doctor fell into a reverie, and MADEMOISELLE DE L'ESPINASSE said:)

Doctor, you are dreaming.

BORDEU: Yes I was.

MADEMOISELLE DE L'ESPINASSE: What about?

BORDEU: Voltaire.

MADEMOISELLE DE L'ESPINASSE: What about him?

BORDEU: I was thinking of the way great men are made.

MADEMOISELLE DE L'ESPINASSE: How are they made?

BORDEU: How? Sensitivity –

MADEMOISELLE DE L'ESPINASSE: Sensitivity?

BORDEU: – extreme mobility of certain threads is the hall-mark of mediocre people.

MADEMOISELLE DE L'ESPINASSE: Oh, doctor, what an awful thing to say!

BORDEU: I expected you to say that. But what is a sensitive being? One who is a prey to the vagaries of his diaphragm. If a touching word strikes his ear or a strange sight his eye, then at once he is thrown into an inner tumult, every thread in the bundle is stimulated, a shudder runs through him, he is overcome with horror, his tears begin to flow, he is choked with sobs, his voice fails him, and in fact the central point of the network doesn't know what is happening to it; all calm, reason, judgement, instinct, resourcefulness have fled.[21]

MADEMOISELLE DE L'ESPINASSE: That's me exactly!

BORDEU: Now the superior man who has unfortunately been born with this kind of disposition will constantly strive to suppress it, dominate it, master its impulses and to maintain the hegemony of the centre of the network. Then he will keep his self-possession amid the greatest dangers and judge coolly but sanely. He will omit nothing which might fit in with his aim or serve his ends. He will be difficult to take by surprise; by forty-five he will be a great king, statesman, politician, artist and especially a great actor, philosopher, poet, musician, doctor, in fact be master of himself and everything round him. He will have no fear of death, for that kind of fear, as the stoic philosopher has sublimely put it, is a noose that the strong man seizes to drag the weak where he likes, and he will himself have cut that noose and so freed himself from all the tyrannies of this world. The over-sensitive and fools are on the stage, but he will be in the stalls, for he is wise.

MADEMOISELLE DE L'ESPINASSE: Heaven preserve me from the company of that kind of wise man!

BORDEU: It is because you have made no attempt to be like him that you will always hurtle from sorrows to violent joys, will spend your life laughing and crying and will always remain just a child.

MADEMOISELLE DE L'ESPINASSE: I'm quite resigned to it.

BORDEU: Do you really hope to be happier that way?

MADEMOISELLE DE L'ESPINASSE: I couldn't say.

BORDEU: Mademoiselle, this vaunted quality of sensibility, which never leads to anything great, is hardly ever cultivated without causing pain, or dabbled in half-heartedly without causing boredom: you either yawn or are intoxicated. You give yourself up unreservedly to the delicious sensation of some lovely music, or let yourself be carried away by some touching scene in a play, and then your diaphragm contracts, the pleasure has gone, and all you have left is a stifling feeling that lasts all the evening.

MADEMOISELLE DE L'ESPINASSE: But suppose that is the only way I can enjoy sublime music or a touching scene?

BORDEU: You are mistaken. I am equally capable of enjoyment or admiration, but I don't ever get upset, except with the colic. My pleasure is pure, my criticism is thereby more searching and my praise more worth while and thought out. Can any tragedy be badly written for such volatile souls as yours? How many times, when reading it over, have you blushed at the transports of emotion you went through at the performance, and vice versa?

MADEMOISELLE DE L'ESPINASSE: I admit it has happened to me.

BORDEU: So that it is not the emotional person like you, but the calm and cool one like me who has the right to say: this is true, good, beautiful. . . . So let us build up the centre of the network, it is the best thing we can do. Don't you realize that life itself depends on it?

MADEMOISELLE DE L'ESPINASSE: Life itself! This is serious, doctor.

BORDEU: Yes, life itself. There is hardly anybody who has not been tired of life at some time. A single event can suffice to make this mood involuntary and habitual, and then, in spite of distractions and amusements of all kinds, the advice of friends and one's own efforts, the threads obstinately go on conveying harmful shocks to the centre. The wretched victim, struggle as he will, sees the spectacle of this world growing blacker and blacker, is dogged at every turn by a train of lugubrious thoughts which haunt him ceaselessly, and he ends by doing away with himself.

MADEMOISELLE DE L'ESPINASSE: Doctor, you terrify me.

D'ALEMBERT (appearing in his dressing-gown and night-cap): And what do you say about sleep, doctor? It's a good thing, isn't it?

BORDEU: Sleep, that state in which either through weariness or habit the whole network relaxes and is still; then, as in illness, each thread of the network becomes taut, vibrates, transmits to the common centre a multitude of sensations often discordant, disconnected and muddled, but at other times so well arranged, logical and clearly set out that even a man awake could show no more reason, eloquence or imagination; sometimes these sensations are so lifelike that after waking the man is still uncertain whether the thing really –

MADEMOISELLE DE L'ESPINASSE: All right, but what *is* sleep, then?

BORDEU: It is a condition during which the animal no longer exists as a coherent whole and in which any collaboration or subordination between parts is suspended. The master is given over to the good pleasure of his vassals and the uncontrolled energy of his own activity. If the optic nerve has been stimulated, then the centre of the network can see; it can hear if the auditory thread bids it. Action and reaction are the only things remaining between them: it is a consequence of the properties of the centre, of the law of continuity and habit. If the process begins in the erotic thread intended by nature for the pleasures of love and the propagation of the species, the reaction at the centre of the network will conjure up a vision of the loved one. If, on the contrary, this vision originates at the centre, the consequences of the reaction will be tension of that erotic thread, erection and emission of seminal fluid.[22]

D'ALEMBERT: So there are coming-up and going-down dreams. I had one of the former last night, but I don't know what route it took.

BORDEU: In the waking state the network is governed by impressions made by external objects. In sleep everything is prompted by one's own sensitivity. There are no distractions in a dream, hence its intensity; it is almost always the product of some erethism or temporary disorder. In a dream the centre of the network is alternately active and passive in countless ways, hence its incoherence. Sometimes, however, the concepts are as logically connected and clear as if the person were looking at the real things going on in nature: hence the impression of truth and the impossibility of telling whether those things are being re-lived in imagination or actually being seen in the waking state. The one state doesn't seem any more likely than the other, and there is no way of recognizing one's mistake except by experience.

MADEMOISELLE DE L'ESPINASSE: But can experience always be had?

BORDEU: No.

MADEMOISELLE DE L'ESPINASSE: Suppose that in a dream I see a friend I have lost, and I see him as clearly as if he were still alive; suppose he speaks to me and I hear him, I touch him and my hands feel something solid. Then suppose I wake up feeling full of tenderness and grief, with my eyes filled with tears and my arms still held out towards the direction from which he appeared – what is to prove I haven't really seen, heard and touched him?

BORDEU: His absence, of course. But if it is impossible to distinguish waking from sleeping, who can appreciate its duration either? Peaceful sleep is an unnoticed interval between going to bed and getting up; troubled sleep sometimes goes on for years, it seems. In the first case at any rate, consciousness of self is suspended altogether. Can you tell me what kind of dream nobody has ever had nor ever will have?

MADEMOISELLE DE L'ESPINASSE: Yes, that one is somebody else.

D'ALEMBERT: And in that second kind of sleep one is conscious not only of self, but also of will-power and freedom of action. What exactly is this sense of will-power and freedom in a man who is dreaming?

BORDEU: Why, the same as that in a man awake: the most recent impulse of desire or aversion, the total to date of everything one has been from birth until that very moment. And I defy the most nimble wit to find the slightest difference.

D'ALEMBERT: You really think so?

BORDEU: Fancy that question coming from you! You

who, buried in your abstruse speculations, have spent two-thirds of your life dreaming with your eyes open and acting quite without volition; yes, with far less volition than when you dream. In this dream-state you issued commands, gave orders and were obeyed, you were displeased or satisfied, ran up against contradictions and obstacles, you were annoyed, you loved, hated, blamed, approved, denied, wept, came and went. While carrying out your researches, scarcely were your eyes open in the morning before you were wholly taken up again by yesterday's ideas, and you dressed, sat at your desk, meditated, drew diagrams, worked out calculations, had your dinner, went back to your problems, sometimes leaving your desk to verify, you talked to people, gave orders to the servants, had supper, went to bed and to sleep without ever having exercised the slightest will-power. Through all this you have been just a single point, acting without volition. And has one any volition if left to oneself? An act of will is always provoked by some inside or outside motive, whether present impression or memory of the past, some passion or some project for the future. And after that there is only one thing I can say about freedom of action: it is that the most recent of our acts is the necessary effect of one single cause – ourselves – a very complicated cause, but a single one.

MADEMOISELLE DE L'ESPINASSE: A necessary one?

BORDEU: Yes indeed. Try to imagine any other action taking place, assuming the person acting to be the same.

MADEMOISELLE DE L'ESPINASSE: Yes, he's right. Since I am the person acting in this way, somebody acting differently cannot still be me, and to affirm that, at the very moment I am doing or saying one thing, I can be saying or doing another is to affirm that I can be both myself and somebody else. But what about vice and virtue, doctor? Virtue, that most holy word in all languages, most sacred idea in all nations!

BORDEU: We must transform it into the words doing good and its opposite, doing harm. One is born fortunate or unfortunate, and each of us is imperceptibly carried along by the general current which leads one to glory and another to ignominy.

MADEMOISELLE DE L'ESPINASSE: What about self-respect, a sense of shame, remorse?

BORDEU: Childish notions founded on the ignorance and vanity of a person who takes upon himself the credit or blame for a quite unavoidable moment of evolution.

MADEMOISELLE DE L'ESPINASSE: And rewards and punishments?

BORDEU: Methods of correcting the modifiable person we call evil and encouraging the one we call good.

MADEMOISELLE DE L'ESPINASSE: Isn't there something dangerous in all this?

BORDEU: Is it true or is it false?

MADEMOISELLE DE L'ESPINASSE: True, I think.

BORDEU: That is to say you think falsehood has its advantages and truth its drawbacks?

MADEMOISELLE DE L'ESPINASSE: It seems so to me.

BORDEU: And to me, but the advantages of the lie are only for the moment, while those of truth are eternal; the unpleasant consequences of truth, if any, soon pass, but those of the lie can only end with the lie itself. Consider the effects of lying upon a man's mind and upon his behaviour: in his mind either the lie is more or less mixed up with the truth and he is incapable of clear thought, or else it all fits in beautifully and he is wrongheaded. Now what sort of behaviour can you expect from a mind either thoroughly illogical in its reasoning or logical in its errors?

MADEMOISELLE DE L'ESPINASSE: The second of these two vices, though less despicable, is perhaps more to be feared than the first.

D'ALEMBERT: Right, and that brings everything back to sensitivity, memory and organic functions. That suits me. But what about imagination or abstract thought?

BORDEU: Imagination –

MADEMOISELLE DE L'ESPINASSE: Just a minute, doctor, let us recapitulate. According to your principles it seems to me that with a series of purely mechanical operations I could reduce the greatest genius in the world to a mass of unorganized flesh; and given that this formless mass retained nothing but sensitivity to things of the moment it could be brought back from the most utterly stupid state imaginable to that of a man of genius. The first of these operations would consist of depriving the original bundle of some of its threads and shuffling up the rest, and the second and opposite operation of replacing the detached threads in the bundle and allowing the whole organism to develop properly. Example: take away from Newton the two auditory threads, and he loses all sense of sound; the olfactory ones, and he has no sense of smell; the optic ones and he has no notion of colours; the taste threads and he cannot distinguish flavours. The others I destroy or jumble up, and so much for the organization of the man's brain, memory, judgement, desires, aversions, passions, willpower, consciousness of self; there is nothing left but a hulk retaining only life and sensitivity.

BORDEU: Which are almost identical qualities. Life is the whole and sensitivity a part.

MADEMOISELLE DE L'ESPINASSE: Well then, I take this hulk and return its olfactory threads, and it starts to sniff, its auditory threads and it listens, optic threads and it can see, taste threads and it can taste. By sorting out the rest of the skein and allowing the other threads to develop normally I see the revival of memory, ability to make comparisons, judgement, reason, desires, aversions, passions, natural aptitudes, talent, and lo! my man of genius again.

And all that without the intervention of any unintelligible outside agency.

BORDEU: Yes, perfect. Leave it at that, for the rest is all mumbo-jumbo. But what about abstract thought and imagination? Imagination is recollection of forms and colours. The visual impression made by a scene or object necessarily winds up the sensitive instrument in a certain way; either it winds itself up or is wound up by some outside agency. Then it either vibrates inwardly or emits some sound outwardly; either silently records impressions received or publishes them abroad in conventional sounds.

D'ALEMBERT: But its narrative is usually exaggerated; it omits some circumstances and adds others, disfigures the story or embellishes it, so that the sensitive instruments close at hand receive impressions which are certainly those expressed by the instrument emitting the sounds, but not those of the thing as it really happened.

BORDEU: Yes, that's true, the story can be historical or poetic.

D'ALEMBERT: But how does this poetry or untruth get into the story at all?

BORDEU: Because ideas awaken each other, and they do so because they have always been related. Since you have taken the liberty of comparing an animal to a keyboard instrument you can surely let me compare the poet's story to music.

D'ALEMBERT: That's reasonable enough.

BORDEU: For every tune there is a scale, and the scale has its intervals; each of these strings has its harmonics, and these harmonics have harmonics of their own. Thus there come into the tune various modulations and the tune is enriched and lengthened. The real happening is a set theme which each musician interprets as he feels.

MADEMOISELLE DE L'ESPINASSE: Why confuse the issue with this figurative language? I would put it that each person sees with his own eyes and narrates differently. I would say that each idea awakens others and that according to his type of mind or character a person either keeps to those ideas which faithfully represent the fact, or adds to them other ideas thus awakened. I would say that these latter ideas open up a wide field of choice, and that . . . well, this subject alone, if properly explored, would fill a large tome.

D'ALEMBERT: You are right, but that doesn't prevent our asking the doctor if he is really sure that the imagination could never conjure up the form of a thing quite unrelated to anything else, and that such a form might not be put into a story.

BORDEU: I think I am. The wildest flights of this faculty called imagination boil down to that trick of the charlatans who take parts of cut-up animals and put them together to make an oddity never seen in nature.

D'ALEMBERT: But what about those abstractions?

BORDEU: There's no such thing. There are only habitual omissions or ellipses which make propositions more generalized and speech quicker and less cumbersome. The abstract sciences have evolved from linguistic symbols. Some quality common to many different acts has produced the words vice and virtue, some quality shared by many people has produced the words ugliness and beauty. Once they said one man, one horse, two animals, and later they said one, two, three, and all the science of numbers was born. We have no mental picture of an abstract word. In every body three dimensions have been observed: length, breadth and depth; each of these dimensions has been studied, and hence all the mathematical sciences. Every abstraction is merely a symbol devoid of particularized meaning. Every abstract science is simply juggling with symbols. The exact picture was dropped when the symbol was separated from the physical object, and it is only when the symbol and the physical object are brought together again that science once again becomes a matter of real things. Hence our need, so frequent in conversation and in writing, to get down to examples. When, after a long series of symbols, you ask for an example, all you are asking the speaker to do is to give body, form, reality, some specific meaning, to the succession of noises he has been making, by linking them up with known sensations.

D'ALEMBERT: Is that quite clear to you, Mademoiselle?

MADEMOISELLE DE L'ESPINASSE: Not terribly, but the doctor will explain.

BORDEU: Nice of you to say so. Not that there isn't probably a good deal to be rectified in what I have said, and many things to be added, but it is half past eleven, and I have a consultation in the Marais at noon.

D'ALEMBERT: 'Speech quicker and less cumbersome,' you said. Doctor, do we understand what we are saying ourselves? Are we understood?

BORDEU: Almost all conversations are like accounts (where on earth is my stick?) – I mean you have no clear idea in your mind (oh, and my hat?). And for the obvious reason that no two of us are exactly alike, we never understand exactly and are never exactly understood. There is always an element of more or less, our speech falls short of the real sensation or overshoots it. We realize how much variety there is in people's opinions, and there is a thousand times more that we don't notice and fortunately cannot notice. . . . Good-bye, good-bye.

MADEMOISELLE DE L'ESPINASSE: Just one more word, please.

BORDEU: Well, be quick.

MADEMOISELLE DE L'ESPINASSE: You remember those leaps you told me about?

BORDEU: Yes.

MADEMOISELLE DE L'ESPINASSE: Do you think that

fools and men of genius have leaps of that kind in their ancestry?

BORDEU: Why not?

MADEMOISELLE DE L'ESPINASSE: All the better for our grandchildren. Perhaps we shall have another Henri IV.

BORDEU: Perhaps he has come already.

MADEMOISELLE DE L'ESPINASSE: Doctor, you ought to come to dinner with us.

BORDEU: I'll do my best, but I can't promise. Expect me when you see me.

MADEMOISELLE DE L'ESPINASSE: We'll wait until two.

BORDEU: Agreed.

SEQUEL TO THE CONVERSATION

SPEAKERS: Mademoiselle de L'Espinasse, Bordeu

(*The doctor returned at two. D'Alembert had gone out to dinner and so the doctor was alone with Mademoiselle de L'Espinasse. Dinner was served, and they talked about nothing in particular until dessert, but when the servants had gone Mademoiselle de L'Espinasse said to the doctor:*)

MADEMOISELLE DE L'ESPINASSE: Come along, doctor, have a glass of malaga, and then you can answer a question which has been going round and round in my mind and which I wouldn't dare ask anyone else but you.

BORDEU: This malaga is excellent. . . . Well, your question?

MADEMOISELLE DE L'ESPINASSE: What do you think about cross-breeding between species?

BORDEU: Well, that's a good question! I think that man has ascribed a great deal of importance to the act of procreation, and rightly, but I don't think much of his civil and religious laws about it.

MADEMOISELLE DE L'ESPINASSE: What do you find wrong with them?

BORDEU: That they were made without regard for equity, without any clear object and without attention being paid to the nature of things or public usefulness.

MADEMOISELLE DE L'ESPINASSE: Will you try and explain?

BORDEU: That's what I am trying to do. . . . But just a moment (looks at his watch). Yes, I can still give you a good hour and that will do if I go quickly. We are alone, you are no prude and so won't imagine I have any wish to appear lacking in due respect for you. And whatever you may think about my ideas, I on my side hope you won't jump to any unfavourable conclusions about my personal morals.

MADEMOISELLE DE L'ESPINASSE: Of course I shan't, but your opening rather disturbs me.

BORDEU: In that case let us change the subject.

MADEMOISELLE DE L'ESPINASSE: No, no, say just what you like. One of your friends, who was casting round for suitable husbands for my two sisters and me, awarded a sylph to the youngest, a great Angel of the Annunciation to the eldest and a disciple of Diogenes to me; he knew all three of us well. And yet, doctor, keep some veils, please, let us have a certain amount of veiling![23]

BORDEU: Naturally – that is, as far as the subject and my profession allow.

MADEMOISELLE DE L'ESPINASSE: It won't be all that difficult. But here is your coffee . . . drink your coffee first.

BORDEU (having drunk his coffee): Your question involves physical science, morals and poetics.

MADEMOISELLE DE L'ESPINASSE: Poetics!

BORDEU: Why not? The art of creating fictional beings in imitation of real ones is true poetry. So this time, as a change from Hippocrates, will you let me quote Horace? This poet, or creator, says somewhere: *Omne tulit punctum qui miscuit utile dulci*; supreme merit is to have combined the agreeable with the useful. Perfection comes from reconciling these two things. An action which is both agreeable and useful must be the summit of aesthetic achievement. We cannot deny the second place to the useful alone, and the third place will be for the agreeable alone. We shall relegate to the lowest rank the action which gives neither pleasure nor profit.

MADEMOISELLE DE L'ESPINASSE: So far I can share your opinions without a blush, but where is this going to lead us?

BORDEU: You will see. Mademoiselle, could you tell me

what benefit or pleasure chastity and absolute continence yield either to the individual practising them or to society?

MADEMOISELLE DE L'ESPINASSE: Well, none, of course.

BORDEU: Therefore, in spite of the magnificent paeons of praise sung by fanatics, and in spite of civil laws which protect them, we shall strike these things off our list of virtues and agree that with the exception of positive evil there is nothing so puerile, ridiculous, absurd, harmful, contemptible and bad as these two rare qualities. . . .[24]

MADEMOISELLE DE L'ESPINASSE: Yes, we can grant that.

BORDEU: Be careful. I warn you, you will be beating a retreat in a minute!

MADEMOISELLE DE L'ESPINASSE: No, I never retreat.

BORDEU: What about solitary acts, then?

MADEMOISELLE DE L'ESPINASSE: Well, what about them?

BORDEU: Well, at least they give pleasure to the individual, and either our principle is false or –

MADEMOISELLE DE L'ESPINASSE: Really, doctor!

BORDEU: Oh yes, Mademoiselle, oh yes, and for the reason that these acts are just as harmless but not so useless. It is a need, and even if it were not it is a pleasant sensation. I want people to be healthy, and I think that is of paramount importance, don't you see? I blame any excess, but in a state of society like ours if there is one there are a hundred reasonable considerations (leaving out the fact of desire and the unfortunate effects of rigorous continence, especially in the young), lack of money, a man's fear of bitter regrets and a woman's of dishonour, which reduce a wretched creature dying of languor and boredom, a poor devil who doesn't know where to turn, to finish it off himself in the Cynic's way. Would Cato, who said to a young man on the point of going into a brothel: 'Courage, my boy', say the same thing today? If, on the other hand, he caught him alone in the act, might he not also say: 'That is better than corrupting another man's wife or risking one's own honour and health?' Because circumstances deprive me of the greatest joy imaginable, that of mingling senses, ecstasy and soul with those of a companion chosen for me by my heart, and of reproducing myself in and through her, because I cannot hallow my action with the seal of utility, must I deny myself a necessary and delightful moment? When we are in a plethoric condition we have ourselves bled – what does it matter what the superabundant humour is, its colour, and how we get rid of it? In each of these indispositions there is too much fluid, and if after being pumped up out of its reservoirs and sent all over the system it eventually is discharged in a longer, more painful and more dangerous way, it is lost just the same, isn't it? Nature puts up with nothing useless, and how can I be guilty if I assist her when she is asking for my help by the most unmistakable symptoms? We must never force nature, but we can give her a helping hand when need arises. Refusal to do so or inaction seem to me just silliness and loss of enjoyment. Exercise self-control, they tell me, and tire yourself out with physical exertion. I suppose this means go without one pleasure and put myself to a lot of inconvenience in order to keep another pleasure at bay! There's reasoning for you![25]

MADEMOISELLE DE L'ESPINASSE: That's not a good doctrine to preach to children.

BORDEU: Nor to anybody else. However, will you let me pretend something? Suppose you have a nice daughter – too nice; innocent – too innocent; and she has reached the age when the amorous instincts begin to develop. Her mind becomes affected and nature does nothing to cure it. You call me in. I see at once that all the symptoms that frighten you so much come from superabundance and repression of sexual desire. I warn you that she is in danger of losing her reason, a state which is easily preventable but sometimes impossible to cure. I tell you what the remedy is. What do you do?

MADEMOISELLE DE L'ESPINASSE: To tell you the truth I . . . but it never happens!

BORDEU: Don't you believe it; it is not rare at all, and it would be quite frequent if the laxity of our morals didn't prevent it. But whatever the truth of the matter, to spread these principles abroad would be to trample all decency underfoot, draw the most odious suspicions upon oneself, and commit a crime against society. But you are thinking of something else.

MADEMOISELLE DE L'ESPINASSE: Yes, I was wondering if I could ask you whether you had ever had to communicate this secret to the mothers of young people.

BORDEU: Oh yes.

MADEMOISELLE DE L'ESPINASSE: And what line did these mothers take?

BORDEU: Every one, without exception, took the right and sensible line. . . . I wouldn't raise my hat in the street to a man suspected of practising my doctrine, and wouldn't mind hearing him called infamous. But we are talking between ourselves and without any practical implications, and I would say of my philosophy what Diogenes, stark naked, said to the young and chaste Athenian against whom he was to contend: 'There's nothing to be afraid of, my boy. I'm not as bad as that fellow over there.'

MADEMOISELLE DE L'ESPINASSE (holding her hand in front of her eyes): Doctor, I see the drift of what you are saying, and I bet you –

BORDEU: I won't take it on because you would win. Yes, Mademoiselle, that is my opinion.

MADEMOISELLE DE L'ESPINASSE: What, whether one keeps to one's own species or not?

BORDEU: That's right.

MADEMOISELLE DE L'ESPINASSE: You really are dreadful!

BORDEU: No, not me; it's either nature or society. Now listen, Mademoiselle. I'm not taken in by words, and I express myself all the more freely because I say what I mean and the well known purity of my personal life gives nobody any grounds for attack. So this is the question I will put to you: take two acts, both of which are concerned with pleasure alone, both of which can only give pleasure without usefulness, but one of which only gives pleasure to the person performing it while the other shares the pleasure with a fellow creature, male or female (for in this matter the sex makes no difference, nor even who does what with what), and tell me what the verdict of common sense will be between the two.[26]

MADEMOISELLE DE L'ESPINASSE: These questions are too abstruse for me.

BORDEU: Aha! Having been a man for four minutes you take to your cap and petticoats and go all feminine again. Very well, then, we must treat you as such. . . . That's that. . . . Nowadays nobody says anything about Madame Du Barry. . . . You see, everything works out all right; we thought the Court would be turned upside down, but the master has behaved like a sensible man – *omne tulit punctum* – and has kept both the woman he has his fun with and the minister he finds useful. . . . But you aren't listening. . . . What are you thinking about now?[27]

MADEMOISELLE DE L'ESPINASSE: These unions that all strike me as being against nature.

BORDEU: Nothing that exists can be against nature or outside nature, and I don't even exclude chastity and voluntary continence which, if it were possible to sin against nature, would be the greatest of crimes against her as well as being the most serious offences against the social laws of any country in which acts were weighed in scales other than those of fanaticism and prejudice.

MADEMOISELLE DE L'ESPINASSE: I keep coming back to your hateful syllogisms, and I can't see any middle course – I must either deny everything or agree with everything. But look, doctor, the most straightforward course and the quickest is to jump over the quagmire and get back to my first question: what do you think about cross-breeding between species?

BORDEU: There's no need to jump to get back to that; we have been there all along. Is your question a scientific or moral one?

MADEMOISELLE DE L'ESPINASSE: Oh, scientific, scientific.

BORDEU: All to the good. The moral question comes first, and you have settled that already. So . . .

MADEMOISELLE DE L'ESPINASSE: We are agreed . . . no doubt the moral question has to come first, but I wish . . . that you would separate cause and effect. Let's leave the ugly cause out of it.

BORDEU: But that is asking me to begin at the end. However, since that is how you want it, I will tell you that thanks to our pusillanimity, our repugnances, our laws and prejudices, very few experiments have been made, and we don't know which copulations would be quite sterile or which cases would combine usefulness with pleasure, what kinds of species might be expected to result from varied and prolonged experiments. We don't know whether Fauns are real or mythical creatures, whether the types of mules could be multiplied a hundred times and whether those we know are truly sterile. But here is a strange story which many educated people will guarantee is true, but which is false. They claim to have seen in the Archduke's farmyard an abominable rabbit which acted as cock to a score of shameless hens who seemed quite willing to put up with it, and they will add that they have been shown chickens covered with fur which were the fruit of this bestiality. Of course they were laughed at.

MADEMOISELLE DE L'ESPINASSE: But what do you mean by prolonged experiments?

BORDEU: I mean that the differentiation of beings is graduated, and that assimilations between them would have to be prepared for; also that for success in experiments of this kind there would have to be long-term preliminaries and much work put in on bringing the animals closer to each other by similar diet.

MADEMOISELLE DE L'ESPINASSE: But it would be a job to reduce a man to grazing in the field.

BORDEU: But not to get him used to taking a lot of goat's milk, and the goat could easily be induced to live on bread. I have chosen the goat for reasons of my own.

MADEMOISELLE DE L'ESPINASSE: Which are . . .?

BORDEU: You are being very daring indeed! Well . . . that we might get in that way a vigorous, intelligent, tireless and fleet-footed race which we could train to be excellent servants.

MADEMOISELLE DE L'ESPINASSE: That's a fine idea. I already seem to see our duchesses' coaches followed by five or six great louts with goat-legs, and that delights me.

BORDEU: But also we should no longer be degrading our fellow men by forcing them to perform functions unworthy of them or of us.

MADEMOISELLE DE L'ESPINASSE: Better and better!

BORDEU: And in our colonies we should stop bringing men down to the level of beasts of burden.

MADEMOISELLE DE L'ESPINASSE: Quick, quick, doctor, get to work and make us some goat-men.

BORDEU: And you would allow that without any moral scruples?

MADEMOISELLE DE L'ESPINASSE: Just a moment, I've

thought of one. These goat-men of yours would be terrible lechers.

BORDEU: I cannot guarantee that they would be very moral.

MADEMOISELLE DE L'ESPINASSE: Then there would be no more safety for respectable women, and they would breed like mad and in the end we should have to kill them off or obey them. No, I don't want it any more. Don't worry.

BORDEU (going off): And what about baptizing them?

MADEMOISELLE DE L'ESPINASSE: That would make a rare hullaballoo in the Sorbonne.

BORDEU: Have you noticed in the Zoo, in a glass cage, the orang-outang that looks like St John preaching in the wilderness?

MADEMOISELLE DE L'ESPINASSE: Yes, I have seen him.

BORDEU: One day Cardinal de Polignac said to him: 'If you will speak, old chap, I will baptize you.'

MADEMOISELLE DE L'ESPINASSE: Well, good-bye, doctor. Don't stay away for ages, as you usually do, and remember sometimes that I'm madly in love with you. If people only knew all the horrors you have been telling me!

BORDEU: I'm quite sure you will keep them to yourself.

MADEMOISELLE DE L'ESPINASSE: Don't you be too sure. I only listen for the pleasure of passing things on. But just one word more, and I'll never bring the subject up again as long as I live.

BORDEU: Well?

MADEMOISELLE DE L'ESPINASSE: Where do these abominable tastes come from?

BORDEU: Always from some abnormality of the nervous system in young people, softening of the brain in the old, from the attraction of beauty in Athens, shortage of women in Rome, fear of the pox in Paris. Good-bye, good-bye.

NOTES ON *D'ALEMBERT'S DREAM*

1. Diderot here carries to its logical conclusion the idea of the 'chain of beings', favoured by many eighteenth-century scientists, including Buffon, and pushes the argument beyond the 'chain' from man down through the animals to the simplest marine creatures. If this is true why not go on to the vegetable and mineral kingdoms? The idea will be elaborated in this first dialogue and recapitulated in the second.

2. Falconet (1716–91), one of the greatest French sculptors of his age and greatly admired by Diderot, which clearly Huez was not. The little exchange which follows is an interesting indication of the typical eighteenth-century attitude towards the artist, who is regarded simply as a master craftsman, not as a divinely inspired being. That will be an invention of Romanticism.

3. See biographical note on D'Alembert. The father's name was really Destouches. The object of this somewhat ponderous speech is to insist on the purely mechanical nature of animal reproduction.

4. 'Pre-existent germs', now called preformation or encasement, is the theory that the ovule and sperm-cell contain all future generations one within the other, like onion-skins. Diderot ridicules this notion and champions epigenesis, i.e. the formation of an entirely new organic germ.

5. Another example of Diderot's analogical method. As a materialist he has to eliminate any external agency, and here he gets round the difficulty of memory, consciousness, individuality, etc., by analogy with sympathetic vibrating strings.

6. i.e. matter and spirit, body and soul. Diderot and eighteenth-century materialists such as La Mettrie and D'Holbach are naturally opposed to the Cartesian dichotomy.

7. This speech makes it clear why Diderot adopts the theory of sensitive matter. It is essential to his atheistic argument.

8. *Ressembler à l'âne de Buridan* is a proverbial expression meaning to be incapable of making up one's mind.

9. From this point Diderot advances the theory of the cellular organization of living creatures. He had already discussed the theory in the *Interprétation de la nature*. The ensuing parable of the swarm of bees is an attempt by analogy to circumvent the problem of individuality, personal identity in a creature made up of separate, living cells.

10. John Turberville Needham (1713–81). English Catholic priest and scientist. He published *New Microscopical Discoveries* in 1745. Needham

advanced the theory of spontaneous generation, alleging that tiny
eel-like creatures develop in fermenting organic matter, such as flour.
Voltaire opposed this idea, hence his derisive nickname. But it
appealed to Diderot as logically eliminating the necessity for outside
(divine?) agency.

11. A vague recollection of Lucretius, *De rerum natura* (V, vv. 1323–5):

> *Jactabantque suos tauri pedibusque terebant . . .*
> *. . . . . minitanti mente ruebant.*

But Diderot has either misconstrued or misremembered, for the
meaning is anything but clear.

12. A beautiful, succinct expression of the relative and ephemeral nature
of man and his ideas. From Fontenelle's *Entretien sur la pluralité des
mondes* (1686).

13. Here Diderot introduces the famous analogy of the spider and its
web, representing the nervous system and its centre. It will be
developed at some length after the interruption caused by D'Alembert,
who wakes up at this moment.

14. Fr Castel, a Jesuit, had suggested a system of coloured ribbons to
represent musical notes for the benefit of the deaf. Used as a symbol
of the indefinite and interchangeable in nature, where one thing
merges into another.

15. In this and the next long speech Bordeu recapitulates the attack on
the theory of preformation ('pre-existent germs'). But there is no
satisfactory explanation of *why* certain 'threads' should develop into
certain highly specialized organs.

16. Having quoted monstrosities and freaks of nature as examples of the
purely mechanical explanation of the 'metaphysical', Diderot
approaches the crucial problems of the brain, the intellectual faculties
and life itself.

17. La Peyronie (1678–1747), surgeon to Louis XV. The trepanning
operation was related in a paper by Quesnay in the *Mémoires de
l'Académie Royale de Chirurgie*, 1761.

18. La Condamine (1701–74), traveller and geographer, was struck
down with paralysis.

19. This example is interesting in more than one way. The case was
recorded in the *Gazette* two days after Diderot had reported having
finished these dialogues (see Introduction). It seems that the example
struck him as too curious to miss. But it is so curious that it is impossible
to visualize clearly how these poor creatures really were joined and
in what positions they could live or die. Diderot appears to have
copied out his example as it was given, and his French is no clearer
than my admittedly unclear English version.

20. A true estimate of the passionate nature of Mlle de L'Espinasse.

21. This and the next speech of Bordeu recall the idea Diderot develops in the *Paradoxe sur le comédien*, namely that mere intensity of emotion is not only not a help but also a positive hindrance to the artist or performer. The intelligence must always observe and remain in control. This theme is applied very shrewdly in the following pages to Mlle de L'Espinasse herself.

22. This turn of the conversation to erotic dreams and seminal losses, i.e. the purely mechanical nature of sexual manifestations irrespective of any outside stimulus, is a preparation for the daring sexual matter of the third dialogue. Similarly the ensuing dismissal of conventional ideas of virtue and vice.

23. This passage, and the preceding apologies of Bordeu for his outspokenness, show how little Diderot really knew of Mlle de L'Espinasse at this time. Her family circumstances were quite different from the tale here made up by Diderot (in reality Julie kept the secret of her origins to herself), and the prudishness hardly corresponds to what we know of the absolute freedom of the conversation in her *salon*. She and D'Alembert were well advised, on personal grounds, in demanding the suppression of these dialogues.

24. The eighteenth-century writers, since the time of the *Lettres persanes* of Montesquieu, were all opposed to celibacy as being patently unnatural. See article *Célibat* in the *Encyclopédie*.

25. In this statement that no *moral* issue is involved in masturbation Diderot is astonishingly modern. See article *Manustupration* in the *Encyclopédie*, in which Diderot had to take a more prudent 'official' line.

26. The next step in the argument is a plea for common sense about homosexual relationships. Again Diderot's attitude is strikingly modern, but it is interesting to note how Bordeu frequently dissociates himself *personally* from all this, and that after this speech Mlle de L'Espinasse dodges the whole issue, and is teased by Bordeu for so doing.

27. Allusion to the hostility between Mme du Barry, last and most notorious mistress of Louis XV, and the minister Choiseul.

THE STORY OF PENGUIN CLASSICS

Before 1946 ...'Classics' are mainly the domain of academics and students, without readable editions for everyone else. This all changes when a little-known classicist, E. V. Rieu, presents Penguin founder Allen Lane with the translation of Homer's *Odyssey* that he has been working on and reading to his wife Nelly in his spare time.

1946 *The Odyssey* becomes the first Penguin Classic published, and promptly sells three million copies. Suddenly, classic books are no longer for the privileged few.

1950s Rieu, now series editor, turns to professional writers for the best modern, readable translations, including Dorothy L. Sayers's *Inferno* and Robert Graves's *The Twelve Caesars*, which revives the salacious original.

1960s The Classics are given the distinctive black jackets that have remained a constant throughout the series's various looks. Rieu retires in 1964, hailing the Penguin Classics list as 'the greatest educative force of the 20th century'.

1970s A new generation of translators arrives to swell the Penguin Classics ranks, and the list grows to encompass more philosophy, religion, science, history and politics.

1980s The Penguin American Library joins the Classics stable, with titles such as *The Last of the Mohicans* safeguarded. Penguin Classics now offers the most comprehensive library of world literature available.

1990s The launch of Penguin Audiobooks brings the classics to a listening audience for the first time, and in 1999 the launch of the Penguin Classics website takes them online to a larger global readership than ever before.

The 21st Century Penguin Classics are rejacketed for the first time in nearly twenty years. This world famous series now consists of more than 1300 titles, making the widest range of the best books ever written available to millions – and constantly redefining the meaning of what makes a 'classic'.

The Odyssey continues ...

The best books ever written

P E N G U I N ⓟ C L A S S I C S

SINCE 1946

Find out more at www.penguinclassics.com